NOVAK'S VERDICT

JAMES H LEWIS

CONTENTS

Also by James H Lewis — vii

1. Friday, November 19 — 1
2. Saturday, November 20 — 19
3. Sunday, November 21 — 38
4. Monday, November 22 — 56
5. Tuesday, November 23 — 78
6. Wednesday, November 24 — 101
7. Thanksgiving, November 25-26 — 119
8. Saturday, November 27 — 141
9. Sunday, November 28 — 158
10. Monday, November 29 — 174
11. Tuesday, November 30 — 192
12. Early December, 2021 — 215

About the Author — 233

NOVAK'S VERDICT

James H Lewis

ALSO BY JAMES H LEWIS

Sins of Omission: Racism, politics, conspiracy, and justice in Florida

Breaking News

Novak's Mission

Novak's Quest

The Quadrant Conspiracy: The Plot to Kill FDR

Belonging

FRED TIFTON SHIFTED the plastic bag from his right hand to his left, peeled off his right-hand glove with his teeth to reach in the pocket of his Navy blue slacks, and withdrew a ring of keys. He inserted one into the lock of the front door but, before turning it, glowered from one end of Pennfield Avenue to the other. His clouded gray eyes were weighed down by sagging bags that, with his drooping earlobes, reminded others of a basset hound. He had once been known for his optimism and boosterism during his several terms as mayor of Boyleston Borough. Now, having lost his office in a scandal, he carried a look of permanent disappointment. On this brisk Friday evening, having satisfied himself that no suspicious characters lurked nearby, he turned the key and entered the small real estate agency that bore his name.

Locking the door behind him, he passed through the reception area whose two armchairs and a sofa faced a modular wall panel displaying flyers of homes and properties in plastic holders, a third of which were empty. He glanced at the desk of Amanda Naughton, his assistant, making certain she'd left no sensitive papers on her desk before leaving for a week-long Thanksgiving visit with her parents in Somerset. He made a similar inspection of the three cubicles for his agents, one of which was unoccupied, and entered his own office at the rear of the building. Tossing his keys onto the desk and hanging his wool jacket on a hook behind the door, he entered the small kitchenette across the hallway, opened the plastic bag, and extracted two white cardboard containers bearing images of a red pagoda. He took a plastic plate from the shelf above the sink, spooned white rice from one container onto the plate, then filled it with chicken and snow peas from the other. He closed both containers, placed them on the mini-refrigerator's top shelf, reached in the bag for the sleeve of chopsticks, and returned to his office. After setting his plate on the wing of his desk, he returned to the kitchen, drew a glass of wine from the box inside the refrigerator, resumed his seat, and began eating.

Tifton tapped his keyboard to coax his computer to life. He logged onto Pandora and called up his seventies playlist. The sound of Mungo Jerry's "In the Summertime" poured out of the twin speakers flanking the monitor. He turned the sound loud enough to compensate for his hearing loss.

He paged through his agents' notes as he ate, hoping one or the other had come up with an offer or a new listing. During his years as mayor, he had promoted Boyleston to all who would listen. The borough lay close to Pittsburgh, just off Parkway West, yet had a charm all its own. Stately old homes lined its tree-lined streets. All they needed was a bit of care to restore them to their past grandeur. Boyleston offered convenience and affordability, he'd argued. The old community was poised to become one of Pittsburgh's most sought-after neighborhoods. Homebuyers listened, and the borough managed a slow gentrification without driving away those who had lived here for generations.

The turnaround worked so well that other real estate firms, those much larger and with greater resources, began paying attention. Their dozens of agents spread throughout Allegheny County knew what was coming on the market before he did. Tifton and his two remaining agents now picked up crumbs others had left. He was a victim of his success.

Returning to the kitchen, Tifton dropped the plastic plate into the garbage. The cleaning crew would arrive later in the evening to clean up. He opened the back door of the one-story structure, collected four open house signs from the storage closet, and carried them out to the driveway where he'd parked his blue Buick Riviera. He loaded the placards into the trunk and returned inside, leaving the rear door unlocked. This is stupid, he thought as he studied the listing for the one showing he'd scheduled for Sunday. Pitt, led by Kenny Pickett, was playing Virginia at Heinz Field on Saturday for the ACC Coastal Title. The Steelers had a Sunday night game against the Chargers that could put them in the playoffs. No one would go house-hunting on a cold, blustery weekend before Thanksgiving, but the homeowner had threatened to take his listing elsewhere if Tifton didn't hold an open house. He would spend Sunday afternoon sitting alone at the dining room table, waiting for no one at all.

Tifton had embarked on another venture and now turned his attention to it. The scandal that had forced him from office had also ended his forty-eight-year marriage to Erica. When she took his house in the divorce, along with nearly everything he owned, Tifton had purchased a two-bedroom flat in a condominium overlooking Boyleston. The fifty-year-old building needed a host of improvements, but seeing an opportunity, he purchased two more units and rented them out, generating enough income to offset all three mortgage payments.

He'd worked his way onto the homeowners association board and become president. In this position, he directed maintenance projects to a firm he'd established, a side-hustle that was becoming lucrative. With his duties came the usual griping and moaning. He paged through the day's emails as Chicago's "Lowdown" filled the room. One owner complained about the noise workers made as they installed a new carpet in her hallway. Another groused about a water leak from the apartment above, even though it had been repaired two weeks before. Still another wanted her assigned parking place moved closer to the garage elevator. To all three, Tifton promised he'd address it the following week, though he had no intention of doing so.

It was almost eight o'clock, and Tifton was on his third glass of wine. From the speakers, David Clayton-Thomas belted out the lyrics to the Blood, Sweat & Tears hit, "When I Die." The music was so loud Tifton failed to sense the movement behind him until a shadow fell over his keyboard. He turned and looked up. "What are you doing here?" he said. His surprise turned to apprehension. "What are you doing with that sign?"

Tifton gasped as the twin prongs loomed over him. His hand shook, wine spilling down his shirt and onto his pants. He leaned back in his swivel chair and raised his arms to ward off the attack. His weight sent the chair reeling backward, his head colliding with the edge of his desk, then the floor.

"I can swear there ain't no heaven," Clayton-Thomas sang, "but I pray there ain't no hell."

Two RIVERS JOIN forces in Pittsburgh. From the high bluff on Grandview Avenue, one can see the muddy brown waters of the Allegheny River as it flows southwest from the mountainous chain that bears its name, merging with the dark waters of the Monongahela as it flows north from farmlands in West Virginia. They squeeze the city of Pittsburgh to a point as they travel west to their confluence, where they form the Ohio River.

From this point, the Ohio flows a thousand miles to Cairo, Illinois where it joins the Mississippi River, dividing Pennsylvania, West Virginia, and Kentucky from Ohio, Indiana, and Illinois—or, at an earlier time—slave states from free. It passes a dozen river cities, including Cincinnati, Louisville, Evansville, and Paducah. Ninety miles downriver from Pittsburgh but only fifty-nine miles by car, the city of Wheeling, West Virginia, slopes gently toward the river.

At the moment Fred Tifton was fighting to defend himself, a figure sat in a parked Chevy Malibu on 14th Street, a block west of Wood Street. He was nearing sixty, and his head of white hair receded at the crown. His thick neck hinted at a muscular body, for he once had been an amateur athlete. Tonight, as he sat behind the steering wheel, his dark brown eyes shifted from his rearview mirror to the door of a two-story brick townhouse three doors away. During its heyday, when the city was known for its steel industry and cigars, this row of houses had been part of a fashionable neighborhood. Since then, Wheeling's industrial base had collapsed, its population declined with each census, and this once-thriving street had fallen into decay. Someone in a neighboring townhouse had placed a pair of plastic chairs on the sidewalk outside the entry. Who would use them with winter approaching was an open question, but one the watcher didn't trouble himself to ask.

He hunched in his seat, trying to minimize his six-foot-two height, not just to get a good look at the front door, but to keep from drawing attention to himself should someone pass by. Not that anyone was likely to do so on this night. The temperature had dropped below freezing and would plunge into the mid-twenties by midnight. Few people were likely to be abroad, which made his presence even more of a fool's errand. He shivered as he watched the street, for he'd turned off the engine and cracked the passenger side window to keep the windshield from fogging. His right calf froze in a spasm from sitting too long in this position. He reached down to massage it, his eyes never leaving the front door of the home with its peeling white paint.

This was his third trip to Wheeling in the past month, and he had yet to find what he was after. Perhaps the tip Father Murray had given him was incorrect. Had the priest lied to him, or had he been lied to? Had his quarry moved on? The watcher had searched all the databases at his disposal—which were many—but found no trace of the man, only the address sent to him in an unmarked envelope two months before, without a name or any clue as to the sender. But he knew the priest was responsible, repaying him for a favor he'd done weeks before.

He jerked to attention as the door of the townhouse opened. A single figure emerged, clad in a dark parka, the hood pulled over his head. The watcher couldn't make out the man's features from this distance and seemed shorter and thicker than he remembered. But a half-century had passed.

The watcher turned on his engine to close the car's window, shut it off, and opened his door. As he stepped out of his seat, he stretched as his muscles complained from his hour of inactivity. Leaning against the hood of the Chevy with his right hand, he tested his balance, which had been a problem in recent years, then began following the man, who was now halfway down the block.

As he did so, a voice from behind said, "Sir, my captain would like you to come with me."

The watcher turned and looked at the uniformed officer. "I'm—"

"Chief Novak from Boyleston PD," the patrolman said. "We know, sir. We ran your plates. Captain Nelson would like a word."

Karol Novak looked after the retreating figure, shrugged, and followed the officer to his waiting squad car.

A WOMAN SAT ALONE at a bar on Braddock Avenue in Rankin, hunched over a ginger ale the bartender had poured into an Iron City glass. She was in her twenties with tight blond curls and a prominent nose, taller than average at 5-foot-9, and slender by the standards of most women of her age in Pittsburgh. She wore tight blue jeans and a long-sleeved Pittsburgh Steelers T-shirt that clung to her body. What most impressed those who glanced at her, however, were deep-set blue eyes that seemed to peer into anyone with whom she spoke, a feature that put many men off.

Not the beefy guy with slicked-back brown hair and a beard flecked with red who now straddled the stool next to her. Over the sound of Kenny Chesney's "Wasted," he said, "Can I buy you a drink?"

She studied him without smiling, noting the light, indented circle around the base of his ring finger. "No, thank you," she said.

"You sure?"

"I have one," she said, raising her no-proof glass as proof.

"You from around here?" he asked.

"No." She intended her curt reply to discourage him, but he didn't take the hint.

"I didn't think so. I stop by here most nights." When she didn't respond, he asked, "Waiting for someone?"

"Yeah," she said. "Godot."

The man shrugged. "Don't know him. He must not be a local either." The woman remained silent. "Busy tonight," he said, twisting in his bar stool and casting a look around the room. Twin television screens above them carried a high school football game. A mirror over the bar was festooned with a strand of artificial evergreens studded with tiny red bulbs, whether in anticipation of Christmas or a permanent fixture she couldn't tell. To the right of the bar, three machines churned containers of garishly colored alcoholic slush.

She stared straight ahead without speaking, sipped her drink, and set it back on the counter. A man at a corner table rose from his chair, but when she shook her head, he resumed his seat.

Her interrogator gave her one last look, shrugged, and hoisted himself off the chair, joining two friends sitting near the pool table. He spoke to them and was rewarded with a round of raucous laughter.

The woman allowed herself a contemptuous smirk, suspecting what he'd said to salve his wounded ego. She appeared to study the single row of bottles lining the mirror as she upended her glass, but for an instant, between a bottle of Knob Creek and Four Roses, she caught the reflection of a figure at a table behind her. He sat alone, seemingly oblivious to what had transpired, but she knew he'd watched the exchange and had been studying her from the moment she entered the bar. Widow's peaks cut twin swaths through his black hair like a pair of racing boats leaving rooster tails. His thick eyebrows met over a nose canted to one side, the result of a fight. This was not a supposition. She knew this and more about the man. His thin lips were locked in a grimace, and his eyes darted around the bar as though plotting an escape route. He was on his second beer but didn't run a tab, paying the server both times she brought his glass. And the woman sitting at the bar knew why.

On the electronic jukebox along the wall, Kenny Chesney gave way to an unintelligible voice deepened by a synthesizer of some sort. Everyone in the bar was white, but someone liked hip-hop enough to inflict it on the crowd.

Another woman slipped into the seat the burly man had vacated. She might have been in her late thirties, but the wrinkles in her neck put the lie to that. Despite the chilly November weather, she wore a short skirt and a salmon-colored blouse with cut-out shoulders and a scoop neckline. Her blond hair gave way to brown at the roots, and her thick lips were red as traffic lights. Or, during an earlier time, a bulb advertising its purpose over a doorway.

The younger woman smiled to herself as she rose from her seat, sliding a twenty toward the bartender. At another time, she might have paid more attention to the hooker, waiting to see what john she picked up—perhaps the guy who fashioned himself a beefcake. But tonight, her mind was elsewhere.

She left the bar without a glance, trying to ignore the smell of urine at the entrance, turned right on Braddock, and walked toward her car. Without turning, she knew the man with the broken nose was behind her. She also knew unseen others were on the street, but this gave her little comfort. For the first time, she wondered why she'd put herself in this situation. Her pulse quickened as she fished in her crossbody handbag for her keys, but rather than quickening her pace, she slowed as she spotted her gray Honda parked in a darkened spot midway between the nearest street lights.

As she felt her follower draw closer, her breath came in quick gasps. She hooked her keyring around the index finger of her left hand, closing her fist around it to keep her right hand free. Her pulse pounded in her temples, but she struggled to appear calm. He was now close enough that she could hear his steps. As she turned toward her car door, she imagined his breath on her neck.

Now, she thought. Any second, he'll wrap his arm around my throat and reach beneath my shirt and down my jeans, as he's done to three other women in the neighborhood over the past month. She was ready for him. She widened her stance to balance herself, prepared to grab his hand, pull him toward her as she leaned forward, and slam him against the pavement.

Instead, he brushed past her, his shoulder almost touching hers. In a gravelly, mocking voice, he said, "Have a good evening, officer."

<hr>

Patrolman David Kimrey was working the night shift when they got the call. At first, he'd resented working these hours, but the weeknights were quiet enough that he could study for the detective's exam on Boyleston's time.

Friday nights were different. The end of the work week brought people pouring into Boyleston's bars, frittering away their paychecks and, for a few, tangling with each other at closing time. Too often, someone drew a weapon, spiraling the night out of control.

This Friday evening had so far been uneventful, a fact Kimrey ascribed to the upcoming holiday. The patrolman had come a long way from months of poor performance reviews, disciplinary work plans, and attendant fears for his job. He'd worked hard to regain the trust of his superiors, doing everything by the book. When Deputy Chief Calvin Mayfield assigned him to train Norville Chastain, the department's newly recruited Black patrol officer, he took it as a sign he was back on the team.

Kimrey had taken the month-long assignment without complaint and almost regretted returning to a day shift the following week, for he'd have to study on his own time.

Allegheny County's 9-1-1 Center interrupted his concentration. "Neighbors report a domestic dispute at 625 Barker Street." Chastain acknowledged the call, and the two officers donned their parkas and headed out in the cruiser.

The address lay in the middle of a side street off Noblestown Road. In the dim light afforded by street lamps, Kimrey made out a two-story brick house with white trim, identical to its neighbors set fifteen yards apart. Lights blazed on both floors, but through the slapping of the windshield wipers, the officers saw no sign that anything was amiss.

Once they opened their car doors, however, they heard a man shouting. His voice was shrill, and while they couldn't make out the words, these were howls of panic. "Heads down," they heard as they approached the door. "Incoming!"

Kimrey motioned Chastain to stand away from the door while he rang the bell. The bellowing came to an abrupt stop, and they heard nothing from inside. To Kimrey, the sudden silence was even more menacing. He rang again and then knocked.

The timid sound of a woman's voice asked, "Who's there?"

"Police," Kimrey said. "We've had a report of a disturbance. Open up."

A hurried discussion took place, the woman pleading, a man breaking into sobs. "No, no," he bawled.

Kimrey opened the clasp on his Taser with his left hand and knocked on the door again with his right. "Please open up," he said in a softer voice. "We want to make certain everyone's all right."

The door opened a crack, and Kimrey inched it forward. The woman stood in a pink housecoat, her straight, lusterless hair tangled like strands of vermicelli. She held a toddler who buried his face in his mother's shoulder. A girl of about three clung to her leg.

"I'm sorry," she said in a timorous voice. "Brock's having a flashback."

"May I come in?" Kimrey asked, not waiting for an answer as he entered the house. Beyond the entry, a man sat huddled on a gray sofa, nestled between twin pillows, his legs drawn up. His hands covered his eyes, and he rocked back and forth to some internal melody. Kimrey introduced himself. "And what is your name?" he asked. The man didn't respond, continuing his rocking motion.

"Brock Gifford," the woman responded. She answered Kimrey's follow-up question with the single word, "Shari."

"What's going on?" the officer said. Officer Chastain stood off to the side, observing, but saying nothing.

"He thinks the Taliban is attacking us," the woman said. "He did four tours. The VA's trying to help him, but ..."

Kimrey made a low moan to show he understood. "Are you all right? Has he harmed you or the kids?"

"No, he'd never do that." Her voice rose an octave as she added, "He's just frightened." She broke down in tears, then sniffled as she tried to recover. Kimrey realized she was struggling to stay strong for her children. Had she been alone, she would have been shaking with fear.

Kimrey told Chastain to take the family into the kitchen. "See if the kids need milk or something." While the officer led them away, Kimrey sat alongside the man. "Brock," he said in his softest voice, "I'm David Kimrey. I'm a police officer, but I'm not here to harm you. I want to help you get hold of yourself."

The man stopped rocking. He cupped his mouth in his hand, shook his head, but said nothing.

"You're not in Afghanistan," Kimrey said. "You're home in the US, in Pennsylvania, in Boyleston. You're safe. Your wife and kids are here to protect you."

The officer spent ten minutes speaking to Gifford, reassuring him in a soft voice. Once he'd calmed down, he leaned sideways on the sofa with his head on the armrest, his energy spent. "Why don't you turn in for the night?" Kimrey said. "Sleep will do you good."

He didn't know whether that was true. Did the terror return as nightmares? But Gifford muttered a word of thanks and stumbled up the stairs.

Kimrey returned to the kitchen, where Shari Gifford and her children were devouring a bag of microwave popcorn Chastain had prepared. "He's settled down," he said. "I've sent him to bed."

"Thank you," she said.

"Do you and the kids have a place you can stay tonight? It might be safer."

"No," she said, putting her arm around her daughter. "These come on every few weeks. He'll be fine for a while. I'll take him to the VA on Monday."

"Mrs. Gifford, does he have any weapons in the house?"

She shook her head.

"Because someone with mental and emotional problems shouldn't have guns around."

"He doesn't," she said. "I don't allow them. Even if he didn't have these spells, I wouldn't permit it with two young kids in the house."

"That was impressive," Chastain said as they drove back to headquarters. "Where'd you learn to do that?"

"It's part of being a cop," he said. "You just listen to hear what people have to say. The rest comes naturally."

GRETA GEILKE PULLED into the driveway and inched toward the rear door of the office building. She was surprised to find a Buick blocking her path. This was a private drive; no one should be parking here. Whoever had done so might return while she was inside and demand that she stop work so he could leave. *Inconsiderate idiot!*

She opened the trunk of her Nissan and removed a sizable rectangular bucket filled with cleaning supplies. Mr. Tifton kept his office stocked with sprays and cleaning rags, but she preferred her own. Greta hoped he'd repaired the vacuum cleaner. Last week it had made a strange noise, and she'd smelled something burning.

Shivering against the evening cold, she reached for her keys, then realized the door was unlocked. Someone had left it open, and the kitchen light was on.

"Hello?" She shuddered as a chill raced through her body. "Who's there?" Hearing no answer, she stepped inside. Light shone beneath the office door. Placing her bucket on the kitchen floor, she advanced toward the door and tapped. Hearing nothing, she knocked, then pounded, calling out to whoever was inside.

Greta stepped back from the door while she considered the situation. She was alone here, while someone in the office was playing music at peak volume. Was this who had parked in the driveway and left the back door unlocked? She should call for help, but who should she disturb at this hour? And what if she was mistaken?

She stepped into the darkened hallway, turned on the light switch, and opened the storage closet to her left. The broom and mop were in their usual places, the latter having the stouter handle. She advanced on the closed office door, wielding the handle like a sword. Leaning forward, she turned the handle and pushed the door open with her left hand while wielding the mop with her right.

She stared in front of her, not comprehending the scene. What first struck her was the For Sale sign tilted at an angle toward the desk. Then the pool of dried blood surrounding the upended chair. For an instant, mental muscle memory made her wonder how she could clean this up. Then the outstretched body registered. All this in the space of less than a second.

Greta Geilke screamed, which only added to the tumult of AC/DC's "Back In Black."

THE FIVE-BLOCK DRIVE from 14th Street to the Wheeling City Hall on Chapline Street took only two minutes. The patrolman parked on 15th Street in front of St. Matthew's Episcopal Church and led Novak through the side entrance of the block-long building, which also housed the Ohio County Courthouse. Stairways to other city offices flanked the entrance to the department along a long lobby that let in natural light through windows spanning both floors. Novak took it all in, envious at the modern facility that made the aging police wing of Boyleston's municipal building seem even more decayed.

A uniformed captain stood inside the entrance to police head-quarters. He was about 5-10, bald, and heavyset, but Novak suspected his bulk was muscle. He introduced himself as Captain Donald Nelson. His high tenor voice belied his formidable appear-ance. He shook Novak's hand and, without another word, led him through the bullpen to a windowed office at the back. Motioning Novak into a chair, he took his seat, folded his hands, and asked, "What brings you here, Chief?"

Novak had spent the short drive wondering how best to answer this question. "I'm looking for a priest."

"We have lots of those," Nelson said.

"We do, too," Novak replied. He looked above the captain's head while gathering his thoughts. "This one's retired. I have information he lives at this address. I'm trying to confirm it."

"What's he wanted for?" the captain asked.

"There's no warrant for him," Novak said. "This is unofficial. Personal."

"I take it you're not trying to make your confession."

"No. It's nothing like that." Novak rubbed both eyes. "Timothy Dacey was a Catholic priest who served in the Pittsburgh diocese years ago. He was in his late twenties then, so I guess he's well into his seventies now."

Captain Nelson made a sound in his throat meant to stand in for uh-huh, nodded his head, and waited.

"He was a predator," Novak said. "The state grand jury named him in its report three years ago. You may have heard about it."

"We had a few of our own," Nelson said. "I'm sure you heard about that."

"I suspect Dacey was among them," Novak replied. "The Pittsburgh diocese transferred him to Charleston ... after they'd finished transferring him from one parish to another in Pittsburgh."

"Yeah," Nelson said, his voice communicating his distaste. "So why are you trying to find him after all this time?"

"I just want to know where he is, what he's doing."

"You said this is personal, not professional."

"Yes."

Nelson ran a thick hand across his bald pate. "You're not out for revenge, are you?"

"No, no, nothing like that. I just want to confront him," Novak said.

"And then what?"

"I, uh—" Novak bobbed his head several times while he looked off to the side. "I haven't figured that out. But I don't intend to hurt him."

"Good, because if you were to do so—threaten him, assault him, whatever—I'd be forced to arrest you. And I'd do it."

"I'd expect you to do so," Novak said.

"It's customary, as you know, for an officer operating out of his jurisdiction to notify the locals when operating in their area."

"I know. I'm sorry."

"It's not required. Nothing in the law says you have to. But it's a courtesy. It avoids situations like this."

"I apologize. I wasn't acting in an official capacity. Still, I should have," Novak said. "I assume a neighbor reported me."

"No. Officer Riley patrols that area. It's a high-crime neighborhood, so he keeps his eyes open. He spotted you tonight and remembered seeing you here two weeks ago. He ran your plates and," Nelson spread his hands, "here we are."

The captain waited for Novak's response and, getting none, said, "Are you going to pursue this?"

"I don't know. I thought I'd spotted him leaving the house just before your officer stopped me. But I'm not sure."

"Because there's nothing legally you can do to him. Like Pennsylvania, West Virginia doesn't have a look-back window." Nelson referred to a provision some states had adopted extending the statute of limitations in cases of child abuse. "And even if we did, it's only applies to civil cases, not criminal."

"I know that, and even if we had such a law, the statute wouldn't have been extended indefinitely." Novak studied the captain, debating how much to tell him. As Nelson returned his gaze, wearing a look of concern, he decided to trust the man. "My best friend committed suicide because of this man's abuse. I intend to make him face what he did." *To him and to me*, Novak thought, unwilling to show all his cards.

Nelson rubbed the fingers of each hand with the other. "Let me check with my chief," he said, "but if you promise not to attack him ... if you pledge you won't threaten him in any way...." Novak shook his head as the officer spoke. "Then I'll find out what I can about this Dacey character. After all, we may not want him in our community."

Novak thanked him and left, refusing the offer to drive him to his car and walking up 14th Street in the brisk night air.

***

Boyleston Borough Detective Lydia Barnwell uncapped her omnipresent water bottle and took a swim before closing it again. Every other officer sitting around the conference table at Allegheny County Police headquarters on Greentree Road gulped mugs of coffee or bottles of cola, but the last thing Barnwell needed at 10:30 on a Friday night was caffeine. County detectives and patrol officers passed a box of chocolate chip cookies from hand to hand, but when it came her turn, she slid the box along without grabbing one.

"What went wrong?" she asked. "How did he know?"

Detective Sergeant Lyle Jeffrey, sitting at the head of the table, said, "We have no idea."

"The bartender?" she said.

"No," another officer responded. "Jerry's solid. We've used him before."

"Who then?" No one had an answer to her question.

Marvin Milford was suspected of having assaulted multiple women over the past few months, three in Rankin and Braddock in the last thirty days. He attacked at night and always from behind, so none of his victims could identify him. Milford liked a certain type: younger women, tall, blond, and well-built. When the ACPD had decided on a sting operation, Jeffrey recalled the Boyleston officer from a case he'd worked months before and asked if she'd be willing to work as a decoy.

Lydia Barnwell welcomed the assignment. As a new detective, she longed for a case of her own. She had nearly bungled her last investigation, one that wasn't even hers. When a mother had reported her child missing from a local thrift shop, Lydia inserted herself into the county's investigation despite Jeffrey's objections. She befriended the mother, accepting her story without questioning it. As they talked, the woman made an inadvertent disclosure that led Lydia to suspect the woman's boyfriend had murdered the child. Sergeant Jeffrey made the arrest, but Lydia knew she'd slipped up. By identifying with the woman's supposed plight, she'd hampered the investigation. Chief Novak had been understanding—she had cracked the case, after all—but Lydia was not as forgiving. She had become more objective, doubting anything a witness told her.

Jeffrey had also pardoned her. She'd allowed him to claim credit for solving the case. Now, he'd invited her to lure Milford into another attack, giving her an opportunity for redemption.

But something had gone wrong tonight. Milford had seemed to swallow the bait, but he'd recognized her as soon as she entered, then had the audacity to mock her effort.

"What do we do now?" she asked.

Jeffrey turned to the other officers without looking at her. "It's back to the drawing board," he said. "Let's review every victim's story and see if we've missed anything. We know he's the guy. We just don't have enough to charge him."

"What can I do?" Lydia asked.

Jeffrey cleared his throat. "Nothing, I'm afraid. You did a good job tonight. We couldn't have asked for more. But he sniffed you out, and there's nothing you can do about it. We're grateful."

The other officers nodded their heads, but the message was clear. She'd only served as bait. They had no further use for her. Suppressing a sigh, she remained stoic, unwilling to share her disappointment. She would have to find another way to prove herself to these men.

KIMREY AND CHASTAIN responded to Greta Geilke's frantic midnight call, entering the office building through the rear door. The cleaning woman sat at a small table in the kitchen, her body trembling and tears streaming down her face. He introduced himself and Chastain, showed his ID, and asked her where she'd found the body.

"In there," she said, waving him in the general direction of the office. He told the new patrolman to remain with her, stepped into the hall, and peered into the room. The scene was unlike anything he'd ever encountered. A man lay on his back, his left arm extended, his right lodged upright against a metal file cabinet. Dried blood pooled at his side, and a sign bearing the bright red words "For Sale" seemed to be propped against the desk.

Kimrey donned white booties and disposable rubber gloves and entered the room, stepping around the body to avoid the blood. On closer examination, he realized the sign was not resting against the desk but had impaled the victim's body. One prong went through his right eye, the other through his stomach. The patrolman reached down to feel for a pulse in the man's throat, but the action was futile. He was dead and had been for some time.

Kimrey peered again at the sign, noting the agency's name, then looked at what remained of the victim's face. Recognizing the implications, he broke protocol and tried to raise Chief Novak on his shoulder-mounted two-way. Getting no response, he reached for his cell phone and called the deputy chief.

Mayfield listened, then asked, "Have you notified county?"

"I was about to, but seeing how this is the former mayor, I thought I'd better let you know first."

"Do it now," Mayfield ordered. "I'll be there in fifteen."

DETECTIVE SERGEANT LYLE JEFFREY stood over the cleaning woman. At over six feet, with the build of a college wrestler and dark, deep-set eyes, he was an intimidating presence. "Did you touch anything?" he asked.

She looked up at him with pleading eyes. "No, sir. It's like I told the officer," she said, nodding toward Kimrey. "I opened the door, found him lying there, and backed right out."

"You're sure?" he asked, and she repeated her assurance. "How often do you see him?"

"Almost never," she said. "I work for his maintenance company. We do Boyleston Arms and sometimes one of his listings. Rita—she's supposed to work with me, but she was busy tonight, and since this is usually such a quick job...." Her voice trailed off without completing the thought.

A white-coated photographer interrupted the conversation, walking through the kitchen toward the back door. "They still at it in there?" Jeffrey asked him.

"Yeah. It'll take a while, this one."

The photographer left. Jeffrey returned his attention to Greta Gielke, who continued her explanation. "We have our schedule. I see him coming and going at the condo—"

"The Boyleston Arms?" he asked.

"That's what I said. I see him coming out of the building in the morning sometimes. He never speaks to me, but I always say, 'Hi, Mr. Mayor.' He's not very friendly these days."

"He's Boyleston's mayor?" Jeffrey asked, turning to the deputy chief.

"Was," Calvin Mayfield answered. "He resigned a couple of years ago after—"

"Could there be a political motive?" Jeffrey interrupted.

Mayfield shrugged. "Anything's possible, but he's been out of the picture for some time. Chief Novak can tell you more about that."

"And where's he tonight?" Jeffrey asked.

"He's off duty. A personal matter of some sort."

Jeffrey snorted and turned to Officer Kimrey. "When you recognized Tifton, you called your deputy chief before notifying us."

"Y-yes," Kimrey stammered.

"Relax," Jeffrey said. "I would have done the same."

Returning his attention to the cleaning woman, he said, "You say the rear door was open when you arrived. Is that typical?"

"No," she said. "They lock the doorknob and secure the bolt when they leave. I need two keys to get in. They've never left it open."

"Have you ever found him at the office at this hour?"

She shook her thinning gray hair. "Like I keep saying, I only see him when I'm arriving at the Arms and he's leaving. I've come across him three, maybe four times in the year I've worked here. Honest."

Jeffrey had a crime lab technician take her fingerprints and swab her cheek for her DNA, "Just to exclude you from other samples we collect," he told her. Kimrey's were already on file. He posed a few more questions, but since the woman had nothing more to offer, he sent her home. He told Mayfield and Kimrey that she was "just a cleaning lady."

Mayfield stiffened but held his tongue. His mother had spent her life cleaning for white people. She wasn't "just" a cleaning lady. He dismissed Kimrey, and the two officers sat at the kitchen table, waiting for the crime lab to finish its work. Jeffrey questioned him about Tifton's relationship with other council members while he was mayor, but Mayfield deflected him. "I don't get into borough politics," he said. "And I was still a detective when he was in office."

A member of the white-suited crime crew poked his head into the kitchen. "Since he was working at his computer when he died, we're taking it for forensic evidence."

"No objection," Jeffrey said. After they wrapped up, another team from the medical examiner's office entered, placed Tifton's corpse in a long body bag, and left. Jeffrey entered the office. The crime lab had removed the carpet stained with dried blood, allowing the pair to approach the desk without disturbing the scene. Mayfield was amazed Jeffrey allowed him to remain on the scene. Crimes of violence were the county's job, since the Boyleston force lacked the resources to pursue them on its own. Months before, Jeffrey had fought Lydia Barnwell's effort to help search for a missing child. Only the mother's continued phone calls and visits to the officer had kept her involved, leading her to the tragic solution to the case. Had that experience softened Jeffrey's antipathy toward the borough?

The detective removed everything from the desk drawers, one at a time. They examined each item, finding nothing interesting except a notebook in which Tifton kept names and addresses. They would leave the file drawers for the next day.

When they heard the rear door open, they returned to the kitchen to find a haggard-looking Chief Novak standing there. "You heard," Mayfield said, stating the obvious.

"Kimrey called and told me. What do we know so far?"

Jeffrey led him into the office and told him what little he'd learned. "The cleaning woman found the back door unlocked, so either the killer had a key, or Tifton was expecting him."

"Or he got careless," Novak said. "Any sign of a struggle?"

Mayfield described the position in which they'd found the body. "Otherwise," he said, "the room seems undisturbed. Nothing was overturned, and there's no sign the killer went through his desk or rifled through his files."

Novak studied the office, trying to reconstruct the scene. He wandered from one side to the other, examining the desk and over-turned chair from several angles. He stopped, crossing his right arm before him, stroking his chin with his left. "The two weren't at eye level. The killer stood over him. This wasn't a conversation that got out of hand. The assailant approached him from behind," he said, demonstrating, "holding the sign over him like so."

Jeffrey nodded in agreement. "He took Tifton by surprise," he said.

"A For Sale sign?" Novak continued. "What an odd weapon. It could be a statement of some sort, in which case it was premeditated. Or else his killer grabbed the closest thing at hand. But the kitchen is just steps away."

He left the room, and Jeffrey and Mayfield could hear him opening drawers. "There are plenty of knives," he called. "So why use the sign? It's an awkward way to kill someone."

"It makes no sense," Jeffrey said. "Mayfield says he used to be mayor."

"For years," Novak said. "Remember the Thomas Walsh case? The man who was falsely accused of killing his wife years ago?"

"Detective Matt Harries screwed up that case," Jeffrey said. "You proved he was innocent. That was also two years ago, wasn't it?"

Novak nodded. "From the moment we reopened it, Tifton threw every roadblock he could in our way. I couldn't figure out why. As we dug into it, we discovered he and Tom Walsh had been friends since grade school. The weekend Walsh's wife was murdered, they and two others were on a fishing trip up at Bessemer Lake."

Novak combed his hair back with both hands as he recalled the details. "Walsh slept in one room, while Tifton and two others enter-tained a group of hookers in a separate suite. Tifton and his friends concealed this information from Harris to keep his wife from finding out. For twenty years, he kept silent, allowing an innocent man to sit on death row for a crime he didn't commit. When we discovered all this and told the council how he tried to restrict our investigation, they forced him to resign."

"I remember the case," Jeffrey said, "but didn't connect it to Tifton."

"The council chose not to publicize his involvement," Novak said. "It didn't exactly put them in a favorable light. But for Tifton, it didn't end there. When his wife learned the truth, she divorced him. She took the house with her."

"Maybe there's a connection between Tifton's murder and the Walsh case," Jeffrey said. "Do any of the council members bear him a grudge?"

Novak thought a moment before speaking. "I haven't seen Fred at the borough building since he resigned. About a third of the council is new since then. I'm not saying there's no link, but I don't know of one."

"How about Walsh?" Jeffrey said. "He must have it in for Tifton."

Novak uttered a low moan and buried his face in his hands. "I'm sure he does, but murder him for revenge? I'd hate to think that. Still, he's the only one I know who has a motive."

Jeffrey began to reply, but Novak interrupted him. "I know this is your investigation. I understand we have no role here. But we knew Tifton, I know Walsh, and we can provide a lot of background as things move forward. I'd like us to stay involved."

He remembered Jeffrey's objections to Lydia helping with the search for young Rosie Fallon. But to his surprise, Jeffrey said, "I'll ask Superintendent Starr for permission. You folks have been helpful in the past, and Barnwell did a great job serving as a decoy tonight. I'll see if we can arrange it."

BERNIE JACKSON, Boyleston's only Black council member, sat at the council table of neighboring Alston Township. He was a big man, standing over six feet tall with a rugged build slightly dimmed by the ravages of six decades and too much pizza, but dark brown skin concealed his wrinkles. With reading glasses perched on his nose, Jackson read pages from a folder before him. He had done his homework before today's meeting, but wanted to ensure he had all the facts in mind.

Jackson was the borough's representative on a three-person committee meeting planning the consolidation of the police departments of Boyleston Borough and Alston and Byers townships. The group met weekly, led by Peter Watson of the state's Department of Community and Economic Development, with the meeting site rotating among the three municipalities. The idea of merging the three small departments had arisen earlier in the year after a police officer in Byers had fatally shot an unarmed Black youth. The town faced nights of protest after the young man's death, leading to the Byers council disbanding its police force. ACPD now patrolled the borough, but the Byers council hoped that by joining the other municipalities, they could provide faster response to emergencies.

As the Alston representative took her seat alongside him, Jackson's cell phone rang. He picked it up and stared at it, ready to decline the call, but when he saw it was from Chief Novak, he answered it with a cheery hello.

Novak dispensed with the usual pleasantries. "Fred Tifton was killed last night. I thought you should know."

"Killed?" Bernie said, "How?"

"He was murdered. Someone came up behind him while he was working and speared him with one of those yard signs they use. It was pretty damn gruesome."

"Jesus!" Bernie said. That explained the sirens he'd heard around midnight. "Who did it?"

"No idea. County police are in charge, but they're allowing us to work with them. All we know is when it happened." Li Wan, who owned the Chinese restaurant across the street, told them Tifton had entered his restaurant minutes before seven and ordered takeout. An hour-and-a-laugh later, Li heard the screech of tires as a vehicle backed out of the driveway onto busy Pennfield Avenue. He hadn't seen the car, only heard the sound, and a customer had told him the driver had nearly caused an accident. "I'll let you know what I can," Novak said.

As chair of the borough's public safety committee, Bernie knew the limitations on sharing information about active investigations, but he trusted Novak to give him a general idea of progress. "It's hard to feel sorry for Tifton after what he did to the borough," he said, "but I do. I've noticed how few of his signs are going up in the neighborhood, so he wasn't getting the listings. I suspect he'd fallen on hard times."

Which Bernie's portrait studio had as well. Novak's wife had gotten him back into the borough's schools, but the work wasn't enough to rescue his business. People relied more on selfies and group photos taken with phones. They felt they didn't need him. Times were changing, and Jackson found himself unable to keep up.

He thanked Novak again and ended the call as the man from the state called the meeting to order.

NOVAK PULLED his unmarked cruiser to the curb and studied the home across the street. He recalled the first time he'd visited the house two years before. It had been run down, aluminum siding coming off one corner, the concrete steps at an angle, the front lawn a jungle. Over the year since Thomas Walsh had walked free, he'd slowly restored the place, cleaning up the yard and contractors to repair the front steps and replace the siding. Novak had visited the man twice. He was now working at a big box hardware store, the kind that had put his small shop out of business years before, and appeared to be doing well. He couldn't imagine the man being stupid enough to risk his freedom by attacking Tifton, but a lifetime of police work had taught him to assume nothing.

He stepped from the vehicle, crossed the street, and took the steps, but before he reached the door, Bridey O'Connor swung it open, a grin on her face. "I saw you pull up," she said. "How are you doing, Chief?"

Thomas Walsh's daughter also seemed to have a fresh coat of paint. The woman, who for years had maintained her father was guilty of murdering her mother, had seemed a decade older than her thirty-four years when they'd first met. She worked in a doughnut shop, raising her daughter on her own, and the long hours and dark clouds hanging over her family's past had weighed her down. Now she looked like a new person.

He assured her he was fine and asked to come in. "Is your dad here?" he asked.

"No, he's at work. Everyone has weekend projects, you know."

"Even the week before Thanksgiving?" he said. He glanced around the room, deciding whether to approach the subject with Bridey. Novak had caught only a few hours of sleep, not enough for a man still struggling with the aftermath of a traumatic brain injury that had caused him to retire from Pittsburgh's Police Bureau three years before.

"What brings you here?" she said. "What do you want with him?"

Trying to keep his tone neutral, Novak asked, "Where was he last night?"

Bridey frowned. "Why do you want to know?"

"Was he home, Bridey?"

She crossed her arms and stepped back. "He worked late and came about nine with takeout from the Chinese restaurant. What's this about?"

"Someone murdered Fred Tifton last night. Given the history between them, I need to account for Tom's whereabouts."

She stiffened, the fingers of her right hand playing a rhythm on her left shoulder. "I can't believe you're asking that after all he's been through."

"In a case like this, everyone who knew the man is a suspect. We're questioning all his employees, clients, and anyone at the borough offices with whom he was in contact. Tom isn't alone, but because of what Tifton did to him all those years ago, we have to ask the question."

"Well, he was at work. You can ask them yourself."

"Fine, I will. I want to cross him off the list."

"You do that," she said.

He almost preferred that she shout at him rather than fix him with her icy stare. He thanked her, drew his lined coat around him against the chilly wind of late fall, and left without another word.

***

Detective Lydia Barnwell arrived at the real estate office at ten, summoned by Deputy Chief Mayfield, who had given her a quick rundown on what had occurred. The morning news had already carried news of the murder while providing no details, not even the victim's identity. She hadn't known Tifton well; Chief Novak kept his officers insulated from the borough council's politics. But what she knew of him, she hadn't liked.

The sign on the agency's front door read closed, and a uniformed officer stood outside. Barnwell noticed a black Jaguar SUV parked at the curb and wondered to whom it belonged. When she identified herself to the officer, he opened the door, ushered her past three empty cubicles and a closed office door adorned with crime tape, and into the small kitchen at the rear.

"I haven't seen you in hours," Detective Sergeant Jeffrey said. "Come join us." He didn't rise to greet her but introduced her to another detective, Bill Thurmond, and a woman who sat across from them. "Evelyn Scowcroft is one of two agents here," he said. "We've just begun speaking to her."

She was a middle-aged woman, perhaps in her early fifties, wearing a tight fitting green dress around a slender figure. Her dyed hair was so blond it appeared white and was cut in the current Pittsburgh style, bobbed and cut close in the back. Her tiny pearl earrings and a double-looped string of pearls told Barnwell the woman had done well for herself. She had no doubt who owned the Jag.

"We're trying to contact both agents and the secretary," Jeffrey said. "Ms. Scowcroft came in on her own."

"I saw the story on the news," she said. "While they didn't identify the victim, I suspected who it was."

"How so?" Barnwell said.

"That's what I was telling these gentlemen," she said. "He was here when I left. Fred often works late. Since his wife left him, he's had nothing else to do with himself."

"One other agent works here, Walter Dwyer," Jeffrey said. "He has an open house at noon but promises to come in when he's through. Their assistant, Amanda Naughton, is taking the week off."

"She left for Somerset yesterday afternoon," the agent said. "I doubt she's heard about this. She'll be shocked when she finds out. I doubt she'll want to come back to work. This neighborhood!" She shook her head and stared below at her shoes. Lydia had already spotted them beneath the table. Ferragamo, unless she missed her guess.

"Tell us about Tifton," Jeffrey said. "What sort of boss was he?"

The woman let out a long sigh. "I don't like to speak ill of the dead," she said, though Lydia knew she was about to, "but he'd become a hard man."

"'Become?'" Lydia said.

"He used to exude optimism, always looking for the silver lining. And he loved Boyleston." She sniffed, leading Lydia to decide the woman didn't live here. "Always talking up the town, what potential it had. He was a one-man chamber of commerce and a joy to work with."

She frowned and held up an index finger. "Perhaps that's putting it a bit strongly. We got along well. That's all I'll say."

"But then?" Lydia prompted, surprised that Jeffrey was letting her take the lead. Did she think a female detective could get more out of this woman than he could? She wondered what had come over this man who, only months before, had bawled her out for interfering in his investigation.

The agent paused and took a long swallow from a glass of water that had so far remained untouched. "He resigned as mayor. Forced to do so, from what I heard. I don't know what caused it. Then his wife divorced him." She held her left palm against her ear and pushed it forward. "And he just changed."

Lydia opened her aluminum water bottle and took a sip while she waited. "He became quite ... unpleasant," Scowcroft said, pausing as though censoring herself. When Lydia continued to stare at her, she continued. "The agency is failing. I think you can see that. But did that change his personality or was it the result? I've never been able to decide. But he became abrupt, distant, and testy. He'd erupt at the slightest thing."

"Abusive?" Lydia asked.

"He didn't call names, if that's what you mean. He just made life difficult. We avoided him whenever we could. I took to working from home."

"How did the others feel about him?" Detective Thurmond asked.

"Oh, we all hated — disliked working around him. He treated some of us unethically. Not me. He wouldn't have pulled any of that on me. But you'll want to speak to Troy."

"Troy...?" Jeffrey prompted.

"Stuart," she supplied. "Troy Stuart. Do you know how real estate commissions work?"

"Tell us," Thurmond said.

She folded her hands and stretched them out on the table. "When a property changes hands, the seller pays a 6 percent commission. Half of that goes to the listing agency, the one that found and marketed it. The other half goes to the selling agency. So 3 percent to each. And of that, half goes to the agent and half to the agency itself.

So if I list a property and it sells, I get one-and-a-half percent of the sales price, and Tifton gets the other half. You follow?"

All three nodded. "Troy came up with this beautiful property over on Hillcrest. Century-old three-story house—almost a mansion—built by the owner of a small steel mill back in the day. Troy listed it and then found a buyer for it. This is unusual, one agent handling both sides of the deal. It requires a lot of disclosures to make certain both buyer and seller agree."

"So Troy earned 3 percent?" Barnwell said.

"He should have, but Fred thought the sale part of the deal was too complicated for him, that this needed to be more of an arms-length transaction, so he inserted himself, moved Troy aside, and took his end of the sales commission. Troy ended up with one-and-a-half percent, and Fred took the rest. We're talking about a $15,000 difference."

Lydia looked at her in disbelief, but Jeffrey didn't miss a beat. "What did he do?"

"He hired an attorney and tried to sue, but Walt and I sat him down and explained that if he did so, he'd be persona non grata with every other agency in town. We advised him to take his share and leave for a larger firm. That's what he did."

"How do we get in touch with him?" Jeffrey asked.

She hesitated, as though considering how to answer. "You can get his name and number on half the For Sale signs in town. Bradley Real Estate took him on and encouraged him to work listings in Boyleston first, then branch out. I hear they gave him a big bonus, but maybe that's just a rumor."

"And Tifton, I'm sure, resented it," Barnwell said.

"Don't you know it?"

Jeffrey leaned forward, resting his chin on his paw. "Did Tifton have any other enemies that you know of?"

"Enemies? Who said Troy was his enemy? He came out smelling like a rose. He'd no need to kill him."

"I'll rephrase it. Did he have any enemies?"

She seemed to think for a moment. "There was something having to do with a high-rise condo he's involved in. He's president of their HOA. Someone came in yelling at him a year ago. I wasn't here, but Walt was. Ask him."

"We will," Jeffrey said. "Meanwhile, where were you between roughly seven and nine last night?"

She flashed a tight-lipped smile. "Attending the opening of the Phipps Winter Flower Show with my husband. They had a reception for donors before the opening. I'm sure you'll find us on the guest list."

Jeffrey made a note of it and thanked her.

"One thing," she said. "KDKA said you're not releasing his name until you've notified his next-of-kin, but who's that? He's divorced, and their only child died in a car crash several years ago. I never heard him speak of brothers or sisters."

"We'll figure it out," Lydia told her. Recalling the words of a fundraising executive she'd once dated, she said, "Where there's a will, there's a relative."

Novak wandered the aisles of the Busy Builder store on Washington Pike until he found Tom Walsh helping a customer in the plumbing aisle. Walsh looked younger than when Novak had seen him in prison. His hair was still shock white, and deep creases lined his face, but he wore a confident expression and stepped with a lightness unlike the shuffling figure he'd first encountered. Walsh's face brightened as he saw the man whose efforts had rescued him from a death sentence for a murder he'd not committed. "Be with you in a moment, Chief."

Novak pretended to study lengths of PVC pipe. A home improvement project might be hiding here, but at the moment, he couldn't think of one. The customer couldn't decide what he wanted, and Walsh kept urging him, showing impatience. Novak raised both palms to signal he had time. The conversation with the customer droned on.

He had helped Walsh secure his job here. Busy Builder had a reputation for giving those with a checkered past a second chance. The chief had vouched for him, assuring first the store manager, then the district manager, that Walsh not only had done nothing wrong, but that his background as the owner of his own hardware store brought skills this chain needed. Walsh hadn't let him down.

The customer finally wandered off, having bought nothing. Walsh shrugged, smiled, and said, "What can I do for you, Chief?"

"Is there somewhere we can talk?"

"The break room. I'm due." He muttered a few words into an electronic instrument hanging at his side and led Novak to a long room off the rear of the store, across from the restrooms. "Coffee?" he asked.

Novak agreed and straddled a bench affixed to a long white picnic table while Walsh poured two cups from a large carafe resting on a stainless steel machine. He returned carrying the two paper cups and extracted small packs of sugar and ersatz creamer from his pocket. Novak waved them off and took a long sip before speaking.

"I have to ask you some questions, Tom. Where were you last night?"

Did Walsh's eyes flicker before answering? "Here," he said. "Why?"

"What time did you get off?"

"We close at nine," he said.

"And is that when you left?"

"I always stay until closing on Friday night," he said. "They scheduled me for a double yesterday."

Walsh hadn't directly answered the question. Novak chose not to pursue it. Evasiveness was a survival mechanism Walsh had learned during his years behind bars. Prison changed people. Novak could confirm the story with the store manager.

"What's this about?" Walsh asked.

"Someone murdered Fred Tifton last night," Novak said, watching Walsh's reaction.

The man flinched, drawing back from his side of the table and knitting his brows. "And you think I had something to do with it?"

"We're interviewing everyone with a motive, crossing each person off our list. You had reason to hate him. Tifton did you in."

Walsh crossed his arms and studied the cop for several seconds. "Well, I didn't, Chief. I've never hurt anyone in my life, and I'm not about to start now. You believe me, don't you?"

"I want to, Tom. You know that. I'm just doing my job."

"Speaking of that," Walsh said, "I need to return to my own."

Novak let him go, dissatisfied with the way the conversation had gone. Walsh was hiding something. He was sure of it.

WALTER DWYER, the other agent in the office, joined detectives Jeffrey, Thurmond, and Barnwell in mid-afternoon following his open house. Jeffrey had moved the interview to ACPD headquarters in Greentree, just two miles from the real estate office. Dwyer was a short, squat man, almost bald on top, but with a fringe of greasy black hair ending in tight ringlets around his neck. He wheezed as the guard at the front desk escorted him into the interview room. Lydia Barnwell couldn't help but feel this was not a man who inspired confidence among his clients.

Jeffrey made the introductions and asked Dwyer how long he'd worked at the agency. "Over twenty years," he said. And to Jeffrey's question as to how he'd gotten along with Tifton, Dwyer replied, "He was all right."

"Just all right?" Jeffrey asked.

"Okay, he was hard to get along with. I'd learned to stay out of his way, do my job, keep my head down." Under questioning, Dwyer told much the same story as Evelyn Scowcroft, how the once-ebullient leader of the agency had become a crotchety boss, finding fault with everything and everybody, making their lives miserable. "I should have left," he said, "but I'm too old to start over someplace else."

"A third agent left about eighteen months ago."

Dwyer nodded. "Troy," he said. "Tifton did him dirt, cheated him out of part of his commission. It was a shitty thing to do." Dwyer's story matched that of the other agent. "He was about to get married," he said. "He needed that money."

"Did he bear a grudge against Tifton?" Thurmond asked.

"Maybe," Dwyer said, "but he got the last laugh. He went with Bradley Real Estate and became one of their stars. I hear he moved over twelve million dollars last year—his first full year there. That's nearly two hundred thou in commissions. It's unheard of. He took everything he learned here and put it to work for himself. And good for him."

"Would he still be angry enough to want to kill Tifton?" Jeffrey asked.

Dwyer shook his round head. "Naw. He didn't need to look back. He made out like a bandit. We worked together on a property a few months ago—my listing, his sale. He offered to put in a word for me with Bradley. They gave me an interview, but...." He left the thought unfinished.

"Did Tifton have any other enemies?" Thurmond asked.

"He wasn't at the top of anyone's hit parade," he said, "but naw."

"We're told someone came in a year ago and argued with him."

Dwyer seemed to think it over for a moment. "The contractor, you mean? Yeah, that got pretty nasty."

"What's his name?" Lydia asked. It was the first time she'd spoken up during the interview.

He tapped the table as though trying to jog his memory. "Cranwell?" he said. "No, Craddock. Benny Craddock. I only know that 'cause I heard him introduce himself to Amanda. You know, the secretary? My desk is closest to hers, so I hear everything that goes on out there."

"What was the nature of their dispute?" she asked.

"I don't know much about it. It's that other thing he's involved in. The condo?"

Lydia recalled Evelyn Scowcroft mentioning a high-rise condominium but realized the three detectives hadn't pursued it. "Boyleston Arms," Dwyer said in response to her question. "He bought into it a couple years back and now runs the board or something. You'll have to ask Amanda about it. I don't know the details. He seems to have replaced this contractor, Craddock, with another fellow. The man was livid. Tifton's office door was closed, but I heard them yelling at each other. 'You ruined me,'" Dwyer said, imitating the sound of the conversation. "'You still owe me money.'"

"And how did Tifton respond?"

"I couldn't hear his end of it. Craddock just kept yelling, but Tifton must have answered quiet-like, to calm him down, you know?" Dwyer paused for breath, puffing as though he'd been running. "Last I knew, he yelled, 'I'll see you in court, you bastard.' He was all hot when he left, head hunched down, red in the face."

The three detectives didn't share a glance, but they took it in. Here was a new angle. Thurmond asked Dwyer where he'd been the night before. "For the record," he said.

Dwyer brightened and grinned. "Me and Sonya went out to dinner."

"And Sonya is your wife?"

"Naw, she's what you might call a girlfriend. Nothing serious. We just hang out together. We go to Eat 'n Park every Friday evening for their cod dinner. You ever tried it? They do a nice job."

Thurmond told him he hadn't had the pleasure and got the woman's full name and number. "Can you think of anyone else who was at odds with him? A disgruntled seller or a buyer?"

Dwyer shook his head. "I don't know anyone who'd want to hurt the man. But you won't find anyone praising him at his funeral."

When Novak finished interviewing Walsh, he asked to speak to the store manager. Told he would return at 3:30, Novak drove to the Boyleston municipal building, which housed council offices, the branch of the county library, and the police station, and caught up on paperwork.

When he returned to Busy Builder at 3:30, Ralph Norris, the manager, was waiting for him. The two greeted each other, and Norris asked what he could do for the chief. "I need to find out when Tom Walsh left work yesterday."

"What's he done?" the manager asked.

"Nothing that I know of, but it is official. He's one of several people whose whereabouts we need to check on. Just marking folks off a list," Novak said, making it sound a tedious necessity.

Norris frowned as though he didn't buy the explanation. "I hope so," he said. "We've come to depend on him."

"I told you he was a good man," Novak replied.

"Yes, you did. Wait here a moment." He left his small office, returning a minute later with a printout. "Here it is," he said. "Tom clocked out at a quarter past five yesterday afternoon."

Novak fought to hide his reaction. "Five-fifteen? You're sure of it?"

"Five-thirteen, to be precise. Why? What's the matter?"

"Nothing," Novak said. "As I said, we're checking on lots of people." He thanked the man and left, not bothering to search the store for Walsh. He needed to think this over.

AS NOVAK DELIVERED his mother to Sunday morning Mass at St. Cyril and Methodius Church, one of Pittsburgh's traditional Slovakian parishes, he suppressed a pang of guilt. She'd become less steady on her feet in recent months and now required a walker to help her get around. Rather than dropping her at the door, he ought to walk her down the aisle and sit alongside her. After all this time, however, he still couldn't bring himself to attend. He'd entered the sanctuary half a year before, but that was on police business, a case involving theft from the alms box that Patrolman Kimrey had solved. No service had been underway during his visit, no rituals to make his forehead sweat and his hands tremble. While over four decades had passed, he still imagined Father Dacey officiating, pretending to be a man of God while he preyed on Novak, his best friend Henry Sutton, and dozens of other altar boys over the years.

He compromised by leading Izabela up the ramp to the right of the stairs, through the vestibule, and into the narthex, then left her to make her way alone. An usher guided her to a pew, casting a perturbed glance at Novak as he took her arm. He knew the man, and the usher certainly knew the chief. Novak's humiliation was second only to his remorse over his inability to do this one small favor for the woman who had done so much for him.

Novak returned to his house. Barbara was finishing a lavish breakfast of a mushroom omelet, leftover steak, crescent rolls she'd made by hand, and a fruit tray. This had become their Sunday morning ritual: a quiet chat during the hour when Izabela was out of the house and they could speak in private without the competition of a blaring TV. He placed the Sunday paper before her, and she glanced at the front page, which carried the story of Tifton's murder below the fold. She ignored it, saying, "You look terrible," as she poured orange juice into their glasses. "I take it you didn't sleep well."

"I did not," he said, matching her pedantic tone. He reached for his pill container, dropped the prescriptions into his hand, then shoveled his hand to his mouth as he considered how much to tell her. Most cops keep details of their investigations away from their families, fearing the details will turn up as neighborhood gossip and shielding their spouses from the temptation. The relationship between Barbara and Karol was different. He shared a great deal with her, and she often redirected his thinking when it wandered in the wrong direction. She also used him as a sounding board for whatever was troubling her, which was usually a conflict between her role as a middle school principal and the administration.

He followed the orange juice with a swig of coffee, then, setting his cup down, said, "Tom Walsh has no alibi for Friday night. He lied to me, told me he was working late when he wasn't."

"Oh, God," Barbara said, knitting her brows in anguish. "Do you think he killed Fred Tifton?"

"No," Novak said, responding almost before she'd finished. "Tom's not stupid. He knows he'd been the obvious suspect. If he had killed him, he would have thought up a better explanation than one so easily disproven."

"Then why do you think—?" she said.

"What I think doesn't matter. The facts are," he said, ticking them off on his fingers, "someone murdered Tifton and wasn't subtle about it; his was a gruesome death. Walsh has a motive; Tifton put him away for twenty years. And Walsh can't account for where he was at the time of the murder; he lied about it. Those are the facts, and if I'm the county detective in charge of the case, I'll reach the obvious conclusion."

"Have you told him Walsh lied?" she asked. He shoveled a mouthful of egg into his mouth and shook his head. "Aren't you obligated to do so?"

"I want to talk to Tom first, confront him with what I've learned, and see what he has to say for himself. Meanwhile," he said, "what's the latest on your teacher?"

Three students had complained to Barbara that her eighth-grade science instructor, George Rollins, had been making off-color remarks. It had begun with playful comments one month into the term about why the boys in his class couldn't wait to get their driving licenses. "We know why they want to drive, don't we girls?" He could have meant to go racing, but he kept at it. "But you can't steer the car from the back seat."

"The way he looked when he said it," one girl told Barbara, "we knew what he meant."

Barbara had met with Rollins and suggested he needed to watch what he said because "some students took it the wrong way." This gentle approach, designed to redirect his behavior without making an accusation, proved too subtle. A few weeks later, he returned to a discussion about driving, telling the class, "I know you boys want to get behind the wheel so you can take the curves. Most of you love curves." And, referring to one young man believed to be gay, he said, "Except for Timmy, here. He likes the straight and narrow."

When Barbara heard this, she lambasted him, but he denied saying anything wrong. "I was telling them how to take the driving test," he said.

"That's at least two years off for the oldest of them," Barbara responded.

"I know that, but they're curious about the process. They know I'm a driving instructor at the high school." He chuckled as though he'd maneuvered his king out of check. "These kids," he said. "They have only one thing on their minds."

"And I understand you made a passing reference to Gary's sexual orientation in front of the others," Barbara told Novak. "Do you know what he replied? 'Are you saying he's gay?' As though I were the one out of line."

"Has he done something more?" Novak asked.

"No, but the way he looks at me in the hall or during meetings ... He's testing me." She tossed her fork onto the plate with a long clatter. "I wish he'd either shape up or screw up."

Novak's cell phone interrupted his reply. He listened for a moment, interrupting with occasional questions that told Barbara nothing of what was being discussed. He thanked his caller and disconnected, burying his face in both hands.

"Who was that?" she asked.

"Walsh's boss, the manager at Busy Builder. Walsh left a voice mail Saturday afternoon, asking him to lie about when he left work the night before, but he didn't listen to it until after I'd left. It's been eating on him ever since."

"It took him long enough to tell you."

"Uh-huh," he said as he pulled on his jacket, ready to leave for the church to pick up his mother. "I think he's more worried about who he's hired than about advancing the cause of justice."

***

BOYLESTON DETECTIVE GORDON HORVATH stood behind his county counterpart, Bill Thurmond, who rang the doorbell of the two-story row house on Princeton Avenue. Chief Novak had awakened Horvath at seven, asking him to accompany the ACPD detective sergeant to interview a suspect in Tifton's murder. Horvath was a large man, six-foot-four and all muscle. He'd played linebacker at

Penn State and prided himself on keeping in shape. His jet black hair and a face with features as sharp as those on Mount Rushmore made him a formidable presence. The county detective was glad to have him along, for Bennie Craddock had a record. Back when he was a union carpenter, he'd assaulted a fellow worker, been convicted, and done time.

The contractor answered the door and looked the two up and down. "What?" he said.

"Are you Benny Craddock?" Thurmond asked.

"Who wants to know?"

Thurmond showed his ID and introduced Horvath. "We need to ask you a few questions. May we come in?"

"You can ask me right here," he said.

Horvath pushed his way in. "Too cold," he said. "Pretend you're a good citizen, why not?" Craddock followed him into a living room crammed with furniture, and Thurmond tagged along. Horvath looked the room over. Brocade peeled away from the walls. The blue carpet had a large red stain in the middle. A venetian blind hung at an odd angle around one of the two front windows. Cobbler's children, Horvath thought. "Have a seat," he said.

Craddock did as he was told. "What's this about?"

"Where were you between seven and eight-thirty Friday night?" Thurmond asked.

"Here," Craddock said. "You can ask my wife when she gets home from church. We watched that TV show with the magicians." He had lost his defiance, and Horvath wondered if this meant he was telling the truth. "What's this about?" he repeated.

"How well do you know Fred Tifton?" the county detective asked.

"That bastard," Craddock spat out. "Too well. What of it?"

"You two had a fight in his office a year ago. What was that about?"

Craddock shook his head. "That prick. You know Boyleston Arms, that high-rise condo atop Fletcher's Bluff?" Horvath nodded, although as long as he'd worked in the borough, he'd never known the name of the tall hill on which the building stood. "I did maintenance for them for twenty years. Me and my workers did a great job. Anything that needed fixing, we fixed. So Tifton took over about a year back—"

"Took over?" Thurmond said. "What does that mean?"

"He and some other owners got elected to the board. Tifton became president. I don't know the details. You'll have to ask others."

Craddock's nostrils flared, reminding Horvath of a bull preparing to charge. "When my contract came up in October last year, he told me he wasn't renewing. Said our work was substandard. That was bullshit," he shouted, shaking a fist at them. "That place is fifty years old and needs constant work. Whatever problems they have, it's due to the age of the place, not us."

"So you confronted him?" Horvath said.

"I wouldn't put it that way. He didn't have the decency to talk to me about it. Just sent an email saying the association wasn't renewing. No notice. No thanks for all your hard work. I went by to ask him why, and he said, 'Because your work is shoddy.'

"You don't tell me that," Craddock said, pointing to his chest. "Whenever they needed me, I was there, twenty-four-seven, like they say. Our work was first-class. You can ask anyone who lives there. Anyone!"

His voice had risen to a shout. Horvath detected a hair-trigger temper and didn't doubt the man had earned his reputation for violence. "Did you threaten him?" he asked.

"With what? What am I going to do to him? No, I tried to reason with him, but he wouldn't listen. I asked for a three-month extension. 'Give us time to wind down and land another contract,' I said. We had nothing else, see? Boyleston Arms was my only client."

"And what was his answer?" Thurmond said.

"He wouldn't budge. 'You're making your problem my problem,' he says."

"And what did you do?"

"I called him a name. Bastard, I think. Prick, maybe. He's both."

"Did you threaten him?" Thurmond repeated.

Craddock, whose answers had come rapid-fire, hesitated long enough to suggest to the detectives that he had done just that. "No," he said.

"Told him you'd see him in court?"

Craddock grunted. "As though I have money to hire an attorney?"

"What did you say?" the county detective asked. "We have a witness."

"So ... maybe I told him he'd live to regret it. But nothing more." He looked from one to the other as though gauging their reaction. "What's this about?" he said for the third time. "What's happened to him?"

"Haven't you heard?" Horvath said. "Someone murdered him Friday night."

Craddock drew back as though shocked, but Horvath thought the man must have suspected as much from their questions.

"Good," he said. "I had nothing to do with it, but he had it coming. I'm glad someone did."

***

Novak wasn't the only one suffering from a sleepless night. Bernie Jackson had tossed and turned until two in the morning, then awakened before six. As he sat over his third cup of coffee, his wife LaDonna said, "What's going on with you?"

He looked up at her with a mournful expression. "I've messed up." He had a more colorful term for what he was feeling, but she wouldn't allow that kind of language in the house.

"It can't be that bad," she said. "You married me." He tried a laugh but coughed instead.

"It's about the consolidation, isn't it?" she asked.

"Yeah," he said. "The three of us have agreed on the framework. Byers fired all its men after the shooting last spring, and Alston has just the one officer, the chief." He snorted at the idea that the small township had a leader in charge of no one. "So we've agreed to expand the force, adopted a governance arrangement, and set a budget we'll recommend to all three councils. Things were going pretty smoothly."

He planted his fists on the dinette set and stared at the surface. She waited, knowing he would get around to it. "Yesterday, the subject of leadership came up. Peter Watson, the fellow from Harrisburg who's leading us through all this, has known from the outset we want Chief Novak to lead the department. That was a condition on which Byers Township came in with us, and Alston has never objected. It was all settled. But Watson asked me a question: 'Hasn't the chief resigned?' I said yeah, but we've talked him into staying on.

"'For how long?' he asks. I say, for as long as we need him. I can tell this is news to May Pinckney—she represents Alston. She starts asking me questions about his background. I explain he'd retired from Pittsburgh and we'd pressed him into service after Chief Russell was arrested. 'So he's retired before?' she says. The way she puts it, I know I'm in trouble."

He peered into his empty cup. LaDonna took the hint and refilled it, cutting him another slice of banana bread. Food, she knew, kept her husband's mouth going. "Watson picks up on it. He starts talking about fresh leadership, someone who's in it for the long haul. He can't mention Karol's age, but that's what he means. May goes along, saying this is an opportunity for the three communities. 'Let's get it right,' she says. Stan Sabol, the mayor of Byers Township, chimes right in.

"I argue with them. 'Chief Novak was part of the deal,' I tell them. Wrong thing to say. Sabol says how he respects Novak, knows what a fine job he's done for us, 'But this isn't about what's best for him,' he says. 'It's about what's best for us.'"

He stuffed the remaining half slice into his mouth. "I've lost them," he said.

She covered one of his hands with her own. "I don't know what else you could have said. This Mr. Watson asked you a question. You answered it. What were you going to do, lie?"

"No, but I might have put it better if I'd seen what was coming. Hedged a bit."

"I don't see how," she said. Bernie muttered what sounded to her like agreement. "What will you do now?"

"I don't know." He looked up and stared at the ceiling.

"Has this been decided for sure?" she asked.

"No. It was just a discussion. We didn't vote on it. But I see the way it's going."

"Then keep it to yourself," she said. "Maybe you can change their minds. This thing with Mayor Tifton. Maybe the chief can solve it. He'll look so great, it will turn the others around."

"That's a strange one," he said. "It makes my skin crawl. For someone to just walk in on you like that..." He gave an involuntary shudder.

"Perhaps you're right," he said. "But I don't like carrying this around with me. As chair of the public safety committee, I meet with Karol twice a week. I don't think I can look him in the eye."

"You will," she said, "because you have to."

Novak climbed the steps to Bridey O'Conner's house, hoping her father was home and she was still at church. For once, he was in luck. Thomas Walsh answered the door wearing blue dungarees, a long sleeve Steelers T-shirt, and black sneakers. He expressed no surprise on seeing the chief at his door but said, "I'm about to leave for work."

"You'll have to wait, Tom," Novak said.

Wearing a look of defeat, Walsh backed into the house, his shoulders bent over as they had been when Novak first interviewed him at the SCI Greene prison facility. He collapsed into a seat at the dining room table. Novak stood over him, "You know why I'm here, Tom." He made it as a statement rather than a question. Walsh stared at his hands without speaking. "You lied to me yesterday. You must have known I'd check your story."

"I didn't kill him," Walsh said. "I didn't go anywhere near his office. I haven't spoken to him since I got out. And I didn't lie."

"Your manager says you clocked out a bit after five."

"I said the store closes at nine. That's true. I told you they'd assigned me a double shift. That's also true. Things were slow, so they let me off early. I let you draw your own conclusions."

"You misled me," Novak said, amending his charge. "And you did so before I told you Tifton was dead. You already knew that, didn't you?"

"No," he said. "It was a complete surprise."

"And if you didn't exactly lie to me, you asked your manager to do so. You were covering your tracks. You went to Tifton's office to have it out with him, lost your temper, grabbed the nearest thing at hand, and killed him."

"I didn't. Do you think I'm that dumb?"

"For the last time, Tom, where were you between seven and eight-thirty on Friday night?"

"Promise you won't tell Bridey?"

"Tell me what, exactly?" his daughter said from the front door.

Walsh closed his eyes and shook his head. "What is it you don't want me to know, Dad? Did you have something to do with that man's death?"

Novak stepped back, figuring she might prove to be a better interrogator than he was at the moment.

"No," he said, his voice cracking.

"Then what?" she demanded.

"I promised you I wouldn't visit her again," he said.

Bridey knelt beside him and placed her hand on his knee. "Only because I see what it does to you. You know what Dr. Paulus said. You have to let it go."

"But it was her birthday," Walsh said, tears streaming down his cheeks. "I couldn't — I had to visit. Had to be with her."

Bridey looked up at Novak. "He visits her grave site. He used to spend all his waking hours there, except for work. The times I had to go out there to make him come home." She shook her head. "He worried me sick. I thought he might...." She left the sentence unfinished.

"Are you trying to tell me you sat by Becky's tombstone in the dark, with the temperature in the thirties?" Novak said. "I find it hard to believe."

"Believe it," Bridey said. "He's obsessed."

"I don't suppose there were any witnesses," Novak said. If this was an act, he thought, it deserved an Oscar.

"Of course not," he said. "But ... flowers. I bought flowers at Giant Eagle."

"Do you have the receipt?"

He shook his head. "I didn't want Bridey to find out, so I tore it up." Looking down at his daughter, he laid a hand on her head. "I'd promised I'd stay away. I'm sorry." He was blubbering now, his breath coming in quick gasps.

"Leave him alone," Bridey said, her voice dripping with venom.

Novak stared her down, enunciating each word. "This is a murder investigation. A man is dead. Someone killed him. No one had a better reason than your father. I did my job when I cleared him. I'm doing my job now."

Turning to the heaving shell of a man, he said, "I'm going to check out your story, Tom. If I find you've lied to me again, trust me, I will bring you in. Meanwhile, stop being a damn fool. You once confessed to a crime you didn't commit. Now you've misled me when you could have answered my simple question. You've involved your boss in this, and he isn't happy. I'm not sure you still have a job. Wise up."

He left before they could say another word, angry that the man he'd gone out on a limb to protect had failed to trust him.

———

Troy Stewart appeared at the front desk of ACPD headquarters at 12:45. Though this was fifteen minutes earlier than expected, Lydia Barnwell and Lyle Jeffrey were ready for him. "I have an open house at two," he said. "I want to make sure you had enough time."

He appeared to be in his late twenties, slender, just under six feet, with neatly combed dark brown hair, a studious expression, and a light blue sport coat that clung to his trim figure like a wrapper. "I wouldn't think this is a good weekend for selling houses," Lydia said as she ushered him down the hallway to Jeffrey's office.

"On the contrary," Stewart replied. "The market's hot. I send out email blasts to a list of potential buyers and those who've bought with me in the past. They often pass my listings on to others they know. You have to generate traffic, not wait for buyers to come to you."

Jeffrey rose to greet him as they entered the room, and the two detectives sat across from him at a small table. "Are you going to record this?" he asked.

"No," Jeffrey said. "It's informal. We could have spoken to you at the open house."

"Are you in the market?" the agent asked.

"Thankfully not," Jeffrey replied. "But since you asked why we're here, let me get one point out of the way. Where were you Friday night between seven and nine?"

Stewart flashed an amiable smile. "My wife and I have a six-month-old son. Our going-out days are over for a while. Yes," he said to Jeffrey's follow-up question, "I was home with my wife. I do the cooking in the house and the kitchen cleanup."

Why can't I meet a guy like this? Lydia thought. "How long did you work for Fred Tifton?" she asked.

"Three years. He gave me my start. I'll say that for him. But he changed. When I left a year and a half ago, he'd become a different person. "

"Why did you leave?" she asked.

"Opportunity," he said. "Fred runs a small agency that focuses only on Boyleston with a bit of attention to Crafton, Byers, and Allston. The Bradley Agency covers the entire county. It's a big operation with good IT support and a huge ad budget. I saw a chance to branch out."

"Don't you still operate mostly in Boyleston?" Jeffrey said.

"Brighten the corner where you are," he answered, and Lydia was surprised that a millennial would know the song her grandfather used to sing. "I have listings all over—Carnegie, Greentree, Bridgeville, Dormont—even one out in Mount Lebanon. But, yes, I know this area best, and Bradley's marketing clout allowed me to do better here than I did at Tifton's."

"He must have resented that," Jeffrey said.

"He wasn't happy." Stewart looked from one of them to the other. "I'm sure you've heard we didn't get along toward the end."

"Tell us about it."

The agent's story was similar to Evelyn Scowcroft's. Tifton had moved in on the sales end of one of Stewart's listings, insisting that the complexities of being on both sides of the transaction were beyond the younger man's capabilities. "I was angry," he said. "I'm not denying it. It was unfair, and I said so. He held firm, so I just took it. Something was better than nothing. And then I left. I'd dealt with one of Bradley's agents, and she'd recommended me to them."

He smiled and spread both hands out, speaking deliberately. "They gave me a draw. This is unheard of. This business operates on commissions, nothing more. But they gave me an advance against earnings—six months to build my book of business. Within three months, I'd earned it back and more," he proclaimed.

Jeffrey repeated his question. "How did Tifton take this?"

"He was angry, but what could he do?"

"You had words?"

Stewart gave a cunning smile. "He threatened to sue me for taking his agency's leads, claimed I was leaving with proprietary information." He snorted. "I told him I was taking nothing except the reputation I'd earned through fair dealing. As for suing me, I told him he'd acted unethically by cutting himself into my deal. I told him I could have taken him to the real estate commission if I wanted to. He tried to laugh at me, but I could tell I'd hit a target. Not that they would have done anything," he said, "but it wouldn't have helped his reputation."

The pair looked at him as though uncertain what to say next. He saved them the trouble. "You want to know if I had anything to do with his murder? No. I work sixty hours a week. I'm always on call. I work hard, but I'm doing better than I could have done if I'd stayed with him."

Turning from one to the other again, he said, "I don't watch the rearview mirror." He held his hand vertically against his forehead and pointed it forward. "I focus on the road ahead. Fred Tifton is part of my past. I have a wife and son to support, and I'm doing it."

"Still," Lydia said, "you were good enough to give Walter Dwyer a hand." When he shrugged in apparent confusion, she said, "You got him an interview with the Bradley Agency."

He frowned and looked off to the side. "When he learned I was leaving, Walt begged me to take him along. I didn't have the power to do that, and Walt—let's just say he's been doing things the Tifton way for too long. But he was pleading with me. God, it was sad. So I asked one of the Bradley secretaries to give him fifteen minutes. It didn't go well, of course. I had to tell him they couldn't find a spot for him. It crushed him. And things weren't about to get better for him where he was."

He seemed to consider it while they waited. "I feel sorry for the guy. I'd do anything to help him, but..." He held out both hands, palms up. "When you realize you're working for a dishonest man, you need to get out. Otherwise, you'll end up like he is."

After he left, Lydia revisited her earlier impression. No, she did not wish she could meet a guy like him. She had learned her lesson the hard way: don't get close to your witnesses or suspects. Troy Stewart might still be one of the latter.

———

THE WOMAN behind the flower center at Giant Eagle greeted Novak with a smile. "Hello, Chief. What's the occasion? Something for Barbara?"

"Not today, I'm afraid, Sonya. What I'm after is a bit of information. Were you here Friday evening?"

She admitted as much. Drawing Thomas Walsh's photo from his notebook, he asked if a man fitting this description had purchased flowers on Friday evening.

"That's Mr. Walsh, isn't it? Is he in trouble again?" Novak was reminded that Walsh was a local celebrity ... for all the wrong reasons. "Not that I'm aware of. I'm just trying to confirm something he's told me."

"This is about Mayor Tifton's murder, isn't it? Terrible thing. For something like that to happen right in our backyard...." She shuddered. "I hope Mr. Walsh wasn't involved."

"Did you see him Friday evening?" he asked.

"Yes. He called me in the afternoon, asked me to put together an arrangement of long-stem roses. I fixed him up a nice bouquet of pink ones. Like these," she said, pointing to a dozen from one of the many narrow containers behind her. "He came in about two hours later and picked them up. Paid in cash. So I guess that lets him off the hook, right?"

"Do you recall what time this was?"

She thought for a moment. "He had to wait for me to finish with Mrs. Samson. She was picking up a fall arrangement for Thanksgiving, but she didn't like what I'd selected. I had to redo the whole thing for her while he waited."

"Around five, would you say?" Novak prompted.

"No, it was one long arrangement in a canoe-shaped wicker basket she'd brought in three days before. I had to help carry it to her car."

"I'm asking what time you waited on Tom Walsh," he said, feeling as though he were a bit character in "Groundhog Day."

"Well, let's see now. I take a dinner break at 5:30 most nights, but Mrs. Samson took so long I was late by the time I got to Mr. Walsh. So let's say 5:40."

Novak asked her a few more questions, but she asked more than he did, and Novak deflected all of them. She told him Walsh had neither done nor said anything remarkable, but she added one detail. "He's in here at least once a month, always buying roses for someone. I don't know who they're for, but he must think a lot of her."

"He does," Novak said. He left the grocery store and drove to St. John's Cemetery, winding up the single-lane road that looped the hill past headstones and monuments until he reached the area where Becky Walsh lay buried. He pulled onto the grass, as other cars were forced to do, and made his way up the lawn until he reached the grave marked with the simple headstone:

REBECCA WALSH

1962-1989

BELOVED SISTER AND MOTHER

Becky's relatives had paid for this, and with her husband on trial for her murder, they'd blotted his memory from the marker. A dozen pink roses lay at its base, and the cold weather had preserved all but a scattering of petals blown off by the wind.

So Thomas had picked up flowers and brought them to the cemetery. But how long had he remained here in the night air? By eight o'clock, the temperature had dropped to thirty-six degrees.

Novak took one last look at the murdered woman's resting place, returned to his car, and drove the rest of the loop. He stopped at the small guardhouse at the entrance. He parked just beyond it, walked back, and approached the window, where the head of an older, bearded man lay buried in a book. Novak tapped at the window, and Chester Freeman jerked up as though shocked.

"Sorry, Chief. I didn't see you coming," he said.

"That's all right, Chet. Were you on duty Friday night?"

"Sure was. I do six nights a week here," the man said.

"What time did you close the gate Friday evening?" Novak asked.

"Five-thirty," he said. "This time of year, it's dark by then. We don't like teenagers coming in and parking, if you know what I mean. Worse are vandals turning over headstones or spray-painting monuments."

"So hat?" Novak asked.

"Not by driving in," he said.

"But someone could walk in?"

"Sure. We close the archway so cars can't get in, but the walkway's always open."

"On Friday night, did you notice anyone coming in?"

Freeman didn't stop to think about it. "Tom Walsh came in about six o'clock, his arms full of roses. He comes often, but it's usually earlier in the day. I was surprised to see him in this weather, but he said it would have been his wife's birthday, and he always visits on that day. Since he got out, of course."

Novak nodded. "And what time did he leave?"

The guard combed his beard with the fingers of his left hand while he thought about it. "I didn't see him leave."

"But he must have," Novak said. "It was cold out. He couldn't spend the night here."

"I had the heater on." Freeman pointed to a rotating space heater behind him, "and I was reading this book of mine. It's about Harry Truman. The Democratic convention picked him. Did you know that? Henry Wallace was vice president at the time, but delegates knew FDR was sick and a lot of folks hated Wallace, so...."

Novak nodded, thinking while the man gabbled. The guard was so engrossed in his book he'd paid little attention to who was going in

—Novak's taking him by surprise showed that—and none to who was leaving.

Tom Walsh had entered the cemetery to visit his wife's gravesite on the anniversary of her birth, but when he'd departed was anyone's guess. Novak wasn't convinced Walsh would have stood before the grave for two hours in the near-freezing temperature. Walsh had a motive and may well have had the opportunity. He hated to think he'd been mistaken about the man.

SERGEANT JEFFREY WELCOMED the Boyleston officers into a briefing room. Novak was surprised his detectives were still along for the ride. Only last spring, Jeffrey had rejected their efforts to help search for a missing three-year-old girl. Had his turnaround resulted from Novak and Barnwell giving him credit for solving the case?

As though reading his mind, Jeffrey said, "Where's Detective Barnwell this morning?"

"She'll be along," Mayfield answered. "She's checking something at the courthouse. I'll bring her up to date when she gets here."

"All right," Jeffrey said, but it was clear to Novak he was not okay with it. For the first time, Novak suspected the detective had another motive for involving her. He wondered if Lydia was aware of his interest in her. She'd never hinted at it, but even if Jeffrey hadn't asked her out, she didn't miss much. Novak didn't care, but he wanted nothing between them affecting her work or the relationship with the county.

Jeffrey had posted a photo of Fred Tifton on the corkboard lining one wall. Below it were photos of Benny Craddock, Troy Stewart, and Thomas Walsh placed slightly left of center, leaving ample room to the right. "The medical examiner says one of the two prongs of the sign penetrated Tifton's frontal lobe," he said. "The other prong punctured the duodenum. While that caused the heavy bleeding, it was the brain damage that killed him."

Despite his years of experience with gruesome murders, Novak winced as he pictured the scene.

"He'd just consumed half a box of Chinese takeout," Jeffrey continued. "Examination of stomach content narrows the time of death to between 8:00 and 8:30."

The officers scribbled in their notepads, aware that the narrowed timeframe might prove crucial as they interviewed suspects.

"We contacted Tifton's assistant, Amanda Naughton," Jeffrey said, "and she provided the computer's password. We Tifton had been listening to music at high volume because the speakers were still blaring when we arrived. The assistant says he was hard of hearing."

Novak, an assiduous note-taker because of memory issues still dogging him four years after his soccer injury, wrote this down and circled it.

"Tifton fell backward as he was attacked, striking his head on the edge of the file cabinet," he said. "He may have lost consciousness, though that's uncertain." Novak hoped that had been the case.

"From the angle of the sign and direction of the puncture wounds, the ME estimates the attacker was between five-eight and five-ten."

"Did the assailant intend to kill him?" Mayfield asked. "The sign doesn't seem like a natural weapon."

"It's not clear. The sign is heavy-grade plastic, and the framework is aluminum, so the whole thing weighs four pounds. Female agents handle them all the time. The blades are sharp to penetrate hard ground. When Tifton toppled over to ward off the attack, the killer may have stumbled over him and momentum took over, bringing the sign down with unintended force. It didn't take a powerful person to do this damage."

Jeffrey shrugged. "There's no point speculating about that. The district attorney determines the charges. Our job is to find out who did it."

"So we're looking for anyone of medium height?" Thurmond said.

"That's about the size of it." If Jeffrey was aware of the pun, he didn't acknowledge it. Turning to the photos, he said, "Which brings us to these three. Anyone who knew the layout of Tifton's office and saw his car parked in the driveway Friday evening had the means. All he had to do was come through the rear door, pick up the sign from the closet, and step into his office. As for motive, Tifton had cheated Troy Stewart out of part of his commission, but everyone tells us he'd gone on to bigger and better things."

"That was more than a year ago," Thurmond said. "Why would he wait so long to retaliate?"

"His wife confirms his alibi. Although," Jeffrey said with a smirk, "spouses have been known to lie." Thurmond snorted, acknowledging the sarcasm.

Turning to Craddock's photo, he said, "This fellow has a better motive. Tifton ruined his business. He has a record for assault, and he confronted Tifton at the office, so he knows the layout. He has motive and means, but if his wife is telling the truth, no opportunity."

Lydia Barnwell entered the room, carrying a manila envelope she placed before her. She sat at the table, huffing as though she'd been running. Jeffrey welcomed her and, displaying a rare deference. took two minutes summarizing what he'd shared with the others.

"Finally, we have Mr. Walsh," he said. "Tifton put him on death row, so he may have the strongest motive of the three. Chief, you checked him out."

"Yes," Novak said, "but I can't confirm his story." He recounted Walsh's late afternoon trip to Giant Eagle to pick up flowers for Becky's grave and the caretaker seeing him enter the cemetery after dark. "But he didn't see him leave. Now that we know Tifton was killed after eight, it makes his story less credible. Does a man stand at a gravesite in the frigid cold with the wind gusting to thirty mile-per-hour for two hours? On the other hand, Walsh claims he's never visited Tifton's office. So," he ticked off the three key elements on his fingers, "motive and opportunity, yes. Means, not so much."

Jeffrey smiled, "Tell them, sergeant."

"A quarter century ago," Bill Thurmond said, "Walsh provided the materials for the Tifton's office kitchen. This was before his wife's murder, so they were still close friends. He was on the site every morning and evening for a week, making certain the work was done well."

Novak exhaled as though he'd been punched. As bad as he felt poking holes in Walsh's alibi for Friday evening, this was worse.

"Before we get ahead of ourselves," Lydia Barnwell said, "there's something more you should hear." Removing the contents of the manila envelope, she passed them to Jeffrey. "As we know, Fred Tifton served as President of Boyleston Arms Homeowner's Association. A group of owners sued the board eight months ago, claiming Tifton had issued an assessment that fell disproportionately on those who'd owned their apartments the longest. They took him to court and, just last month, lost. You should read some of the language in their suit. They accuse him of misrepresentation, fraud, and breach of trust."

Jeffrey leafed through the lawsuit, turning to the summary judgment on the closing pages. "I gather you want to look into this," he said.

Lydia caught Novak's eye as he nodded. "We do," she said.

Jeffrey glanced around the table, taking in Novak and his detectives. "All right," he said. "You pursue that angle, but keep me informed."

"One more thing," Barnwell said. "Who owns the agency now that Tifton is gone?"

"I've called the attorney who handled his divorce," Jeffrey said. "I'll get back to you on that. Meanwhile, Chief, I'd ask your officers to help Detective Thurmond question these other suspects while I focus on Walsh."

He tapped the man's photo as he spoke. "I consider him our prime suspect."

———

Novak had just returned to headquarters and was pouring himself a cup of coffee when Norma Marks, his assistant, interrupted him. "Sheila Montgomery called from KDKA and wants to talk to you about Fred Tifton."

"County's in charge of the case," he replied. Novak avoided the news media. He was inarticulate in formal settings and, to his mind, appeared a bumbling fool when interviewed. "Refer her to Lyle Jeffrey."

"She knows that. She wants to know why he resigned two years ago."

The chief replaced the glass carafe on the warming pad as he weighed his response. While he was uncomfortable serving as a spokesman, neither did he want to be seen as concealing information from the public. Secrecy was necessary when you didn't want to a suspect to know how much they'd discovered.

Here, however, he had an out. "Refer her to Doug Lentz," he said, referring to the Boyleston council president.

He picked up his phone just as Mayfield entered his office. Novak motioned the deputy chief to sit as he dialed Lentz's extension. When he answered, Novak explained the reporter might call him and what she wanted. "If you can keep Tom Walsh's name out of it, please do," he said.

Mayfield watched as Lentz posed a question. "We're working with the county to question anyone who had grievances with Tifton. Walsh is among them, but given the publicity around his case, I want to avoid a rush to judgment."

That seemed to satisfy the council president. Novak hung up and gave Mayfield a slight shrug. "What do you think?" he asked.

"Jeffrey's put a target on Walsh's back," the deputy chief replied.

"Tom hasn't done himself any favors by misleading me about the time he left work," Novak said. "The man will never learn."

"Is he capable of doing it?" Mayfield asked.

"God, I hope not." Novak considered it for a moment while his deputy waited.

"He had reason, though why he'd wait so long after his release makes little sense. Perhaps some unknown event served as a trigger," he said. "While Jeffrey focuses on Walsh, he's given us free rein to interview everyone else. Perhaps this condo lawsuit will provide fresh leads."

His cell phone chimed, the call coming from the 304 area code. "I have to answer this," he told Mayfield. Taking the hint, the deputy rose and left the office, closing the door behind him.

"This Don Nelson ... from Wheeling PD," the voice added.

"Yes, Captain. I remember you. It hasn't been that long." Although the sixty hours since they'd met seemed longer to Novak.

The West Virginia police officer chuckled. "I spent some time on my own yesterday looking into that old row house you'd staked out. A congregation of Catholic priests owns it. They claim it's a treatment center for those with troubles such as alcoholism, but it seems more like a boarding house. A couple of registered sex offenders live there, so our social service people are familiar with it. There are five priests in all. They live together and care for the place, doing their own cooking and cleaning."

Novak's pulse quickened, and he leaned forward in his chair as though drawing closer to the conversation.

"But here's the thing," the captain said. "One brother says your man, this Timothy Dacey, is no longer there. He moved in three years ago but left in mid-May. So whoever you saw that night and tried to follow, it wasn't your priest."

"Damn!" Novak didn't hide his disappointment. "Mid-May, you say. Can you pin it down a bit?"

"The brother wasn't forthcoming, and I had to press him a bit. He says Dacey left a week before Memorial Day. The move was sudden—I gather Dacey was their unacknowledged leader—and he couldn't tell me where the man went. Or wouldn't," Nelson amended.

"How did he leave?" Novak asked. "Did he own a car, or did he take a bus?"

"A woman came to collect him. Dacey received a call one morning and began packing. He gave no explanation, at least according to this priest. An older woman with gray hair pulled up in mid-afternoon. He didn't notice her license plate, couldn't give me a better description of the woman, and claims not to know who she was. Dacey threw his things into the trunk, told the brothers goodbye, and left without an explanation."

Novak thanked Nelson and disconnected. He leaned back in his chair, his hands locked behind his neck, and thought about what he'd just learned. In early April, he'd done Father Murray a favor. Weeks later, a letter bearing no return address arrived at his home. Inside was a single sheet of paper, unsigned, bearing the address of the Wheeling row house. Although he'd never asked Father Murray whether he'd sent it, Novak believed he was the source. A few weeks later, the predator priest received a phone call in the morning and left the "treatment center" that afternoon with a mystery woman.

Novak didn't believe in coincidences. Someone had alerted the priest Novak was after him. Had Father Murray done so? Novak found it hard to believe. Had Murray requested information from someone at the diocese who alerted Dacey? That was a possibility, but one he'd never be able to explore, such was the wall of secrecy surrounding the church's administration.

Novak's frustration that the man had escaped was tinged with a trace of satisfaction. Dacey was frightened by what Novak might do to him. He'd gotten under the man's skin.

Barnwell and Horvath arrived at Boyleston Arms without calling first. The front door was open, but the entrance to the ground floor hallway was locked. Barnwell ran her finger down the list of residents on the wall opposite a row of mailboxes, pausing at the names Jason and Catherine Lindsell in 5 1 3. Rather than calling them on the house phone, however, she continued until she found a number for the management office. She dialed that extension and waited for over thirty seconds before a woman's voice answered. "Police," Barnwell said. "Please let us in."

"What's this about?" the voice asked.

Barnwell gave an exasperated snort and turned to Horvath. "Police business," he barked.

The woman told them to wait a moment. What else were they to do? Minutes later, she shuffled to the door in house slippers. She was short and round and looked up at them with suspicion. "What do you want?" she asked.

The detectives flashed their credentials and moved past her to the elevator just beyond the door. "Let's go up a floor and walk down," Horvath said. Barnwell chuckled and pressed the button for the sixth floor. The elevator rocked as it ascended. Barnwell wondered when it had last been inspected. She gave a sigh of release when the doors opened. They walked to the end of the hallway, passed through the metal door under the exit sign, and took the flight of stairs to the fifth floor.

Barnwell led her partner up the hallway, which smelled of fresh paint and new carpeting. "Not bad," she said as she reached the seventh door on the right-hand side. She rang the bell and was surprised when the door opened almost immediately.

"Maisie said you were on your way up," the man said. He appeared to be in his seventies but had a trim, athletic build, and a full head of sandy hair that was turning white. He smiled at them, and the skin around his light brown eyes crinkled. "I've been expecting you."

Barnwell introduced the two of them, and Jason Lindsell ushered them in, directing them to a sofa beneath a large painting of what looked like an Italian coastal town. A woman entered the room, about the same age as the man but looking younger. She, too, had a trim figure, toned, Barnwell assumed, by a regular exercise regimen. "Can I get you anything to drink? Ice tea? Sparkling water?"

Both turned down the offer. Lindsell introduced himself and his wife, Catherine, and they took seats in matching, floral-colored, armless chairs. "I'm sure you've come about our suit against the association. This started about eighteen months ago. No, let me back up. Tifton bought his unit here about two years ago."

"Two years and two months," his wife said.

Lindsell nodded. "We heard his wife divorced him and got the house," he said. "He bought a unit on the eighth floor—the building is ten stories high—with a pleasant view of the valley. Tifton did some remodeling, then moved in and made himself at home. He wasn't friendly. Didn't get to know people, but he was quiet and didn't cause any trouble."

Lydia recalled the real estate agent, Evelyn Scowcroft, describing the change in Tifton's personality after losing his wife and his office as mayor. "But then?" she prompted.

"He bought another unit and then a third," Lindsell said. "He rented them out without getting permission from the council."

"Why would he need permission?" Horvath said.

"Our bylaws state only ten percent of units can be used as rental property. When Tifton rented his second unit, we hit the 10 percent mark."

"Actually, a bit above that," Catherine Lindsell said. "Ten-point-two."

"So the third unit put him over the limit?" Linda said.

"Right. When the council called him on it, he claimed the bylaws had no provision for determining how to resolve disputes over the ten percent figure," he said.

"He challenged the whole limit," his wife explained. "Who was the council to tell him he couldn't rent out his unit when Joe Blow could? He claimed that, as a homeowner, he had as much right to rent as anyone else."

"He had the council over a barrel there," her husband continued. "We had this rule, but there was no 'or else,' if you get what I mean. We had no mechanism for dealing with this, so the council let it go."

"Most residents weren't aware of this," Catherine continued. "In our association, about a third do all the work, and another third criticize how they're doing it. The rest pay no attention. They don't attend meetings and don't vote for the board. They just go about their business. Tifton was so sly about his campaign, he pulled it off before we knew what was happening."

"Pulled what off?" Lydia said, the first time she'd had to pose a question in five minutes.

"Staged the coup," Jason said. The expressions of the two detectives conveyed their bewilderment. "He took over the board. You should talk to Bryce Combs about this. He was council president, but Tifton and two others got elected to the board, forming a majority. They ousted Bryce and made Tifton president. The next thing we knew, he'd changed management companies."

"With his own," Catherine said.

"Yes, we didn't learn that until later," Jason said. "We just got an email stating our old managers were out and a new one was coming in. It turned out Tifton had set up that company and granted himself a big contract."

"Is that why you sued him?" Horvath asked.

"Technically, we sued the association," he said, "but we also sued him. The self-dealing was only part of our case. The other was the assessments."

Batting the story back and forth, the two described how Tifton and has council majority had hired an outside firm to conduct a property assessment. It revealed many deferred maintenance issues, ranging from new rooftop air conditioners to overhauling the elevators, repairing a crack in the indoor swimming pool that threatened to become a gaping leak to new hallway carpeting.

"The cost was way above what our monthly dues can cover," he said, "so the report recommended a special assessment. But they proposed a higher amount than what the council could issue on its own."

He explained that the association's bylaws limited an assessment to six times the monthly dues. Anything greater required an affirmative vote by two-thirds of the homeowners. "There was no way enough of us would vote for that," Lindsell said, "so the council issued one assessment at the limit of what they could charge, then followed it six months later with another. They were about to issue a third when our group sued, arguing the council had exceeded its authority."

"Dues and assessments are based on the size of your unit," Catherine said. "Those with two bedrooms pay less than those in three-bedroom apartments. That's only fair, and we understand that when we bought in. But Tifton found a provision hidden in the bylaws. Where the assessment resulted from deferred maintenance, the council could also base its assessment on years of occupancy."

"The idea," her husband said, "was that more recent owners shouldn't have to pay for issues caused by the neglect of those who'd lived here longer."

"I've never heard of a rule like that," Horvath said.

"Neither had we, but it was a seven-word clause in the bylaws," Catherine said. "It had never been applied, so most people didn't even know it was there. Tifton discovered it and turned it against us."

Barnwell chuckled. "Tifton was a new owner, and I suppose his two fellow council members were, too."

"You've got it," Jason said. "He tiered the assessment so most owners got off fairly light while those of us who'd been here longest, particularly those in larger units, were hit hard. We're talking tens of thousands of dollars. When he ganged up on us, we went to court to stop him."

"And?" Lydia said.

The pair looked at each other, and Catherine let out a derisive puff. "We lost," Jason said. "The judge said the fact previous boards hadn't invoked this language in the past made no difference. The bylaws allowed it, and that was that."

"We're going to sell," his wife said.

"Which is too bad," her husband continued, "because this is a desirable location."

Lydia asked where they had been between eight and nine on Friday night. "We were at a Steely Dan concert at the Benedum," he said. Catherine got up, returned with her purse, and flashed her ticket stub.

"I've tossed mine," Lindsell said, "but we went together." He escorted the detectives to the door. "Talk to Bryce. He can tell you how Tifton pulled this off."

Barbara Novak strolled through the hallway of Washington Middle School, greeting students as she made her rounds. Girls returned her smiles, but most of the boys ignored her. She wondered if they would react differently if she were a man. She'd have to ask one of the male principals.

"Mrs. Novak?" She turned to see Marcie Liebowitz, an eighth grader, calling to her in a soft voice from the alcove of a classroom door. "Yes, Marcie."

"May I come speak to you sometime? It's—" She looked around as though fearing she'd be overheard. "It's a personal matter."

"What is your next class?" Barbara asked. When the girl told her it was phys ed, she decided skipping part of the class wouldn't seriously curtail Marcie's prospects of getting into college. She turned toward her office with the girl trailing behind as though she didn't care to be seen with her, piquing Barbara's curiosity. Marcie came from a solid family. Her father was an attorney in the public defender's office, and her mother was the cantor at the synagogue in nearby Dormont. Barbara couldn't imagine what personal matter she couldn't discuss with her parents.

She entered her office, standing aside until Marcie entered, then closed the door. The girl smoothed her skirt and took a seat, then stared at Barbara for a moment as though waiting for her to begin the conversation. "What concerns you?" she asked.

"Can I keep this between us?" Marcie asked. "Where you got it, I mean."

"Of course." The girl drew a deep breath and hesitated.

"You can tell me anything," Barbara said. "I sense this is something I should know."

The girl nodded her head. "The boys—many of them are being nasty."

This was hardly breaking news. "In what way?" she asked.

"They tell some of us we're making them strike noon. Paul says it to Cindy all the time, and it embarrasses her."

"Strike noon?" Barbara asked.

"From Romeo and Juliet," Marcie said. "It's the scene between the nurse and Mercutio."

"I remember," Barbara said, though she only vaguely recalled the scene. "I'm sorry, Marcie, what does it mean?"

"That his ... thing...is, you know?"

Barbara was getting the picture. "Is this just one or two boys?" she asked.

"No, it's like the entire class."

Barbara sighed, knowing the answer to her question before she posed it. "And what class is this?"

"I don't want to get anyone in trouble," the girl said.

She couldn't tell her that wouldn't happen, for it wouldn't be true. How to get the rest of the story out of her? "Is this an English class?" she asked.

"No, ma'am."

"Math?" The girl shook her head. "Science?" Now she looked down without responding.

"Thank you, Marcie. You didn't tell me, did you?" The girl again shook her head without speaking. "I'll keep you out of this. In return, I ask you not to tell Cindy or any of the other girls you've mentioned this to me. Let's keep it between us, okay?"

"Yes. Thank you," she said. "Can I ask one other thing, Mrs. Novak?"

"Of course."

"May I have a pass to get back into class?"

Barbara smiled, entered Marcie's name on the form, and signed her name. After the girl had left, she opened her computer and Googled the play.

"God ye good morrow, gentlemen," the nurse said.

To which Mercutio replied, "God ye good e'en, fair gentlewoman."

"Is it good e'en?" the nurse asked.

"'Tis no less," Mercutio answered, "I tell you, for the bawdy hand of the dial is now upon the prick of noon."

Barnwell and Mayfield knocked at Bryce Combs' door but got no answer. The woman in the management office who'd tried to block their way into the building placed a phone call. She reported that the former association president was working at his accounting office in Dormont and would speak with them there. Fifteen minutes later, they pulled into a small parking lot beside a three-story yellow brick building whose facade held the inlay, *Brockert Bldg., 1925.* Combs's office was on the top floor of the walkup. Lydia took the stairs two at a time, with Mayfield trailing behind her.

She paused before a wooden door halfway down the hall whose frosted glass panel carried the words *Bryce Combs, Accountant* in gold lettering outlined in black. As she knocked, a voice from inside called, "C'mon in." The pair entered and found a short, older man sitting at an L-shaped desk with two chairs before it. "I'd get up and open the door, but my knees take a beating from climbing those stairs," he said. "I'll have to pack it in before long."

"Or get a first-floor office," Mayfield said.

"Can't afford it. I'm down to five clients, plus I do some individual returns come tax time." Combs explained he'd set up this practice to give him something to do after retiring from a major accounting firm in the downtown district. He still handled the books for two consultants and three retail stores in Dormont. "But you didn't come to hear about that," he said. "You've come about Tifton's murder."

"How well did you know him?" Barnwell asked.

"Not at all. That was the strange thing about all this. He moved in, kept to himself, never came to council meetings or the few social events we have. Next thing I knew, he'd formed this little group via email, sending out all sorts of accusations against me and other board members."

"Accusations?" Mayfield said.

"You have to understand this building is fifty years old. It started off as an apartment complex, but the original owners converted it to condominiums five years into its life. There was no reserve fund or anything like that."

He seemed to look into the distance for a moment. "After all those years, we had a lot of deferred maintenance. When I came on the board, we hired a firm out of Cleveland to do what's called a reserve study. They evaluated the condition of the building from the roofs down to the garage. They told us what we needed to do to catch up, so we raised the dues and were making improvements."

"I thought Tifton did a reserve study," Barnwell said.

"I'll get to it," he said, holding up both palms as though to stop her questions. "We were on track, doing a bit each year. On a building this old, though, new problems crop up quicker than we can fix the old ones. Tifton decides we're not doing things fast enough. He gets some of the newer owners together and begins agitating. One owner sent me a couple of his emails. It was nasty stuff."

Barnwell asked for specifics, and Combs opened his email and, after a brief search, began reading. "The value of your unit is declining while surrounding property increases," he read. "The present council is responsible for this. The president has allowed your property to deteriorate because he can't afford to pay an assessment. His management company is holding off repairs to keep costs down while this building decays."

"It got personal," Barnwell said.

"Worse than that," he replied. "He started a whispering campaign saying I was getting a cut of money from the cleaning staff."

"Did you take him to court?" Mayfield asked.

"No, because he never wrote this down. It was word-of-mouth. Three of the five council members were up for reelection that fall. Two couldn't take the abuse and dropped out. One of them was so disgusted he sold his place and moved."

Combs grew still for a moment, avoiding their gaze. He clenched his teeth and straightened a paper clip. "Board service is a volunteer position," he said. "It takes time and effort, and who needs to be treated that way?"

Mayfield shook his head to show he understood.

"Tifton and two of his cohorts swept into office, giving them a majority of the five-member board," Combs said. "They elected him president."

Tifton replaced the management company with a firm no one had heard of, he told them. "I looked into it and learned it was a company he'd set up to maintain other properties he manages. He was lining his pocket, the very thing he'd accused me of doing. Then the assessments began."

He repeated what the Lindsells had told them. Tifton and his hand-picked board members issued a series of assessments to get around the provision in the bylaws limiting a single levy. "And they found a provision that put most of the burden on the longest-tenured residents," Combs said. "A group of them sued the association, but Tifton knew both Pennsylvania's real estate and condominium laws, so they lost." He almost spat the final few words.

"There was no love lost between you and Tifton," Mayfield said.

"No. I hated the man. But I wouldn't hurt anyone, not physically. I was waiting for my opportunity to sue him for something. I admit I wanted to ruin the man. But kill him? Not me. And if you don't believe me, I have three bowling buddies who can tell you where I was and what I was doing Friday night. I scored 194 that night. Haven't done that well in years."

———

George Rollins poked his head through Barbara's door as soon as classes were dismissed for the day. "You asked for me?"

"Yes," she said. "Close the door and take a seat."

The science teacher did as he was told and folded his lanky frame into one of her guest chairs. He flashed a broad grin, which she did not return. "I understand we're teaching Shakespeare in science class now."

The grin relaxed a bit, but didn't leave his face. "Shakespeare?" he said.

"Romeo and Juliet," she replied.

He turned his head from one side to the other. "I'm not sure what you're—"

"The scene where Mercutio informs the nurse that his dial has arisen."

"Oh," he said, forcing a laugh. "Who told you about that?"

"More to the point," she said, "why is a science teacher teaching Shakespeare to his class?"

Rollins chuckled. "It came up in the context of whether Romeo and Juliet's deaths could have been prevented. I like to bring many examples into my teaching. Isn't that what education is all about? I'm a big Shakespeare fan."

Barbara picked up a pen and twirled it as she spoke. "The context, I'm told, was specifically about Shakespeare's use of a rising dial as a metaphor for male arousal. 'Upon the prick of noon,' as he put it."

"Did some kids take it that way?" he asked, feigning innocence.

"They took what you offered them and ran with it," Barbara said. "At least, the boys did."

"One of them must have offended someone. Give me her name, and I'll apologize."

"I've spoken to you before, George, about making comments designed to—" She stopped herself on the verge of saying titillate, not wanting to give him an opening. "Designed to be provocative. These youngsters have enough hormones coursing through their systems without an adult leader encouraging them. It is not all right for you to use your position to spread off-color remarks. Is that clear?"

"I was only—"

"Have I made myself clear, George?"

"Yeah," he said, "okay."

"That's all," she said. But as Rollins rose to leave, she couldn't resist one last shot. "Since you're so enamored of Shakespeare's plays, can you tell me why he called his comedy 'Twelfth Night?'"

He looked back at her in confusion. "I'm afraid I don't know."

"I thought not."

Novak often worked until the dinner hour, but this afternoon he took off early, kissing his mother as she sat in the family room before the TV, watching a game show on a cable channel. Despite the gas log in the fireplace going full blast, she'd draped an Afghan—or "African," as she called it—over her legs. "*Ahoj mami,*" he said in Slovakian.

She held his hand for a moment and smiled at him, then returned her attention to the screen. He left her and opened a can of carbonated water, descending to the finished basement one step at a time while holding onto the wooden handrail. He often felt a rush of vertigo as he descended stairways, one aftereffect of his concussion a few years before. Knowing he couldn't afford a fall, he'd learned to take special precautions.

He turned on his computer and opened the internet browser. He could have done this at work, but never used department resources for personal business. Taking a swallow from the open can, he typed "Timothy Dacey" into the search box. He came up with an attorney, a professor, a major general, an actor, and several others, but no sign of the priest. "Father Dacey" produced a Catholic priest with another first name who was much older than the man for whom he was hunting. Below that, a link to the Pennsylvania Grand Jury report on the sex scandal within the Catholic Church. A bit more exploring produced links to stories about Dacey's ordination and his assignment to various parishes in and around the Pittsburgh area. A photo showed Father Tim standing behind a group of youngsters dressed in baseball uniforms. The caption identified him as the coach.

Novak bookmarked each link and read the descriptions. He slowly pieced together the man's career, his graduation from college seminary in 1969, theological seminary and ordination in 1973, and the string of parishes he had served. He entered each description and date into a spreadsheet, then studied the result. Dacey's career in Western Pennsylvania was documented through 2005, then another eight years in West Virginia when he seemed to disappear. That, Novak assumed, was when one diocese had finally had enough.

What was missing was information about his life before that. No mention of parents or siblings. Rereading the story of his ordination, Novak found a reference to his graduation from St. Francis High School in Johnstown. Novak searched for the school and learned it had closed in 2011.

He finished his drink and crushed the can in his fist. Captain

Nelson had told him an unidentified older woman had come to the Wheeling facility in mid-May, just weeks after Novak had received the anonymous note with Dacey's address. She'd arrived on short notice, taking the disgraced priest and his handful of belongings with her. Who was she? An old friend, parishioner, or relative? And where had she taken him? He had to find her and, through her, Dacey.

The back door opened and closed above him, followed by Barbara's voice ringing out. "I'm down here," he called over the din of the TV.

She bounced down the stairs and gave him a hug. "What are you up to?" she said.

He told her about Captain Nelson's call that morning and described the fruitless results of his online search. "I don't know how to reach his fellow seminarians, and his high school closed years ago. Another dead end."

Barbara placed her hands on the back of his neck and massaged him. "Buy the yearbook," she said.

"From whom?" he asked.

"Go online, type in the school's name and the word 'yearbook.'"

He did as she suggested and was presented with a site offering original and reproduced copies of the St. Francis High School 1965 yearbook. He ordered a copy and paid extra to have it shipped via express mail. "You're brilliant," he said.

"I know," she giggled as she headed up the stairs to start dinner.

Lydia Barnwell answered the door at the first knock, stepped aside, and allowed David Kimrey to enter the apartment they'd shared until she'd thrown him out the previous April. "Thank you for seeing me," he said.

"You were pretty insistent," she said, her arms folded. "I didn't feel I had a choice."

"I'm sorry I came over that way. I offered to meet somewhere for coffee."

"You're here now," she said.

He straddled a stool at the kitchen counter while she stood on the other side. "I don't know where to start," he said.

"At the beginning," she answered.

Kimrey scratched his neck while looking down. "I want to apologize," he said, his voice shaking. "I behaved like a jerk. When you got promoted over me, I just—I guess I lost perspective."

Placing both hands on her side of the counter, she leaned toward him. "I was not promoted *over* you, David. I was promoted. Period. It had nothing to do with you."

"I know," he said. He exhaled and looked off to the side. "It's difficult for a man to live with a woman who outdoes him."

Lydia opened her mouth to speak but stopped. Telling him to get used to it wasn't constructive.

"I've come to apologize. That's all," David said.

That was not all, she suspected, but to forestall further conversation, she said, "Apology accepted."

"Is there any chance we could—"

"No, David. And don't take it personally. I don't have anyone else in my life right now, but when I do, it won't be another cop. I've decided that."

"We had a great time together in our good days," he said.

"We did, but there were too few 'good days,'" she replied.

"Mayfield trusts me again. It's taken me months to earn his respect. He has me partnering with Chastain."

"I know. I'm proud of you," she said.

"I'd studying for the detective's exam."

"Good for you." Once more, she bit her tongue, doubting any opening was imminent on the Boyleston force. Perhaps he'd apply elsewhere. That might be best. "I know you'll do well," she said.

"I miss you." His face took on a pleading look, and his voice cracked. "I love you."

"David, please don't say that. I respect you. I like you as a friend. But I will not resume our relationship." Lowering both hands to the left as though placing something on the counter, she said, "This is my work life. And this," she added as she shifted her hands to the right, "is my personal life. I'm keeping them separate from now on."

He shrugged as though admitting defeat and uncoiled himself from the barstool. "One hug for old times' sake?"

"No," she said. "I'm sorry, David, but I want nothing physical between us. It's over."

He left without saying goodbye looking, she thought, like a little boy whose puppy had died.

DISREGARDING BARBARA'S DIETARY RESTRICTIONS, Novak brought a box of doughnuts to headquarters. His team straggled in over the next quarter hour, gathering in the chief's crowded office. Detective Barnwell and Deputy Chief Mayfield took the two seats before the chief's desk while Gordon Horvath, the last to arrive, went in search of a vacant chair from the bullpen.

While they waited for the detective, Lydia looked over the awards displayed on Novak's bookcase. The man had spent over thirty years with the Pittsburgh Police Bureau, first as a patrol officer, then a detective, before rising to chief of detectives. Her eyes fell on two framed photographs in the bookcase behind Novak's right shoulder. While photos of his wife, daughter, and granddaughter sat to his left, these two had always intrigued her. One was of Petr Čech, a goalkeeper in the English Premier League, who, she'd learned, had suffered the same traumatic brain injury that had forced Novak's retirement from the Pittsburgh force. The other was an aging photograph of a young man who looked nothing like Novak. "A boyhood friend," he'd explained when she asked. "He's gone now." Something in his tone warned her not to pursue the matter.

Horvath wheeled in a chair that creaked as he deposited his bulk into it. "Let's take stock," Novak said, moving to a corkboard he'd also dragged from the bullpen. It mirrored the version Detective Sergeant Jeffrey had assembled at the county. A photo of the victim, Fred Tifton, was pinned to the top with photos of suspects or, in their absence, index cards bearing their names.

"Jason Lindell," he said, turning to Barnwell for an update.

She recounted their interview with the condominium owners who'd sued Tifton. "The homeowners lost," she said, "and had to pay attorney's fees. He and his wife are bitter but say they were at a concert the night Tifton was murdered."

"More interesting," Horvath said while Mayfield scribbled on cards and pinned them under Lindsell's name on the board, "is how Tifton schemed to take over the board. The former president, Bryce Combs, says no one had ever mounted a political campaign for the council. The council members were taken aback."

"Motive?" Novak asked.

"I don't sense the loss angered him as much as Tifton's personal attacks, setting neighbor against neighbor," Barnwell said. "One board member got so upset he sold his unit and moved out. Combs admits he hated Tifton but claims he went bowling with friends."

"Let's check that out," Novak said. "We need to confirm everything we're told. Next is the contractor, Benny Craddock."

"He's a piece of work," Horvath said. "Craddock was in charge of maintenance at Boyleston Arms for years. When his contract came up for renewal, Tifton cut him off without notice, destroying his business. They had words at his office a few weeks ago. One of his agents overheard it. But Craddock claims he was home watching TV the night of the murder and that his wife can vouch for him."

"Tifton formed a separate corporation and gave himself the contract to manage the condo," Barnwell said. "Other homeowners didn't know it at first, but Jason Lindsell got the records from the secretary of state. His management firm then hired another company to perform maintenance. That was also a Tifton shell corporation."

"A real wheeler-dealer," Mayfield said. "We found correspondence in his file cabinet with other HOAs. He was trying to parlay the Boyleston Arms coup into a major association management firm."

"The Lindsell's lawsuit was a matter of public record," Barnwell said. "No HOA was likely to retain him with that going on."

"We need to confirm the Lindsell's alibis," Novak said. "And Bryce Combs's as well. Something about these business dealings smells."

Something in the chief's intensity made Lydia wonder whether the chief was searching for something to clear Thomas Walsh. "This brings us to Troy Stewart, Tifton's former real estate agent and rising star," she said. "Tifton cheated him out of part of a commission he'd earned. But he's turned lemons into lemonade. He lands most of the local listings. If he were going to attack Tifton, he would have done so a year ago, so I don't see he has much of a motive. His alibi is weak, though. He was home with his wife and infant son."

"Let's do what we can to check it out," Novak said as Mayfield continued to post notes on the board. "Finally, we have Thomas Walsh. He has a powerful motive; Tifton lied to protect his reputation, sending Walsh to death row for a crime he didn't commit. His alibi is weak, and he lied to me and asked his manager to cover for him."

Novak paused and wrote himself a note. Had Walsh lost his job at Busy Builder? He'd check.

"Jeffrey is focused on him. We can't place him at Tifton's office, but he worked for him years ago, so he knows the place." Novak raised his eyebrows as a thought occurred to him. "Have Lindsell and Combs ever been there?"

Barnwell and Horvath looked at each other. "You forgot to ask," Novak said. "Okay, follow up on that. Let's check every one of these alibis. We need to make sure these people were where they say they were on Friday night."

"You're worried about Walsh," Barnwell said, putting her suspicions on the table.

Novak ran both hands through his graying hair. "Yes, but I'm not going out on a limb for him. I keep thinking he wouldn't be that stupid, but he proved me wrong by lying to me."

The three rose to leave as Norma Marks rapped at the door. "There's a Walter Dwyer on the phone for you, Lydia. He says it's important."

"Everyone stay put," Novak said. He picked up the phone and turned on the speaker.

"This is Detective Barnwell," she said. "I'm in a conference with my chief and fellow detectives. What do you have to tell us?"

"You asked if Fred had any enemies," he said. "I don't know how important this is, but a couple of months ago, another fellow came in and had words with him. I couldn't remember his name, so I went through our files and found it. Louis Callon." He spelled it out for them. "French Canadian fellow, I think. Fred sold him a house here in Boyleston, and there was some sort of problem. Plumbing, electrical, structural? I don't know. But he was convinced Fred knew about it when he sold it to him. He was boiling when he came in."

"Did he threaten him?"

"I don't know. I just heard them yelling behind the closed door. When he came out, he said, 'You're a cheat and a liar. I'll make sure everyone knows it.' I asked Fred what it was all about, and he said there was a problem with the house, and he thought Tifton should have disclosed it."

Lydia asked for the man's address and phone number and thanked Dwyer for the information. "Calvin, I'd like you to handle this one," Novak said, "while Lydia and Gordon check these other alibis."

BARNWELL STUDIED the list of suspects, deciding where to begin. Bryce Combs claimed he'd been bowling at the time of the murder. She doubted the alley would be open until later in the morning. She was about to move on to Bennie Craddock when Norma Marks told her Detective Jeffrey was on the line. "Yesterday, you asked a question I should have asked myself: Who inherits Tifton's agency?"

In other words, who benefits from his death? she thought. *It's the first question I would have asked.*

"The answer is, we don't know," he said.

She asked him to hold on for a minute, returned to Novak's office, and put him on speakerphone, wondering as she did so why he had called her rather than the chief.

"I contacted his attorney, the one who handled his divorce," Jeffrey told them. "It turns out he died intestate. Tifton had no will when he was married. Under Pennsylvania law, everything would have gone to his wife when he died, so he didn't bother. Once he divorced, his attorney urged him to take care of it. Tifton kept putting him off."

"Why would he be so stupid?" Barnwell asked. "Even I have one. He owned three businesses. You don't leave something like that to chance."

Novak couldn't answer her question, but posed one of his own. "What happens now?"

"Under terms of the divorce, his ex-wife has no standing," Jeffrey said. "The estate would pass to his children, but a drunk driver killed Tifton's only son three years ago; he was single and left no heirs. Tifton's parents would be next in line, but they're both gone. Then his siblings, but his sister died years ago. The attorney is checking to see if she had any children."

"It sounds like the lawyer is the only winner here," Novak said.

"I'm sure you're right," Jeffrey said as Barnwell chuckled, sharing Novak's cynicism. "Lots of billable hours will come out of the estate. And it may still be unclear who inherits. If they find no aunts, uncles, or cousins, the estate passes to the commonwealth."

"Meanwhile," Barnwell said, "who's running things?"

"There are just the two agents left," Jeffrey said. "They're classified as independent contractors, so they appear to be acting on their own. How long that can last is anyone's guess."

They thanked Jeffrey and ended the call. "What a mess," she said.

THE DISPATCHER ALERTED Officers Kimrey and Chastain as they patrolled the borough. "A caller reports a domestic disturbance at 625 Barker Street. A subject is armed and has hostages inside."

Kimrey acknowledged the message and directed Chastain toward the side street where the incident was underway. Neighbors had gathered across from Brock Gifford's house, some with arms folded, two with cell phones trained on the porch.

As the officers emerged from the cruiser, an older man approached. "Be careful," he said. "He has PTSD. Afghanistan. Nice enough most of the time, but when it kicks in...." He finished with an upward motion of his hands and a whooshing sound.

Kimrey knew all this but let him speak, hoping he'd shed light on what was happening inside the house. "Did you call it in?" Chastain asked.

"No. Ruth over there did." He pointed to a middle-aged woman standing nearby, kneading her hands. "She heard the yelling and two shots. That's when we all came out."

"You need to go back inside," Kimrey said. "We don't want him using you for target practice."

As Chastain moved the crowd away, Kimrey spoke to the woman who'd placed the call. "Ruth Sawyer," she said in response to his question. "He's in the house with his wife and two kids. I've begged her to move out."

Kimrey had done the same sixty hours earlier. "Has he hurt anyone?" he asked.

"I don't think so. The two shots I heard, I think he was firing into the air. But I can't be sure. He has these spells when he thinks people are trying to kill him," she said. "He goes berserk."

Kimrey asked a few more questions, but the woman had told him all she knew.

"We should call in the county," Chastain said.

"You're right, but he knows me. I'll try speaking with him first."

"Shouldn't we call the SWAT team?" Chastain asked.

Kimrey shook his head. "I don't want to escalate things. I'll try reasoning with him the way I did Friday night."

"Let's at least suit up," Chastain replied.

This time, the rookie cop won the day. The pair returned to the cruiser and donned bulletproof vest armor.

"Keep your weapons holstered," Kimrey instructed. "I'm just talking to the guy."

"Aren't we supposed to—?"

Kimrey ignored him, walked toward the house, and crossed the street. "Brock," he shouted. "It's Officer Kimrey. We spoke Friday night. Come to the window so we can talk." He held out both hands to show they were empty. "I'm unarmed. No one's going to hurt you."

BARBARA HUDDLED over her weekly report to the superintendent when Bettina Zimmerman interrupted her. "Can you spare a few minutes?" she asked. Barbara invited her in, and the teacher closed the door behind her as she entered. She smoothed her skirt and took a seat. A light-skinned Black woman, Betty, as everyone called her, was in her first year as the art teacher. She was in her early twenties and carried herself with a patrician air. "This is my free period," she said.

Barbara nodded, knowing that whatever bothered her, she would not have left her class unsupervised. "What's on your mind?" she said.

"This is difficult," the teacher said.

"Whatever it is, I'll try to make it easier." Barbara rose from her desk and took the second guest chair, removing the distance between them.

"I understand you spoke with Mr. Rollins yesterday." Barbara said nothing. "It's probably none of my business, but has another teacher complained about him?"

"I'm not at liberty to discuss our conversation," Barbara replied. Theirs had been a private talk, and she wasn't about to let anyone else in on it. "I would extend the same courtesy to you. Please tell me why you're asking."

Betty rubbed her knuckles against each other. Barbara stared at her graceful hands, which reminded her of her own. Karol was always telling her how much he loved her hands. Unless he was admiring her legs.

"He's been coming on to me," the teacher said. "He's not pleasant about it. If he were to ask me out, I'd refuse. He's not my type." She gave an involuntary shrug, as though acknowledging that she was straying from the topic. "He makes remarks."

"What sort of remarks?" Barbara asked when she didn't continue.

"At first, it was about my hair. White people are always going on about our hair. Sometimes they mean it as a compliment, but often it's out of curiosity, a why-are-you-different sort of thing."

"But then?" Barbara prompted.

"He started talking about my face, said it reminded him of the bust of Nefertiti." Barbara got the illusion. She'd made the same observation herself.

"And that made you uncomfortable," she said.

"It was the way he pronounced it," she said. "Not 'Nefer-tee-ce,' but 'Nefer-tit-ee.' And then he said, 'I really like that bust.' And he smiled at me, but it was more of a leer."

"Go on." Barbara sensed she had more to say.

"He keeps calling me the queen. 'How's the queen today?' he says. And last week, he said he wished he were Akhenaten. Do you know who that was?"

"The pharaoh," Barbara said. "Nefertiti's wife. I'm familiar with it. What have you said to him?"

"I've asked him to stop, but always with a smile, in a kidding way.

I didn't want to offend him. But when he said that last week, I was firm. 'Please stop,' I said. 'You're making me uncomfortable.'"

"And he said?"

Betty took a deep breath and closed her eyes. "He asked me why I was offended. He said, 'A beautiful woman like you should be pleased that white men find you attractive.'"

"'White men?' He specifically said white men?" Barbara realized she had leaned forward in her chair, almost nose-to-nose with the young teacher.

"That's what he said."

"Did anyone else hear this?" Barbara asked.

The teacher shook her head. "No. He's always cautious. He catches me in the hall between classes, hangs back after a teacher meeting, or wanders into the lounge during the third period. I get up and leave."

"To your knowledge," Barbara asked, "has he done this to any other teacher?"

"Fran Nelson, I think. I don't know what he's said to her, but she's warned me to stay away from him."

Barbara asked her to keep their conversation in confidence for the moment. "I need to decide how best to deal with it, but deal with it, I shall."

In the background, she heard sirens blaring. First one, then two, then more. Like every partner of a police officer, her body tensed in fear.

Louis Callon was a small man with a massive build. Powerful arms bulged from his short-sleeve shirt, whose faded lettering was tight against his chest. Despite the cold weather, he wore a pair of shorts, its cuffs straining against his thighs. He was bald, though Mayfield suspected he shaved his head, but had a full beard and a gold ring in his left ear. When Mayfield introduced himself, Callon's response was as frosty as the weather. "I'm busy," he said. His voice was a high treble with a raspiness Mayfield often associated with heavy smokers. The effect was incongruous, as though God had assembled Callon from spare parts lying about His workshop.

"This will just take a few minutes," Mayfield said. "Do you mind if I come in?"

"Suit yourself." Callon stepped aside as the deputy chief entered a room with spartan furnishings, the most prominent of which was a glass-fronted display case filled with photographs and trophies. The adjoining room most people would have used for dining contained a barbell store rack, mats, and a utility bench. Callon's life, Mayfield decided, revolved around an obsession with his body.

"I suppose you're here about Tifton," he said, and Mayfield detected the slight French accent.

"I understand you had some sort of dispute with him."

He snorted. "Some sort? If you mean, was I pissed off at him for misleading me, causing us thousands of dollars and untold hours of work, yeah. But I didn't kill him."

"How did he mislead you?" Mayfield asked.

"I'd never bought a house before. My parents' place had been passed down from my father's family, so I knew nothing about the process. Neither did Steve."

Mayfield absorbed this new information without commenting on it.

"We found this place on our own. It's near work for both of us, and it was affordable. Plus, it's a nice neighborhood. People here are accepting. They leave us alone. Tifton's for sale sign was in the front yard, so what did we know? We made an appointment with him rather than finding our own agent. That was our first mistake."

He gripped one fist and cracked his knuckles, then repeated the process with the other, making Mayfield cringe. "We took a tour, made a full-price offer—mistake number two—and the owner accepted it. Steve knew a bit more than I did and asked if we should have an inspection. Tifton told us it wasn't necessary since we were paying cash. He said only mortgage holders required inspections, and this place was solid. Mistake number three."

"You bought it and then discovered a problem?" Mayfield asked.

"Problem?" Callon repeated his high-pitched snort. "Problems. Where do you want me to start? The water heater gave out in the first two months. Then we discovered the water line was plugged. The previous owners had flushed paper diapers down the drain. You know what that means? You're responsible for everything between your house and the main sewer line. Then we found water in the basement and had to dig a French drain. I did that myself, rented a backhoe, filled the trench with gravel and filler fabric, the whole bit."

"And you took these problems to Tifton?" Mayfield said.

"Yeah." He laughed to himself. "I could tell I intimidated him, but I wouldn't hurt a fly. I started bodybuilding when I was a teenager. No one's messed with me since."

Mayfield got the picture. A small, scrawny, gay kid is bullied by schoolmates and decides no one's kicking sand in his face ever again. "How did he respond?" Mayfield asked.

"He had his secretary pull out the paperwork and showed how we'd waived an inspection. I said, 'That's what you told us to do.'" Callon snorted again and shook his head. "He claimed he'd said nothing of the sort, that we'd told him money was tight. That much was true."

"So, what did you do?"

Again, that high-pitched sound that was now more like a giggle. "Took out a home improvement loan, fixed everything we could on our own, found a plumber friend of Steve's to repair the sewer line. Then I made it my business to tell everyone I knew what a sleaze Tifton is—was. But I didn't hurt him."

"Where were you Friday night between 7:30 and 9:00?" Mayfield asked.

"I was at Mother's."

"Your parents live here?"

"No, they're up in Trois-Rivières. Quebec," he added, as though

Mayfield needed the clarification. "I said I was at Mother's." With that, he pointed to the fading print on his T-shirt. "I work there. I'm an instructor and night manager."

"Okay," Mayfield said, and now it was his turn to laugh. "And I'm sure someone there can confirm this?"

"Dozens of people. Ask Frank. He's at the front desk now. He handed the reins over to me at three. Ask him to share the log with you. People have to scan their passes when they come in. Every one of them has to have seen me. Dozens."

Mayfield heard a siren nearby, then another. As a wailing chorus filled the air, he gave the man a hasty thank you and raced for his cruiser.

BERNIE JACKSON LOOKED across the table at Stan Sabol, president of the Byers Township Council. "We'd agreed," he said. "Karol was to become chief of the new police force. His leadership, how he's turned this department around over the past two years, was one reason you sought this alliance."

"That was before we knew he was on the verge of retirement," Sabol said.

Bernie studied the brown surfaces of his hands, which he'd planted on the desk to calm himself. "You insisted he lead the department. It was a condition of your participation. Doug and I approached him with the idea, and he agreed to stay. Now you're reneging."

"This guy from the state, Peter Watson, makes a valid point," Sabol said. "If we're starting fresh, we need someone who'll stick here for a while. Novak is near retirement age."

"He's fifty-nine, for Christ's sake." Bernie was stretching a point. Novak was less than two months from his sixtieth birthday.

"Don't yell at me. I'm president of my council," Sabol said in a tone underlining that, as a mere council member, Bernie ranked lower. "I have certain responsibilities to my citizens."

"And Doug Lentz is president of ours," he replied. "He supports Chief Novak. You're threatening to pull this entire agreement down."

Sabol leaned back in his chair. "Have you talked to Doug about this?"

"No. I chair the public safety committee. He's put me in charge of these negotiations." Bernie knew that Lentz's support of Novak had little to do with his respect for the man. As the sole borough among these smaller townships, Lentz saw Boyleston as first among equals. Installing his chief as leader of the regional police force could achieve that.

Sabol cocked his head and pursed his lips. "Why?" Bernie said.

"You should speak with him."

"C'mon, Stan. Show your cards."

Sabol held out his hand, palm up, as though holding a globe. "I think you'll find Doug is as concerned about the future as we are," he said.

Bernie felt his pulse quicken. Had Lentz gone behind his back, betraying both Novak and him? "I'll have that conversation," he said. "Novak is part of the package. If he goes, so will we. I've been in this position for three years. I have some pull with my fellow council members."

As he rose to leave, Lentz said, "What the hell is that?"

They both listened as an ambulance roared past the township hall, followed by what sounded like a police car.

NOVAK PARKED a block from the scene and jogged toward it until a county patrol officer stopped him. "Active shooter, chief. We're holding everyone back."

Novak nodded. "And my officer?"

"He's still on the front lawn. Whenever we try to approach him, the shooter opens fire."

"Is he alive?" Novak asked.

"We can't tell, but ...."

"He's not moving," Novak said.

"No, sir."

"And his partner?"

The patrolman turned his head, staring at a figure who sat alongside the curb, partially hidden by a parked car, his head in his hands. "SWAT's here?"

"They're planning how to approach the house. The shooter still has his wife and kids inside. We've evacuated the neighboring homes."

A news van pulled up behind them, and the patrolman rose to block its path. Two helicopters churned overhead. One was the county's, but the other belonged to a television station.

"Thank you," Novak said. "I need to speak with my officer, but I'll stay out of their way."

Novak bent and crept toward Norville Chastain, tripping over the curb and landing alongside him. "How are you doing?" he asked.

The young Black patrolman looked up at him, tears streaming down his face. "Awful," he said. "Terrible."

"What happened?"

"We got the call that there was an active shooter. Neighbors told us he was holding his family hostage. Kimrey had talked him down Friday night when he was screaming at the family. He thought he could do so again."

Chastain looked toward the sky as though praying for guidance. "I tried to get him to wait for backup. I begged him to call in the SWAT team. He insisted he could reason with the guy. He approached the house, identified himself, and told him he was unarmed. The bastard fired one shot, and Kimrey went down."

The rookie officer brushed tears off his cheeks with his sleeve, and Novak handed him a handkerchief. "We were wearing flak jackets, but the shooter got him in the head."

From this angle, Novak could see Kimrey sprawled on his back on the front lawn of the house. He wasn't close enough to see his condition, but, as the county officer had reported, he wasn't moving. With the SWAT team unable to approach him, Kimrey's chances faded by the minute.

"When we answered a call Friday night," Chastain said, "his wife told us he had no firearms in the house. Where did he get them?"

"It's too soon for that," Novak replied, "but we'll find out."

"Why did he do it?" Chastain wailed. "He knew we should call for help, but he insisted on doing it himself. Why?"

Novak had no answer. All the training and five years of service had failed to do their work. Kimrey had done what no officer is supposed to do: go one-on-one with an active shooter without calling for backup or alerting the SWAT team.

Only later would Novak recall he had once done the same thing himself. As a young Pittsburgh police detective, he'd mounted the steps of a home where a man was holding his wife and kids hostage. He'd spoken to the gunman through the screen door, listening to him as he told his story. Novak coaxed him outside and sat with him on the front steps until he calmed down. His act had inspired eight-year-old Lauryn Carter to become a cop. She was now the first Black female to serve on Boyleston's force.

Kimrey's action made no sense, but this was not his chief concern at the moment. "Don't blame yourself," he told the young officer. "He was supposed to be training you, not the other way around. You spoke up. There's nothing more you could have done."

"I should have stopped him."

"Not your place," Novak said. "If you'd been full partners, maybe he would have listened to you, but you weren't. *It is not your fault.*" He shouted the last few words to drive them home.

The review board might not see it that way, but right now, Novak wanted to keep his officer from falling apart so he could talk to him.

He tried to recall Kimrey's emergency contact. He wasn't married and had no children. Novak would have to notify his parents, but at the moment, he couldn't remember who they were or where they lived.

Mayfield approached the pair, and as he did, Detective Barnwell chased after him. "Down!" Novak shouted at her. "Get down. Active shooter."

She paid no heed and arrived at the same time as Mayfield. "What's happened?" she said, out of breath. "How's David?"

"We don't know. The SWAT team can't get near him." He told them what he little he'd learned.

"Why didn't you stop him?" she hissed at Chastain.

"He did," Novak replied. "David didn't listen."

"Why do they leave him lying there?" she cried. "We've got to help him."

She was near hysteria, and it was out of character. Despite being kidnapped by a corrupt police officer in Ohio two years ago, she'd remained calm, insisting on finishing the investigation with Novak instead of returning to Boyleston. She'd never experienced the wounding of a fellow officer before. The closest they'd come was when Mayfield's body armor had saved him from all but a broken rib when he'd taken a shot during the same investigation.

She and Kimrey had once been close. Perhaps still were, for all he knew. "The shooter is still inside and is holding his family hostage. They'll get them out and then attend to David."

A movement caught Mayfield's eye. "There they go," he whispered. "One squad is moving through the alley; another peeled off and is coming around the house next door. This will be over in a minute."

The news helicopter had moved away, ordered to do so by the county to keep the shooter from following the SWAT team's approach on TV. News crews were being held two blocks away for the same reason and for their safety. Mayfield, who was monitoring the terse commands on the ACPD channel, continued whispering to

Barnwell and Chastain, describing the progress of the two teams as though he were a play-by-play announcer.

"Brock," a SWAT officer called over a bullhorn, "let Shari and your kids leave. You don't want them hurt."

"I'm protecting them," a voice from within yelled. "I won't let you get them."

A moment's silence followed. Novak assumed the negotiator was conferring with others on how to address this confusing response. "He's having a flashback," Mayfield whispered. "He thinks we're the Taliban or something."

"We're here to help," the negotiator called. "Why don't you let your wife and kids come out? Let's get them out of this situation. Then we can help you."

"Stand down, or I'll shoot."

Three more exchanges followed. The SWAT team prepared to move in as the negotiator distracted the man's attention. As Mayfield listened to the terse commands, his breathing stopped. He extended his arm as though holding his colleagues back. "Now!" he proclaimed in a harsh, muffled shout.

The four heard nothing at first, then saw two black-clad members of the SWAT team escort a woman and two small children behind their neighbors' homes. From within the house came the crack of gunfire, then silence. The tension vanished like air escaping from a balloon. Uniformed and plainclothes officers advanced on the house. Ambulance attendants surged forward, kneeling at Kimrey's side.

Novak and Mayfield sprang forward as one, while Barnwell remained with Chastain. At first, they could see nothing as county officers and ambulance attendants surrounded the fallen officer. Then the group parted as the attendants pulled a sheet over him, allowing Novak to glimpse Kimrey's body. A pool of blood surrounded his forehead. The attendants could do nothing more than cover his body until a medical examiner arrived.

Vertigo swept over Novak. He crumpled to the ground, holding his face in his palms as he sobbed.

WHILE THE CRIME scene investigators placed evidence markers along the lawn, street, and trees in locations struck by Gifford's bullets, an assistant medical examiner bent over Kimrey's body and pronounced him dead. Investigators took photos of his body while the medical examiner went inside to examine Gifford's. The attendants lifted Kimrey's remains into a body bag, moved it onto a metal stretcher, and placed it in the ambulance.

Thus began a grim journey conducted too often in the Pittsburgh area. Two motorized officers turned on their blue lights and led the ambulance from Barker Street south toward Noblestown Road. Boyleston and ACPD cruisers trailed behind, soon joined by those from Carnegie and Crafton, all with emergency lights on. As they passed the Pittsburgh police substation, the length of the cordon grew. News helicopters flew overhead, sharing aerial views of the flashing snake as it slithered crossed the West End Bridge, turned east on Route 65, then right on Chestnut Street toward the 28th Street Bridge.

"Look at them," Lydia said as she looked out the window. On both sides of Chestnut, onlookers stopped to gaze at the procession. Men and women, Black and white, solemnly stared as they passed, many removing caps and placing them over their hearts. "They're so respectful," she said, her voice catching in her throat

Novak wished people showed the same regard for police every day, not just when one of them had died. But he didn't say so. He was thinking about what lay ahead.

Barnwell had reminded him David's parents lived in nearby Swissvale. He'd have to notify them. And the council, starting with Bernie. He'd have to release a statement to the media, perhaps even meet with them. The ambulance turned onto Penn Avenue and backed up to the county medical examiner's office along The Strip. Novak pulled into the parking lot. "Calvin is two cars back. I have to go in," he told Barnwell.

"Go," she said, waving a hand dismissively. *She's angry with me,* he thought. *Maybe angry at the world.*

Notifying the guard at the front desk where he could find him when the autopsy was completed, he requested a private room with a phone. The guard, who'd been through this before, directed him to a small booth off the reception area. He called Norma Marks on the landline and asked for the names and contact information for David's parents.

"He's dead then?" She burst into tears, and Novak realized how cavalier he'd been in his approach. Had she not known until now, or had she refused to accept it until she heard it from him?

"I'm afraid so," he said. Then, fumbling for the right words: "I'm sorry. It was instantaneous. He didn't suffer."

"It doesn't help," she said in a quavering voice.

"He was trying to help," he said. "It cost him his life." Again, he stopped, not knowing what else to say.

She seemed to collect herself, reeling off the information he needed. "They're quite upset."

"They know?" Novak said.

"When they heard on the news an officer was down, they called to make certain David was all right. I lied. I told them I didn't know who was involved."

"You didn't lie," Novak told her. "You didn't know for sure until I just told you. You said the right thing."

After disconnecting, he sat with his head buried in his folded arms for several minutes. Novak had seen many police officers injured and a few killed during his three decades in law enforcement, but it had never been one of his men. He'd never had to make this call and didn't know how to do it. Finally, he gave up trying to plan and dialed the number.

"Oh, no," a woman's voice said. "Tell me it isn't so."

He was taken aback, then realized caller ID must have shown he was calling from the morgue. "This is Chief Novak," he said. "I'm afraid I have bad news."

"I knew it. The moment I heard the news, I knew it. Wayne," she said in a louder voice. "It's Chief Novak. He says our David is dead."

Novak had said nothing of the sort, but the anxious parent had filled in the blanks. He wasn't surprised, knowing Barbara would have reacted the same. "Hello," Wayne Kimrey said. His voice was composed, businesslike. "Please tell me what's happened."

"There was a domestic dispute, and your son tried to intervene." He led the father through the details.

"They said on the news he lay there for some time."

"Yes, because the shooter fired at any officer who tried to reach him. But it wouldn't have helped," Novak said. "Your son died instantly."

"Thank God for that," he said. "What happens now?"

"We'll need you to identify the—him. I don't think it's something your wife should see. We can send a car."

"I'll drive myself."

"No, I'll have the county pick you up. It will be faster and safer. Can someone stay with your wife?"

"Our son is here, David's brother. We'll want to make funeral arrangements."

"Yes," Novak said, marveling at the man's matter-of-fact tone. Was he in shock, or was this just his nature? "We'll cover all expenses."

"I'm not concerned about that," he said. "I never wanted this, you know. Never wanted him to become a cop. He wouldn't listen. It was all he wanted to do from the time he was a boy. Now look what's happened." With that, his stoic bearing crumpled, and Novak heard him sob.

After extricating himself from the call with one last expression of sorrow, Novak called Bernie. "I know," he said. "I was there. The county wouldn't let me through, but I stood at the police line and listened to the reports on the radio. When the ambulance left and you followed, all of you moving so slowly, I knew. Ewer told me the rest," he said, referring to the third detective in the department. "I've alerted the council. I hope you don't mind."

"On the contrary, Bernie. I appreciate it."

Jackson started to say something, then stopped. "What is it?" Novak asked.

"Nothing," the council member replied. "Nothing that won't keep. You have a job to do."

Novak had nothing to do until David's father arrived. He called Barbara to tell her what had transpired. "I heard the sirens," she said, "and knew it was something bad. I was so worried ... for you."

He told her he was fine. "This time," she said. "His family must be in agony."

They spoke for a few minutes, then Novak went outside to wait for the county to deliver Kimrey's father. He found all three of his detectives—Ewer, Horvath, and Barnwell—standing alongside Mayfield's cruiser. "You should all return," he said. "There's nothing more you can do here. Lydia, you may want to take the day off."

"I'm staying here," she said.

"All right. I'll let the rest of you know if we need anything. It will be a long afternoon."

As the three returned to their cars, a county patrol cruiser pulled to the curb, lights flashing. The officer came around and opened the passenger door. Wayne Kimrey stepped out, looking past Novak at Barnwell. "Lydia," he said. He wrapped her in his arms. "David loved you, you know? He still loved you."

"I know," she said, tears streaming down her face. "And I loved him. We just couldn't...." Her voice trailed off.

The three entered the morgue together. Wayne stood at the window as they pulled back the rubber sheet, revealing what was left of his son's face. "That's him," he said. "That's our David."

They stood outside for a few minutes, the father asking Novak for details of his son's death. He told the man everything he knew. "And the man who killed him, what of him? PTSD, you said?"

"He'd done four tours in Afghanistan," Novak said, repeating what his friend from ACPD, Glen Carpenter, had told him. "After they snuck the family out, the SWAT team crept toward the front of the house. He turned and shot at them, and they returned fire. He's dead."

Kimrey shook his head. "What a waste," he said. "I was in Desert Storm. We had it easy. How is his family?"

"Physically safe, but I don't know how they're doing psychologically."

"What a goddamned waste," he repeated.

The autopsy took three hours. Blood and tissue samples would be sent to a lab to make certain Kimrey had had nothing in his system that would have affected his judgment or performance. *Blame the victim*, Novak thought. He passed the time speaking with county officers while Barnwell sat alone in the cruiser, leaving twice for short walks through the markets and specialty stores lining The Strip.

While she was gone, Novak faced reporters from Pittsburgh's television and radio stations and its two newspapers. "Allegheny County Police are in charge of the investigation," he said, nodding toward Superintendent Albert Starr, who stood alongside him. "I'll defer to them in discussing what happened this afternoon, but I want to speak about my officer. David Kimrey was in his fifth year of service. He was honest, dedicated, and committed to Boyleston Borough. All who knew him held him in high regard. He was a decent man and a fine cop."

Novak choked and stared at the pavement until he regained his composure. "Law officers put their lives on the line every day," he said. "We are human beings and thus are imperfect. We sometimes make mistakes. But the vast majority of us do our jobs to the best of our abilities so every citizen can enjoy peace and safety. That is what David Kimrey was all about. His death is a loss to everyone in Allegheny County. We mourn him. We shall miss him."

Reporters began shouting questions at him, but Novak turned toward Superintendent Starr, allowing him to recount the grim details of the day's events.

A few minutes past six, a longer cordon left the medical examiner's offices, cruisers from throughout Allegheny County trailing the ambulance as it made its way east toward a funeral home in Wilkinsburg. Alongside him, Barnwell sat in silence. "How are you holding up?" he asked.

"Terrible," she said. "I don't know if I'll be able to work again."

"It's tough losing a colleague," he said.

"You don't understand," she replied. Now her voice was firm and gravelly. "This was my fault."

"No," he said, enunciating each word, "it is not your fault."

"Do you know why he did this?" she asked, her tone angry and defiant. "He was trying to be a hero. For me. To prove himself. To me. One hug," she continued. "That's all he asked for. Couldn't I have given that much? One lousy little hug?"

KAROL NOVAK REACHED toward the coffee carafe. "Haven't you had enough?" his wife said. "You've had so much caffeine you'll be bouncing off the walls."

"I suppose you're right," he said, returning the container to the warming tray. "I need something to keep me awake." He'd returned late from work, giving them little time to speak. He was up half the night, lying awake in bed while he stared at the ceiling, then padding around the house in his slippers while writing notes to himself.

"His poor parents must be beside themselves," she said.

"His father alternates between grief and stoicism," Novak replied. He described Wayne Kimrey's initial reaction, breaking down in tears over the phone, and his impassive manner at the morgue. "I suspect it hasn't hit him yet."

"Happy Thanksgiving," Barbara said. Novak grunted in agreement and, despite Barbara's warning, refilled his mug with what was now lukewarm coffee. "How is Lydia taking this?" she asked.

"Personally." He recounted her declaration that Kimrey had taken on the shooter to prove himself to her. "He visited her the night before. Whatever transpired between them, he asked for a hug, and she refused."

"Oh, God," Barbara moaned. "I feel for her. How are the rest of them taking it?"

"Everyone is shell-shocked," he said. "They've seen officers fall in other jurisdictions, but never here. They know this could have been one of them. "

She leaned forward and placed her hand on his. "I worry about this all the time. If something were to happen to you, I don't know how I'd go on."

"I don't intend to let anything happen," he said.

"Neither did David. As you said, it can happen to anyone." He nodded but did not reply. "Twice you've said you were ready to retire, and that doesn't count your injury forcing you to leave the Pittsburgh force. You've put in your thirty years and more. Isn't it time to give it up?"

Novak stroked the stubble on his neck. "I'd like to, but I've promised to manage the merger of the three police forces. Once the transition is complete, I'll bow out."

"How long will this take?" she said.

"Two years, give or take," he said.

"Give," she asked, "or take?" Novak answered with a shrug. Changing the subject, she said, "What will you tell your officers this morning?"

"I've spent half the night trying to work that out," he said. "I hope the right words will come to me when we meet for roll call." He drummed his fingers on the tabletop.

"What about the investigation into Fred Tifton's murder?" she said.

"I can't even think about that now." He buried his face in his hands. "What about your teacher?" he asked.

"The plot thickens," she said. "One of my newer teachers says George is making inappropriate remarks and stalking her around the hallways. Another teacher had warned her about him, so I spoke to her after classes. She gave me an earful. You remember I told you he always seems to stay just inside that red line? He stepped over it here, patting her on the bottom so often she threatened to turn him in."

"Why are you just now learning this?" he asked.

Barbara scoffed. "There's no percentage in a woman claiming sexual harassment, so it has to get unbearable before she'll step forward. Now that I know, however, I'm taking it to the assistant superintendent this morning. I want George Rollins out of the classroom."

"Whew," he said. "Beware tangling with the dragon lady." He chuckled, but she did not share it.

"Can you still pick up the turkey, or do you want me to do it?" she asked.

"I'll take care of it."

"Because we're only in session for half the day," she said. "I have time."

"I'll take care of it," he repeated.

———

At 7:45, officers straggled in for roll call. Most spoke to each other in whispered tones. Norville Chastain, the young officer who had been with Kimrey when he was gunned down, was not present, having been excused from duty for the rest of the week. Lauren Carter, another Black recruit, sat at her desk, her head buried in her hands, one of which clutched a balled-up tissue. Her eyes were red, and she shook her head at irregular intervals as though denying the reality of what had happened.

Lydia Barnwell was the last to arrive. In contrast to Officer Carter, she wore a look of grim determination, her mouth set, her blue eyes searing anything she saw. She stood apart from the others, waiting for the meeting to begin.

Novak rarely led the roll call. That was Mayfield's job. But he was on his feet this morning. "I won't say good morning, because it is not," he said. "We lost a valued friend and colleague yesterday. This department has never suffered this kind of loss. We all feel it. We're all in mourning. David was a young man with his entire life ahead of him. He was trying to help a man suffering a mental health emergency."

The search by ACPD investigators had turned up three semi-automatic weapons, a single-shot bolt-action rifle, four handguns, and a cache of ammunition in a crawl space above Gifford's garage. Shari Gifford insisted she'd known nothing about it.

"You know my attitude toward the proliferation of guns in our society," Novak said. "I also know some of you disagree. But I hope we agree that this man, given his history, should not have had access to any firearms, let alone a small arsenal."

Novak took them through the details of the shooting, empha-sizing that the county's crime lab would be the ultimate arbiter of the sequence of events. "I'm awaiting word from David's family on funeral arrangements and will let you know as soon as I do."

"It's at two Saturday at Eastminster Presbyterian," Lydia said, her voice flat. "The reception is Friday night at Hazelton Funeral Home."

"Thank you," Novak said. Despite their breakup months before, Lydia remained close to Kimrey's family. It must have been an awkward relationship, he thought, almost as though David's parents had sided with her. He set the speculation aside. This was none of his business, and he avoided his officers' personal issues unless they inter-fered with their work.

"I'm sure you will all want to be there," he said. Glancing at the somber faces in the room, he realized they wanted something more, but he couldn't think of what to say. "If anyone wants to say a few words about David, now is the perfect time."

It seemed to hit the right note. One by one, each officer shared a memory of working with Kimrey. Many were inarticulate but sincere, choking back tears as they spoke. A few went on for several minutes, and neither Novak nor Mayfield dissuaded them.

Only Detective Mark Ewer, known for playing class clown,

broke the spell. Even when being serious, Ewer often said the inappropriate thing, and he did so now. "I wish he'd called in the SWAT team," he said. "He knew better. I can't imagine what he was trying to do."

"Oh, shut the fuck up," Gordon Horvath said, turning on him.

Before Novak could intervene, Barnwell said, "I know what he was doing."

Novak interrupted her. During the past sixteen hours, he'd pondered what might have motivated Kimrey to ignore his training. "David was trying to prove himself," he said. "He'd had a rough patch earlier this year, and I'd put him on a work plan. He stuck to it, exceeded every goal, and was studying for the detective's exam. When he got the call yesterday, he may have seen this as a way of distinguishing himself."

He looked around to make sure he had their attention. "I don't want anyone blaming him. The review board will play that role all too well. Just recognize he was attempting to defuse the situation, trying to help."

Novak stared at Ewer, daring him to respond, as he frequently did. The detective hung his head. Indelicate though he had been, Horvath had put the man in his place.

"May I say a word?" Officer Carter said. "David and his family were active at Eastminster. As some of you know, that church is in East Liberty." Although several high-tech companies had located there, changing the area, it remained home to thousands of Black people.

"Many white families have left Eastminster," she said. "My uncle and aunt attend there. They tell me the Kimreys stayed loyal to the church and welcomed everyone who worshipped there. David learned from them. He always treated me with respect." Her eyes scanned the room, and Novak knew she could not say that of every officer. "He was a decent soul."

"Thank you, Lauren," Novak said. "Let this serve as a reminder to all of us. Remember your training whenever you find yourselves in similar situations. Now, we have jobs to do. Deputy Mayfield will hand out assignments."

Mayfield took over the morning roll call. The death of a fellow officer did nothing to halt the obligation of the Boyleston Police Department to protect and serve.

DETECTIVES Jeffrey and Thurmond sat with a trace evidence examiner at the ME's office. "We found fingerprints of both agents throughout the office," she said, "but that's to be expected. Also, numerous prints of unidentified others. When did you say the assistant returns?"

"On Monday," Jeffrey said. "We've spoken to her by phone, but have no reason to ask her to return before that. The Turnpike Authority has her e-pass entering the turnpike at 6:30 and exiting at Somerset at 7:45. That's longer than usual, but the holiday traffic was heavy. There's no way she could have returned to Boyleston at the hour Tifton was killed."

"We'll need her prints when she returns to eliminate her from the unknowns," the examiner said.

"What about DNA?" Jeffrey asked.

"I'll get to that," she said, "but the samples we found on his desk, keyboard, and chair match nothing on file."

Jeffrey muttered an oath under his breath. He'd been expecting more.

"One of the two footprints in the victim's blood belonged to the cleaning woman, Mrs. Geilke. The other is unidentified, but we know it belongs to a male wearing a size 10 Bostix rubber-sole shoe. It was just a partial print, so it tells us nothing more."

A complete set of footprints could estimate a subject's height, weight, and unique characteristics, such as whether the wearer limped. A partial print could mean anything unless they found the shoe. He was about to close his notebook when the examiner said, "We found one significant thing."

The detectives leaned forward, Jeffrey resting his chin on his knuckles. "Both fingerprints and DNA from a known subject." Jeffrey flipped his hand over, inviting her to continue. "A Thomas Walsh, convicted of killing his wife in—"

"We know who Walsh is," Jeffrey said.

"We found his prints on the back of the sign."

"The murder weapon," Thurmond said.

"Yes. The supports and most of the sign had been wiped clean, but whoever did so neglected the back surface. We found impressions of the index, middle, and ring fingers of both hands. We also found traces of his DNA."

"So Walsh first thrust the prongs into Tifton's body, pushed on the top for good measure, then cleaned his prints off the supports, but forgot he'd touched the sign itself."

"It might have happened that way," she said, "but we didn't find his DNA is on the supports themselves. We found traces from Tifton, both agents, and a few others so far unidentified, but none from Walsh."

Jeffrey waved away the objection. "Motive, means, and opportunity," he said.

BARNWELL, Horvath, and Mayfield, gathered in the chief's office at mid-morning. The first winter snow swirled outside, accentuating the somber mood permeating headquarters. Horvath broke the silence. "I'm sorry for my outburst just now. It's just that Ewer—"

"Had it coming," Barnwell said. "Mark is a loudmouth and has no sense of decency. He says whatever comes into his mind."

Novak tried to suppress a smile, but failed. "Consider yourself disciplined, Gordon. Now it's back to work."

Although Novak had just briefed the force, Mayfield asked, "Do we know anything more?"

"I just got off the phone with Glen Carpenter at county," Novak said. The detective sergeant had worked with the Boyleston force on several cases and often served as a conduit to Novak when others at ACPD withheld information. "Gifford served multiple tours in Afghanistan. We know the story. They kept sending these guys back for one tour after another. When Gifford returned from his third tour in 2017, he began suffering nightmares. He'd duck whenever he heard a loud noise. If a heavy truck went by, he'd scream. His wife urged him to seek help, but he shrugged it off and returned for another tour."

Novak flipped a page in his notebook while his officers watched and waited. Their chief was a copious note-taker, and what had once seemed just a quirk they now knew was a defense mechanism. His concussion four years before had left him with frequent memory lapses. Barbara drilled him once a week on important names and dates.

"The Marines returned him involuntarily in 2019, declaring him unfit for service," Novak continued. "He suffered a breakdown after an action involving civilian casualties. The VA has been treating him for two years. When we withdrew and Kabul fell, he began hallucinating, convinced the Taliban were coming for him and his family. Yesterday, he snapped."

"His wife called 9-1-1 for help," Barnwell said. "Have you listened to her call?"

"The district attorney has it, but they haven't turned it over to us. She warned he'd found weapons. As I've said, he shouldn't have even had a handgun."

The four of them looked at one another for a moment. There seemed nothing more to say. "Getting back to Tifton's murder," Novak asked, "what have you learned about Louis Callon?"

"A gay man who took up bodybuilding as a youngster to deal with bullies," Mayfield said. "He and his partner bought a house last year.

Tifton represented the seller, and the buyers made the mistake of representing them as well. Tifton discouraged them from hiring an inspector. After the closing, they discovered a range of problems, drainage outside, water leaks inside."

Novak grunted. These were among the most frequent issues with Pittsburgh's older homes:

"They went back to Tifton, who refused to help," Mayfield said. "When they reminded him he'd discouraged them from getting an inspection, he said it was because they had so little money to put down, that it was their decision. The remediation cost them so much money, they had to take out a loan to cover it."

"Bastard," Barnwell said.

"So, yes, Louis and his partner, Steve Greenleaf, have a motive, but Callon has an alibi. With all that came down yesterday, I haven't had time to confirm it. I also need to speak with his partner. But my guess is," the deputy chief said, "there's nothing there."

Novak shook his head. "All right. Tomorrow's a holiday, and we may find it difficult to talk to some of these folks. We also have David's viewing Friday night and his funeral on Saturday. I know it's asking a lot, but between now and Sunday, let's try to check out every suspect's story."

He seemed about to dismiss them but said, "Everyone we've talked to can account for their time. When was the last time we saw that? Someone's always just sitting home alone with no one to vouch for them. It's too neat. There must be a flaw in one of these alibis. We need to find it."

As they rose to drift off in their own directions, Mayfield laid a hand on Barnwell's shoulder. "I'm sorry," he stammered, withdrawing it as though he'd touched a burning stove.

Turning toward him, she gave a halfhearted smile. "I am, too. We all are."

Assistant Superintendent Alex Northman peered at Barbara over his half-glasses while shooting a glance at his watch. "I hope this is important, Mrs. Novak. My wife and I are heading to Rochester to spend Thanksgiving with her folks. We need to get on the road."

"It is," she said. "One of my male teachers is making suggestive remarks in class and harassing two of my female teachers."

Northman sighed, removed his glasses, and twirled them by the earpiece. "Go on."

Barbara laid out her case, remarks about curves in a co-ed class, encouraging boys to make suggestive remarks through the medium of a Shakespeare reference, and making oblique references to a student's sexual preferences.

"Did he suggest the boy is gay?" the assistant superintendent said.

"No," Barbara admitted, "but the context matters. First, he says how most of the boys like curves, then this one boy sticks to the straight and narrow."

"What's the harm in that?" Northman asked.

Barbara leaned forward and peered into his eyes as though reprimanding a student. "The rest of the boys think he's gay. They constantly bully him. I had to change his homeroom in October, but it only worsened things. And here's a teacher contributing to it."

Northman gave a slight shrug. "But he said 'straight and narrow.' Straight. Aren't you reading too much into this?"

Barbara stared at him until Northman broke off the gaze. "Let me turn to the harassment of my teachers," she said, describing the innuendo he threw at Bettina Zimmerman and his statement that his attention shouldn't bother her. "White men," she said and repeated it.

"Are you certain she didn't mishear it? Were there any witnesses?"

"Of course not," she said. "He's crass but crafty. He doesn't do or say anything incapable of another interpretation. That's his way."

It was Northman's turn to gaze at her, cocking his head to one side in appraisal.

"This is not personal, if that's what you're thinking," she said, finding herself on the defensive. "I've supervised many male teachers as a principal and never had a problem. This one," she said, avoiding the word man, "is toxic. He does not belong in the classroom."

"That's a bit strong," Northman said.

"It is my considered judgment that George Rollins is a danger to students of a certain age," she said through gritted teeth. "He says and acts in ways that are inappropriate and demeaning. These episodes have become more flagrant and frequent. If we do not act, something bad will happen. And we will be responsible."

Northman glanced at his watch. "I've noted your concerns, Mrs. Novak. Thank you for bringing them to my attention."

"You'll look into this?" she said. "Consider what I've told you?"

"Of course," he said as he rose. "And now, let me wish you a happy Thanksgiving."

"It's too late," she said.

He gave her a confused expression. "My husband is the chief of police, as you know. He lost an officer yesterday. We have little to give thanks for."

"I understand," he said. "My sympathies."

After he left, Barbara sat in the outer office and wrote a page of notes. She signed and dated the yellow sheet from her legal pad and asked the lone assistant still on duty to witness it with her signature.

* * *

THE ALLEGHENY COUNTY COURTHOUSE, an imposing structure on Grant Street in Pittsburgh's Downtown, resembles the set for a medieval film. A pair of ten-story towers flank the entrance to the U-shaped stone building, enveloping a courtyard dominated by a circular fountain. Compared to ACPD's modern headquarters in Greentree, Detective Sergeant Lyle Jeffrey found the structure an anachronism, but anything he needed to accomplish, from charging suspects to trials to sentencing, required a visit. He took the stairs to the third floor and told the man at the reception desk he had an appointment with Melissa Dawkins.

While he waited, he paged through a magazine for the legal profession. Five minutes passed, then another five. When a quarter hour had elapsed, Jeffrey approached the desk again to remind the attendant he was waiting. "She knows you're here," he said.

"Please remind her," Jeffrey replied.

The man nodded and dialed her extension. "She says she'll be right out," he said. "She's finishing a pleading."

I'm pleading, he thought as he retook his seat. Another quarter hour passed, and Jeffrey was getting pissed. This was a damn murder case. He was ready to make an arrest and needed the DA's approval. He rechecked his watch, then ran through his notes. Finally, forty minutes after he'd arrived, the assistant DA entered the reception area and said, "Detective Jeffrey?"

He nodded and followed her past the desk and down the narrow hallway, not failing to notice her check her watch as though he had kept her waiting. *Mind games*, he thought. She entered her office and sat behind her desk, motioning to one of her guest chairs with a sweep of her arm. She was a tiny woman whose brown hair was flecked with strands of gray, but her air of self-importance dwarfed her diminutive size. "You're asking for a charge," she said. "Tell me what you have."

"Fred Tifton, real estate agent, former mayor of Boyleston, murdered on Friday evening shortly after eight. Someone caught him at his desk and drove the metal slats of a real estate sign into his head and torso."

"I've read the report," she said.

"We've eliminated all suspects except one, Thomas Walsh."

"*The* Thomas Walsh?" she said.

"The same. He and Tifton used to be close, but they fell out. Tifton helped put him behind bars over twenty years ago to cover his own activities. Since his release, Walsh lives with his daughter. He told two different accounts of his whereabouts on the night of Tifton's death. The first was a lie. We can't verify the second, and it sounds unlikely."

Jeffrey recounted Walsh's story of visiting his wife's grave on Friday evening. "The guard saw him arrive on foot at six, but didn't see him leave. It was cold that night, so it doesn't stand to reason he would have stood by the grave for two hours. It's only ten minutes from the cemetery's front gate to Tifton's office."

"Is that it?" the prosecutor said.

Jeffrey allowed himself a smile. "We got the lab report this morning. Tifton's prints and DNA are on the sign used as a murder weapon."

He handed her the examiner's report. She donned a pair of reading glasses and read through it while Jeffrey waited, his right leg beating a rhythm on the carpet. "This is odd," she said. "It says they found his DNA only on the sign's reverse, not on the shafts. How do you explain that?"

"Perhaps he wore gloves while committing the murder and took them off to wipe the sign clean."

"Why wipe it clean if he was wearing gloves?" she said. "Understand, I'm playing the role of a crafty defense attorney here."

"Leather gloves hold prints," he said. "He removed them to be sure he hadn't transferred some evidence."

"Perhaps," she said, "but gloves also carry DNA. Is there any other physical evidence? Were his prints found in the office itself? Did anyone see him arrive or leave? Any security cameras catch his image?"

To each of these questions, Jeffrey replied no.

"Have you re-interviewed him since getting these results?"

"No," Jeffrey said, "we want to charge him."

"How else could his prints get on the sign? Where was it stored?"

"In a closet in the office. He would have had to enter the building to gain access to it." Jeffrey leaned forward, stacking his fists on the corner of her desk. "Walsh had a powerful motive. The unlocked back door provided him with the opportunity. His alibi doesn't hold water. As for means, his prints are on the murder weapon."

"A defense attorney will come up with all sorts of explanations about how he came to touch that sign," she said. "We need more."

"Ms. Dawkins," Jeffrey said, "Walsh hated Tifton for what he'd done to him. When we asked where he was, he implied he was at work—"

"'Implied,' you say. Did he state he worked that night?"

"Not in so many words. He said he was assigned to the late shift. His boss tells us he asked to leave early, that it was the anniversary of his wife's death and he wanted to visit her grave."

"But he didn't specifically claim he was working late? The distinction is important."

"He asked his boss to cover for him."

She leaned back in her chair and closed her eyes. "I'm not ready to file charges yet. You may be correct, but I need to build a case that will hold up in court. As I said, I'm thinking of what his attorney will tell the jury. 'The county railroaded my client once before,' she said, lowering her voice to sound like a man. 'He spent twenty years on death row for a crime he didn't commit. So when he learned Tifton had been murdered, he knew suspicion would fall on him. He knew they wouldn't accept that he stood by his wife's grave shivering in the cold...' You see how they could twist this?"

"Yes." Jeffrey sighed in exasperation. "But he did it."

"I have no doubt. Bring him in for another interview. Grill him on his story and see if he trips up. If not, face him with this physical evidence and try to break him down."

"We'll do this tonight."

"You are anxious. Are you concerned Walsh will kill again?"
Jeffrey shook his head. "So let him celebrate Thanksgiving. I'm not being tender-hearted. I want to lull him into a false sense of security. Friday morning, after he's slept off the turkey and whatever he's had to drink, pull him in."

Bernie Jackson arrived unannounced at the council office to confront Doug Lentz, the council president. "Is there something you have to tell me?" he asked.

Lentz wrinkled his forehead as though perplexed. "About what? The death of that patrol officer?"

"No," Bernie said. He looked off to one side. "But we should also discuss that."

"It shouldn't have happened," Lentz said. "Last spring, you and Novak leaned on me to expand the force. You said our men shouldn't be making domestic calls alone. If two officers respond, one can back up the other, you told me. There's less chance of one of them getting ambushed, you said."

Bernie didn't recall this precise conversation, but Lentz had the general thrust right.

"So I gave in, and yesterday, one of them was gunned down. While his partner stood idly by, from what the papers say."

The press had said nothing of the sort, but Jackson decided Lentz knew why he'd come and was putting him on defense. "Norville Chastain was not yet Officer Kimrey's partner. He was in training. From what I've been told, Chastain suggested Kimrey call in the county rather than trying to negotiate on his own. For whatever reason, Kimrey didn't listen, God rest his soul."

"That doesn't speak well to his training, does it?"

"Look, Doug, I know what you're trying to say." Jackson kept his voice low. He was unwilling to let Lentz intimidate him, but neither did he want to anger him. "This was not Chief Novak's fault. He'd had problems with Kimrey and was trying to bring him back into line. He's spent hours working with him. Until yesterday, he was making progress. No one knows why Kimrey acted on his own."

"That doesn't change the fact one of our officers died yesterday."

"No, and nothing can bring him back. Meanwhile," he said, "Stan Sabol blindsided me yesterday, telling me he no longer supports

Novak to lead the new department. I reminded him he'd insisted Novak serve as chief. On that basis, you and I pressured him to withdraw his resignation last spring. Sabol now tells me you've changed your position. Is that so?"

Lentz smiled and leaned across his desk as though imparting a confidence. "I like Karol as much as you do, Bernie. He inherited a disaster and has done wonders pulling this department together. But he's getting up there."

"He's younger than we are," Jackson said.

"But we're not cops. He came to us with these problems—memory, vertigo, who knows what else? And he's missing some steps. Yesterday showed that. By your own admission, he'd paired a problem cop with a trainee and sent them to deal with an armed subject on a domestic dispute. I'm not blaming him..."

"Yes, you are."

"That's unfair. I'm merely pointing out the obvious. We need a vigorous leader to make this regional force a success. Pete Watson is convinced Novak's not up to the task."

So the commonwealth's consultant had been speaking with Lentz behind Jackson's back. Bernie folded his paws and looked up for guidance. "You've put me in a difficult position. As chair of the Public Safety Committee, I represent the borough on the study team. You told me to carry the ball. Yet, you've held ex parte negotiations—"

"Ex-what?"

"Off the books, Doug." Jackson raised his voice, no longer attempting to conceal his anger. "Behind my back. Sub rosa. There's more Latin for you. You haven't brought me into this discussion. That's dishonorable."

"Is that it? Are you concerned for Novak, or is this about your wounded pride?" Lentz said.

Jackson sat back in his chair and planted a hand on his hip. "It's a bit of both, Doug. You've betrayed Karol while betraying me."

"Careful now."

"So here's the deal. If Novak goes, so do I, and I won't go quietly. Next election, I'll make damn sure voters know what you've done and how you've done it." He left before Lentz could think of a rejoinder.

———

SOMETHING WAS up at the county. Novak was sure of it. Three days had passed since Jeffrey had given them the green light to question other suspects in Tifton's murder, but he had yet to ask what they'd learned.

He called ACPD and learned the detective was out. "Ten-seven?" he asked, meaning was he out of service, starting the Thanksgiving holiday an hour early?

"No, ten-eight at the DA's," came the answer.

That could mean only one thing. *Wouldn't you want to have all the information before you asked for authority to arrest?* he wondered. Not that Novak's team had anything substantive to share. But Jeffrey didn't know that.

He wandered into Mayfield's office to go over the plans for the holiday. The assistant chief said he'd be on duty—*didn't he have someone to spend the day with?*—along with three patrol officers. Thanksgiving wasn't the worst day of the year for crime. That was Christmas Day when men got a bottle of whiskey under the tree, drank most of it, and terrorized their loved ones. But on Thanksgiving, extended families gathered to resurface old grievances and wage political warfare. Someone had to be on duty, and his deputy chief had volunteered himself.

Satisfied, Novak returned to his office and donned his parka, not noticing the pink note on his desk. He checked out, giving best wishes to everyone still on duty. He was sorry he'd missed Norma Marks. The administrative assistant was often left out of things, and Novak tried to spare a kind word for her at the end of each day.

He drove home in the doldrums, hoping Jeffrey had the decency to allow Walsh to spend Thanksgiving with his family. While Novak didn't know what more the county had found, the circumstantial evidence was troubling. Knowing Walsh, however, he found it hard to believe he would risk his freedom by committing a violent act.

He slouched into the kitchen and was surprised to see Barbara wrestling with a turkey alongside a brine bath. "Can you help me with this?" she said.

He stepped out of his parka, letting it slide to the kitchen floor, grasped the bird, and lowered it into the tub. "I'm glad you got my message," she said. "I was worried I'd miss you and send you off on a fool's errand."

Distracted by everything swirling around him, he'd forgotten his promise to pick up the bird. He would keep this memory lapse to himself.

NOVAK PEERED out the living room window, watching the wind blow the remaining leaves off the trees. Despite the warmth inside, he shivered. Five years before, he and Barbara had walked the neighborhood in shirtsleeves on Thanksgiving Day. Today was payback time.

A gray Toyota stopped outside the house. Before its driver could honk, Novak was out the door, turning the key in the ignition of his Buick and pulling away so the car could take the parking space along the crowded street. He drove through the alley behind their home and pulled into the garage, then jogged through his backyard and up the stairs to the porch, entering through the door alongside the kitchen.

His daughter Mariel stood at the counter digging into the stuffing. She raised her eyes in greeting. "Where's my princess?" he asked.

"I'm right here," she said. "But if you're looking for your granddaughter, chances are she's curled up on an upstairs bed with a book."

He gave her a hug and went off in search of Jennifer, who was right where her mother had suspected. She looked up when he entered the bedroom and smiled. "Hi, Pap," she said, then redirected her attention to a book with a dark blue cover.

"What are you reading?" he asked, scanning the title, *The Girl Who Fell from the Sky*, upside down.

"It's about a half-Black girl who has to live with her Black grandma. She's a piece of work."

"After a plane crash?" he asked.

"No, something else has happened to her, but I haven't figured it out yet. But it's not about that so much as it's about race."

"Good for you," he said. Jennifer was only eleven, but old beyond her years. He stared at her for a moment until she looked up with a puzzled expression. "I'm just remembering when you were little, and we walked hand-in-hand around the block here." Barbara had taken a photo from behind them years before, his hulking figure and the diminutive presence alongside him, grasping his big paw. Their closeness had persisted until a year earlier, when school friends and activities had taken his place.

Suppressing a sigh, he returned to the kitchen. "Anything I can do?" he asked.

"We have everything under control," Barbara said, "until it's time to defrock the bird."

"Defrock," he said. "We need more of that." She ignored his barb at the church and opened the oven to check the temperature of the probe sticking out of the turkey's thigh, leaving Novak to go in search of his mother.

Izabela was easy to find. He had only to follow the sound of the TV at full volume. Novak had tried to get her to wear earphones or earbuds, but she claimed they were too uncomfortable, so he and Barbara were forced to endure the pain of the belching audio throughout most of the day. He found her sitting in a rocking chair, a blanket draped over her knees, as she watched the Hallmark Channel.

"I'm cold," she said in response to his greeting. "Can you turn up the heat?"

"It's seventy-five," he said. "Let me get you a jacket."

"It's my hands," she said.

He was tempted to suggest gloves, but stepped into the hallway and jacked up the thermostat. Izabela suffered from congestive heart failure, and the attendant circulation problems meant she was cold even on all but the hottest days of summer. Novak looked down at her, wondering how long he'd have her. She'd had a hard life, born in Slovakia and trapped with her mother in Nazi-occupied territory throughout the war. She'd arrived in New York harbor on July 3, 1945 on a converted destroyer filled with war brides and spent Independence Day looking at the Statue of Liberty before she could be processed at Ellis Island. When fireworks lit the sky ablaze, and the roar of explosions filled the night, her fellow passengers screamed in terror, convinced they were under attack. After reuniting with her husband, Izabela gave birth to three children and, because of his father's punishing hours at the steel mill, raised Karol almost single-handedly. If she wanted the TV to blare and send their heating bill soaring, who was he to deny her?

"Karol, time to carve, please." Obeying Barbara's call to action, Novak removed the wings and legs from the turkey and sliced the dark meat onto a serving platter. He inserted the thin-bladed knife between the breast and the bone, laid each half-breast on the carving board, and sliced them across the grain. "Masterful," she said. "You can work in a restaurant in your next life."

"Of this one," he said. "It can't come too quickly."

With that, the five of them took their seats around the dining room table. Novak deferred to his mother for the blessing. As they grabbed their cutlery, however, Jennifer spoke up. "I want us all to tell something for which we are thankful."

"That's what the holiday is for," Mariel said. "I'm thankful for you."

"Nanny?" Jennifer said, turning to her great-grandmother. "What?"

Raising her voice, the girl said, "What are you thankful for?"

"Good health," Izabela said.

"My family," Barbara followed, "and my students."

"What about you, Pap?"

"You, your mother, my mother, and my lovely wife," Novak said, leaving his voice in the air as he finished. But nothing more came out. He'd spent the last half-minute racking his brain for something to add, but could come up with nothing. "All of you," he said.

"God, it's hot in here," Mariel said. "Can you turn it down a bit?"

———

TWELVE MILES TO THE EAST, the holiday took on a more somber feel in the Kimrey household. Members of Eastminster had provided the dinner, so they had only to serve the plates.

"I wish I had something to do," Janet Kimrey said. "It would keep my mind off ... things."

David's brother Kurt and sister-in-law Beth were present, and when Lydia Barnwell arrived, she completed a solemn quintet. As she entered, a white West Highland terrier rose from alongside the fireplace and jumped up on her leg. "Down, Howie," Janet said.

"That's all right," Lydia replied. "I've met him before." She reached down and scratched his ears. The dog looked up at her, his tail wagging. When she took a seat on a high-backed chair, the dog curled at her feet.

"That's amazing," Beth said. "He's spent the morning lying in front of the fire. He doesn't respond to anything we do or say."

Howie had been David's dog since he was a teenager, but when he left for college, he'd remained behind. After his graduation, David lived in apartments that didn't allow animals, so he saw Howie only during visits to his parents.

Lydia stroked his ears again and said, "You know, don't you, boy?"

"Yes, he does," Kurt said. "We've been worried about him. I take it he knows you."

"I've only seen him once before," she said. During happier times, David had taken her home to introduce her to his folks.

"Perhaps he smells David on you," Kurt said.

But that was impossible since, discounting their brief encounter three nights before, she hadn't been with David for months. With the dog at her side, she sat apart from the others, fidgeting in the high-backed chair in the living room. "Can you help me with something?" Beth asked.

"Happy to," Lydia said, grateful to be drawn away from David's parents. They sat holding hands on the burgundy-colored sofa beneath a large family portrait taken years before when Kurt was in high school, David still in middle school, and Bianca, who would fly in tomorrow from Denver, was still in pigtails.

Howie followed as Beth led Lydia into the kitchen. Lifting a layer of heavy aluminum foil off one of the aluminum tubs and stirring the sweet potatoes, she said, "I know you feel uncomfortable. Don't be. Wayne wanted you here. It was kind of you to agree."

"He insisted," Lydia said. "I couldn't refuse."

Beth's smile curled at the side of her cheek. "He was always taken with you. It's a wonder Janet isn't jealous." She giggled and tossed her head. "He never forgave David for letting you go."

A strange way to put it, Lydia thought, *since I'm the one who ended it.* "He's a good father," she said.

"That he is, so don't feel uncomfortable," Beth said. "We want you here. You're like family."

Lydia, whose mother was gone and who was estranged from her father, had no family of her own. Beth's reassurance made her feel both grateful and sad. "David came to see me the night before he died—"

"I know. Kurt says it was Wayne's idea. He'd been after David to get back together with you. Instead...." She trailed off without finishing the thought.

Lydia had been on the verge of revealing why she felt responsible for David's death, but held her tongue. Something about this conversation wasn't making sense. Instead, she said, "They're sitting around as though they're waiting for something. I know they have no reason to celebrate, but maybe we should bring them to the table."

"Good idea," Beth said. Leaving Lydia in the kitchen, she returned to the living room. "I know no one's hungry, but you need to eat something. Lydia and I will serve plates."

"Let me help," Janet said. She joined her daughter-in-law in the kitchen while Lydia decanted a bottle of pinot noir she'd brought for the occasion. The five ate in silence for several minutes, their gloom hanging like a pall across the dining room as the Westie curled up at Lydia's feet. Janet pushed food around her plate, not taking a bite. Kurt and Beth discussed who would collect Bianca from the airport in the morning, lamenting she'd had to take a redeye flight. Their conversation dragged on, turning this simple errand into a debate to avoid the unpleasant reality of what had brought them together.

"I want to prepare you for what happens Saturday," Lydia said. "Hundreds of police officers will attend the service. They're not just coming from Allegheny County, but across Pennsylvania and from New York, Ohio, and West Virginia."

"Did David know that many people?" Janet asked in a shaky voice. In the two years since they'd first met, David's mother seemed to have aged two decades.

"It's a mark of respect. Whenever an officer falls in the line of duty, others step forward to honor him. Most won't get in, but they'll stand outside during the service, almost as an honor guard. Hundreds of patrol cars will follow us to the gravesite with their emergency lights blazing." Lydia paused before continuing, thinking about how best to broach what would seem an invasion of their privacy. "There'll also be lots of media. The entire community is in mourning. I'm not trying to frighten you. I just don't want you to be surprised by all the attention."

"David would have liked that," his brother said. "He was proud of what he did. He wanted people to take notice." His voice cracked as the implication of his words came home to him. David had achieved the glory he craved only in death.

"I tried to talk him out of it," his father said. "I never wanted him to become a cop."

"I know, Dad," Kurt said, his tone suggesting he'd heard this many times. "But it was his choice. His life."

Wayne seemed not to have heard. Turning to Lydia, he said, "You were the best thing that ever happened to him. I tried to get him to stay with you. I don't know what got into him."

So great was her shock that she gawked at him. Beth's words came back to her: "He never forgave David for letting you go."

Rather than telling his parents she had thrown him out, David claimed he had ended it. They didn't view her as the rogue in the failed relationship, but as the victim. David had not shown up at her apartment of his own volition Monday night. He'd come to satisfy his father. And if that were the case, perhaps he hadn't been trying to prove something to her when he tried to negotiate with the shooter, but to Wayne.

She pushed her plate back, unable to eat. For the first time since her former lover had been gunned down, tears spilled from her eyes. Oh, David, she thought, always trying to live up to the expectations of others. The other four stared at her but said nothing, unable to comprehend that she wept not in sorrow but in anger.

As she dabbed at her eyes, a steely determination replaced the void in her heart. She was a cop, a good one. David had been out to prove he was the best there was. She would do the same.

FRIDAY MORNING, Novak arose before dawn, slipped into a pair of jeans and a woolen shirt without shaving, and drove to his daughter's house. Jen stood at the front door holding a to-go cup of coffee. "Mom said you'd need this," she said as she raced through the icy drizzle to the car.

"Your mother was right," he said, "again."

"Not always," she said with a giggle.

"Did you throw them away?" he asked as he drove with one hand and swilled coffee with the other.

"All of them," his granddaughter replied, "except what I'm wearing."

They drove west on I-376 and exited at the mall. The parking lot was already full, as thousands of people tried to get Black Friday deals, but Novak's mission was more mundane. On the day after Thanksgiving, He took his granddaughter out to buy socks, replacing all their worn ones. Novak had initiated this pilgrimage when Mariel was a child, back when a local store had a two-for-one sale on socks on this day. This sale no longer existed, nor did the store that had featured it, but Novak continued the tradition.

"I can drop you at the door," he offered as the rain increased.

"I'm a big girl," she said. "I won't break."

Novak was relieved. He didn't care to leave her alone in this crowd. She might be nearing eleven, but the police officer in him still saw her as a vulnerable child, bait for any sick individual out to prey on children.

He found a spot on the periphery of the lot, and they ran toward Macy's, Jen giggling as she went. She ran ahead of him, leaving him huffing and puffing behind her. *I'm out of shape*, he told himself.

Another thought occurred to him. For every year they'd conducted their expedition on this day of the year—and it had started when she was three—she'd held his hand as they crossed the parking lot. Today, she was on her own, floating with the breeze. *I'm almost sixty*, he thought. *And she's nearly a teenager.*

"Are you crying, Pap?" she asked as he entered the store.

"No," he lied, wiping his eyes with his handkerchief. "It's just the rain."

AN HOUR LATER, Jeffrey pulled Thomas Walsh in for questioning. He'd never met the man, but he seemed older and grayer than his sixty-seven years, shuffling as he entered the interview room, as though he'd already been tried, convicted, and sentenced.

"What's this about?" Walsh asked.

"Have a seat," Jeffrey said. He introduced his fellow detective, Bill Thurmond.

"Is this about Tifton?" Walsh asked.

"We have a few questions about your movements the night he was murdered."

"Do I need an attorney? I can't afford one. You people took everything I had years ago."

"We're not charging you with anything. We just want to clarify a few things you told Chief Novak."

Walsh looked from one detective to the other. Prison was full of jailhouse lawyers who'd taught him a lot during his twenty-year incarceration. He didn't have to answer their questions, but he knew failing to do so would increase their suspicions.

"I made a mistake when I first spoke to him," Walsh said. "I didn't know why he'd come to question me, but I didn't want my daughter to know I was visiting Becky's grave. I'd promised to stop."

"You didn't know Tifton had been murdered?"

"Not then," Walsh said. "Chief Novak told me."

"After he left, you asked your manager to lie for you," Jeffrey said.

"Yes," Walsh replied. "Another mistake."

"Why did you do that?" Jeffrey asked.

Walsh hung his head. "I didn't think anyone would believe I'd spend two hours standing out in the cold," he said. "But it's God's honest truth. I go there all the time. Bridey thinks I have an obsession." He folded his hands and stared down at them. "Maybe she's right."

"You must have known your boss would tell the truth." Thurmond said.

Walsh stared at him for a few seconds. This was no good-cop, bad-cop show. They were both after him. "I didn't think. Someone murdered Tifton. I know you'd suspect me. I panicked."

"Years ago, when you were arrested for Becky's murder," Thurmond began.

"When you arrested me," Walsh said.

The detective pushed on as though he hadn't spoken. "Tifton could have provided you with an alibi. He didn't. His silence sent you to prison."

The detective's statement seemed to call for a response, but Walsh remained silent, his legs performing a nervous dance as he fidgeted.

"You must have hated him," Thurmond said.

"I don't have time for hate," Walsh snapped. "Except for the woman who killed Becky. I can't forgive her." A neighbor, Florence O'Rourke, had murdered Rebecca Walsh after learning she was having an affair with her husband.

"And your wife was carrying Terrance O'Rourke's child. Do you want us to believe you spent two hours in near-freezing weather over the grave of a woman who cheated on you?"

Walsh let out his breath in a rush and buried his head in his hands. "Believe what you want," he said. "She was my wife, and I loved her. I don't blame her for what happened between them. I blame O'Rourke."

Raising his head, he looked Thurmond in the eye. "And myself. I blame myself. If I'd been more attentive ..."

"You resented Tifton," Jeffrey said. "He took two decades out of your life."

"His wife left him. His business was failing," Walsh said. "It's divine retribution. I didn't need to hurt him, and I didn't."

"Then why did you go to his office Friday night?" Jeffrey said.

"I didn't. Why would I go there? I don't have the money to buy a house."

"Your phone pinged at a location not one hundred yards from his front door," Jeffrey said.

Walsh shook his head in disbelief. "There's a Chinese restaurant across the street from his office. I went in for takeout at—I don't know. Eight? Eight-thirty? I explained all this to Chief Novak."

"You saw Tifton's car was in his driveway and a light was on in the agency. You left your phone in the car, crossed the street, entered through the back door, and killed him."

"I did not." Walsh's voice was almost a sob. "I didn't cross the street, didn't notice anyone was working late, didn't pay a bit of attention to his office. I haven't spoken to the man since I got out. And I certainly didn't kill him."

"If you didn't center his office," Jeffrey said, "how did your fingerprints and DNA get on the murder weapon?"

"They aren't," Walsh said. "They can't be. What murder weapon? What are you talking about?"

"The For Sale sign you used to stab him. We found your prints all over it. You can't explain this away, Walsh."

"I don't believe you. You're lying, thinking I'll admit to something I didn't do. You bastards got me to do that once, but you're not pulling it on me this time."

Drumming his fingers on the table with each word, Jeffrey said, "You left both your prints and DNA on the sign when you wiped it clean."

"I did not," Walsh said. "You're making it up. I have nothing more to say to the two of you. Either charge me or let me go."

Jeffrey ended the interview, and Walsh walked free, though for how long he didn't know.

Lydia was behind the wheel of an unmarked cruiser pursuing David Kimrey, who was in a patrol car with its emergency lights flashing and siren blaring. She had to give him a message, but he didn't respond to her radio calls. As she drew near, he blew through the intersection, and when she slowed to check on traffic, he sped up. In the distance, she saw him turn to the right down a side street, but when she tried to follow him, a paving crew blocked the road. She sped to the next corner and turned right, spotting his blue, red, and white pulsing lights two blocks ahead. Lydia floored the accelerator, but the road arced to the left. She followed it, turned right at the next intersection, and found herself outside the main gate at Joint Base Fort Sam Houston in San Antonio.

What was David doing here? How had he made it this far? A formation of squad cars blocked the road. She pulled to a stop, her car skewing sideways and almost hitting the roadblock. Leaping from the vehicle, she saw David engaged in animated conversation with an Army colonel. Her father. What was he doing here?

"David," she shouted, "Come here. I need to talk to you."

He turned but didn't acknowledge her, almost looking through her. Her father grabbed David by the arm and led him away. Novak stopped her from pursuing them. "What do you want him for?" he said. "You've missed him." Lydia drew a blank. She had something important to share with David, but ... now she couldn't recall her urgent message. What was happening to her?

She awoke with her heart pounding, unable to recall where she was. Then she did. David was dead. She knew what her dream was about. She wanted to give David the hug he'd asked for. "Too late," she told herself. "Too damn late."

Lydia arose, went to the bathroom, and made a cup of coffee. A heavy wind found its way through the front window of her apartment. "I have to move," she said. "Get out of this barn."

She wrapped a blanket around her, carried her coffee to the bar, and pulled a paper tablet toward her. She thought for a moment, her pen poised, then drew two vertical lines down the page, dividing it into three columns. In the first, she wrote "Benny Craddock," then "Tifton destroyed business by canceling contract w/o notice." She completed the row by writing, "claims spent evening w/wife watching TV." Not only did he have a powerful motive, she thought, he had a weak alibi.

Next was Jason Lindsell, who'd sued Tifton over his string of owner assessments at the condominium. He and his wife claimed they'd attended a concert together, but only his wife could produce a ticket stub. Again, powerful motive, but weak alibi.

Tifton had sold Louis Callon and his partner a house he knew had problems and had covered them up. Callon had called Tifton a sleaze. "That's putting it mildly," she said aloud. It would be easy to check on his whereabouts; if it held up, he was clear. But what about his partner, Steve? Distracted by the sounds of police cars and ambulances, Mayfield hadn't thought to ask where he had been the night of the murder. Was Steven Greenleaf another suspect?

Tifton had squeezed Bryce Combs out as president of the HOA. Was that a motive? He didn't seem to mind that much and claimed to have been bowling with friends at the time of the murder. She'd have no problem checking this.

Finally, she listed Troy Stewart. Tifton had cheated him out of part of a large commission, but he'd moved on. His wife served as his alibi. This wasn't airtight, but Lydia couldn't see him as Tifton's murderer.

Novak had ordered them to check all five alibis. The viewing was scheduled for that evening, and given the turmoil following David's death, she doubted anyone else would follow through. "This is my chance," she said aloud, gritting her teeth and nodding to herself, "my case." Where to start? She bit the tip of her pen and worked her way up from the bottom.

———

NOVAK STARED OUT THE WINDOW, across the parking lot of the police wing and toward the bare trees swaying in the wind, when his cell phone rang. He stared at the caller's name for a moment, debating whether to answer it. "Novak," he said.

"Chief, this is Tom Walsh. I need your help."

"What sort of help?" Novak asked, not bothering to hide his hesitation.

"They're going to arrest me for Tifton's murder. I didn't do this." His voice rose half an octave as he said, "I can't go back to prison. You've got to help me."

Novak was taken aback. What did the man expect him to do? He was a cop. If Jeffrey arrested Walsh, it was out of Novak's hands. He couldn't interfere. "This is the county's investigation, Tom. I have no role in it."

He was met with silence. "Are you still there?" he said after several seconds.

"Yeah. I don't know who else to turn to. They're going to book me. They're tossing the place right now. Bridey's beside herself."

So Jeffrey had a search warrant. This was serious. "If they had enough to arrest you, they would have done so," Novak said to calm the man down.

"No, this guy Jeffrey made it clear." Walsh's words tumbled out in a torrent. "He's trying to frame me. I'll have to go before a judge. Chances are, they'll deny bail or set it so high I can't post bond." He stopped for a moment while Novak waited.

"Do you know what it's like?" Walsh demanded. "You spend years living in a little cell, every minute of your life controlled. This is the extent of your universe, and you come to accept it. When I got out, walking down the street terrified me. The openness of it all. The unrestricted horizon. People I didn't know walking along without a care in the world. What did they want from me? I'd lost the ability to make choices, to decide what to do with my time."

"I understand, Tom, but—"

"It's taken me all this time to recover," he said in a shrill voice, "to accept freedom. I can't return to a cell, even for one night. I cannot face it."

"Do you have an attorney?" Novak said.

"I don't have the money. I lost everything back in ninety-nine. Bridey lives paycheck-to-paycheck. Now I've lost my job."

Novak had feared as much when he questioned the manager at Busy Builders about when Tom had left work the night of Tifton's murder. "If you are charged," he said, "the court will appoint a public defender."

"What good that will do?" Walsh shouted. "They'll just help me enter my plea, argue for no bail, and shrug when the motion's denied."

Novak knew he was right. Public defenders weren't callous; they were overworked. They would do their best when the case came to trial, but didn't have time to waste on pre-trial motions.

"I need to ask you some tough questions, and you need to be honest with me," Novak said. "If they call me as a witness, I'll have to testify truthfully, but until then, I won't volunteer we've spoken. Knowing all that, if you don't want to answer, just remain silent. Okay?"

"Go ahead," Walsh said.

"Did you kill Fred Tifton?"

"No. I've already told you that."

"Attack him? Have any sort of physical altercation with him."

"No."

"Have you threatened him?" Novak asked.

Again, Walsh said he had not.

"Have you been in contact with him since you got out?"

"No."

"I don't just mean in person. Have you called him, written him, sent him a text message?"

"No. I've had no dealings with the man. None."

"Have you visited his office, even when he wasn't around?"

"I haven't gone into the place. I told you I got takeout from the Chinese restaurant. But I went nowhere near his office. They claim my fingerprints are on the murder weapon, one of the yard signs his agents use. But that's impossible."

This was news to Novak. Did Jeffrey have such evidence, or had he lied to force a confession? It wasn't unheard of, nor was it illegal. He drummed the fingers of his free hand on his desk while he thought. "What size shoe do you wear?"

"What?" Walsh asked. "What kind of question is that?"

"Just answer my question. What size, Tom?"

"Eleven. What difference does it make?"

Novak made up his mind. "Let me call a few defense attorneys to see if I can get someone to help. I'm not promising anything. All I can do is ask."

"Thank you," he said.

"Don't get your hopes up," Novak said, "And for God's sake, if I do find someone, I don't want you broadcasting that I had anything to do with it."

"I understand."

After they disconnected, Novak thought about what he'd promised. While it wasn't illegal to help a suspect he believed innocent, it was unorthodox. If he succeeded in getting an attorney to help Walsh and if the ACPD found out, it could mean the end of his relationship with them. And likely the end of his career. It all depended on whether he believed Walsh, a man who had already lied to him during this investigation.

Lydia emerged from the AMF bowling alley on Noblestown Road and slid behind the wheel of her unmarked cruiser. Opening her notebook, she wrote, "Manager Otis Allard confirms Combs and friends at the alley between 7:00 and 9:30 11/19."

The manager had been positive about the fact. "They're here every Friday night. They always take Lane 11. It's not that I remember they were here. I would have recalled if they'd missed."

He'd given her the names of Combs's three friends, but Allard had been so sure she saw no need to question them.

She'd also struck out at Troy Stewart's home. Joan Stewart had been annoyed at her intrusion. "I just put the baby down for his nap," she said. "He was up all night with a tummy ache, and I was hoping to get an hour myself." But when Lydia insisted on questioning her about her husband's whereabouts on the evening of the murder, she relented. "He was with me the whole night long," she said, adding in a whiny voice, "We don't go anywhere these days."

It wasn't unusual for a witness to lie to protect their spouse, but her exhaustion and exasperation led Barnwell to accept her word.

She pulled into the lot alongside Mother's to find Gordon Horvath's cruiser parked in a spot. She considered waiting for him, but the icy wind would penetrate her vehicle as soon as she turned off the ignition, and she was not about to sit there running the engine. Zipping up her parka, she entered the building and spotted her fellow detective standing before a man with dyed blond hair. He wore a gray cotton T-shirt with faded lettering on the back, its cuffs stretched taut against his muscled arms.

Horvath saw her and raised his eyebrows in inquiry. Barnwell shook her head to show she hadn't come to summon him to something more important. She chose not to interrupt their conversation but stared across the floor where a dozen clients strained under barbells, sweated as they hefted dumbbells, or pulled and prodded at various machines. Most were men, but one woman held a kettlebell with both hands, swinging it between her legs, then standing as she lifted it to her chest. Her leg and arm muscles were so well-defined she looked more like a man than a woman. As Lydia gaped at her, the woman grinned and hefted the kettlebell as though it were as light as a rolling pin. The detective gave an involuntary shudder and returned her attention to Horvath and his witness.

"You're certain," she heard him say.

"Absolutely," the young man replied. "Louis never leaves the desk except to pee, clean the equipment, or wash and dry the towels. There's always someone calling on you. If he'd left the building, I'd have heard about it."

Horvath thanked him, but Barnwell interrupted and introduced herself. "What about Steven Greenleaf?" she asked.

"Steve?" The man sneered. "He's not one of us, but he hangs around a lot when Louis's on duty."

"How about last Friday?" she asked.

"I dunno," he said. Then, turning to scan the room, he shouted, "Hey, Nico, were you here a week ago tonight?"

"Nah," a man answered.

"But I was," the weightlifting woman answered.

"Was Stevie here with Louis?"

She dropped the kettlebell and padded across the floor to join them. "Yeah, come to think of it," she said. "He was doing the laundry and watching the front desk so Louis could spend time on the weights."

"Were they both here all night?" she asked.

"You cops?" she asked. Lydia introduced both of them. "I don't know if they were here all night," she said, "but they were when I left around nine. Why?"

"If you're sure they were here, no reason," Lydia said.

In the parking lot, Horvath joined her in the front seat of her cruiser. "You following me?" he said.

"No, I'm just chasing down these alibis.," she said, unwilling to tell him she'd decided to devote herself to this investigation. "I need something to occupy myself."

"Me, too," he said. "Lindsell and his wife did attend that concert. I checked her ticket and got the Benedum to give me the names of those on either side. When I showed them their photos, both couples remembered them."

"Which leaves Benny Craddock," Barnwell said. "I'm going to speak with his wife."

"It's only eight minutes away," he said. "Let's do it together."

They found her at home, a short, round woman with a face shaped like the full moon on which lines of worry stood out like its crater rays. "I don't know if I should speak to you with Benny away," she said.

"This'll just take a minute," Horvath said, no more willing to be put off by her than he'd been for her husband. "Where was Benny last Friday night?"

"With me," she said. "We watched Penn and Teller on the tube. We never miss it. They had this kid on who did card tricks. He didn't fool them, but he was damned cute."

"You're sure?" the woman said.

"Didn't I just tell you?" she snapped back.

Returning to their cruisers, Horvath said, "You ever notice how the longer people live together, the more they act alike?"

"Like people and their dogs," she said.

They returned to headquarters, knowing they'd batted zero. All five suspects could account for their movements on the night the man they hated had been murdered. And where, they wondered aloud, did that leave Thomas Walsh?

BEHIND HER HUSBAND as a column of mourners snaked from the reception area into the visitation room of the funeral home. She wore a knee-length black dress while her husband was in his dress uniform. "Shouldn't we get in line?" she asked.

"I suppose so," Novak replied. She understood his reluctance. He'd never been good with words, and the knowledge he would have to say something meaningful to the family made this difficult for him.

"You'll do fine," she told him, squeezing his hand for reassurance. They took their places, rejecting the invitations of other officers to let them break in line. A few grabbed Novak's hand, expressing their condolences as though he were part of the family.

"He was a fine officer," one said.

"That he was," Novak replied, though that wasn't quite the case. "None better." About half the group was in uniform—from Pennsylvania State Police and Allegheny County Police Department to the smallest townships and boroughs in western Pennsylvania. Novak even recognized two FBI officers. The rest ranged from local government officials and Boyleston citizens to others he didn't recognize, friends of the family and church members, he assumed.

It took ten minutes before the line inched forward enough that they left the reception area and entered what the funeral home euphemistically called the "parlor." A solid oak casket lay atop a metal stand, shielded in a white border with ruffles laced in gold trim. The coffin was closed, such were the facial wounds the gunman had inflicted, but an array of photos was arrayed on its surface—David in uniform on the day he graduated from the academy, his official portrait on the Boyleston force, his college graduation photo, and a half-dozen shots taken throughout his earlier days, from his baby photo to a picture of him on the high school basketball team.

Beyond them stood his mother and father, brother and sister, and their spouses. Novak gripped Wayne's hand but said nothing. To Janet, he said, "I'm so sorry for your loss. He was such a fine young man." She harrumphed and glowered at him through eyes red with weeping. *She needs someone to blame*, he thought, *and here I am*.

Barbara engaged her in conversation, making it about her, the mother who had raised such an outstanding son. Once again, Novak blessed his luck for having met, courted, and married this remarkable woman.

After they expressed their sorrow to the rest of the family, they peeled off to join others standing around the room, holding cups of coffee or plastic glasses of non-alcoholic punch. This was not an Irish wake, though Novak was sure there would be much drinking elsewhere later in the evening.

Barbara nudged him. Following the direction she was looking, he saw Lyle Jeffrey hovering over Lydia Barnwell in a corner of the room. "I wonder what that's about," she said in a low voice. Having no answer for her, he said nothing.

A few yards away, Stan Sabol chatted with one of his fellow council members. Taking Barbara's hand, Novak guided her in his direction. "Hello, Stan," he said. "Thank you for coming."

"It seemed the right thing to do," the Byers council chair said. "He soon would have been one of our own."

Novak's shoulders dropped. "We're going to miss him," he said. "He'll be hard to replace."

Sabol averted his gaze, scanning the room. "Well, good to see you, Karol, even under these circumstances. Take care." He moved off without another word, joining a huddle of men but not engaging in their conversation.

"What was that about?" Barbara said. "He seemed embarrassed to see you."

"I have no idea." Frowning, Novak pushed his hair back from his forehead with both hands. As Barbara reached up to smooth it, he spotted Bernie Jackson coming through the line. He made a mental note to ask if he knew what was bothering Sabol. But not here, he decided.

They wandered through the crowd for a few minutes, Novak thanking other officers for their presence, when he spotted a familiar face standing alone at the back of the parlor. He pulled Barbara toward her, introducing Ceil Adams, a defense attorney with whom he'd occasionally jousted while on the witness stand. She was tall and overweight, and her flaming red hair and loud voice made her an imposing figure. He greeted her, introduced Barbara, and said, "I have a favor to ask."

She gave a raucous laugh. "I'm not letting one of your officers off the hook."

Novak lowered his voice. "Nothing like that," he said, turning so his back was to the room. "Quite the opposite, in fact."

"I'm listening," she said.

"You remember Thomas Walsh, the man who was falsely convicted of murdering his wife in the late nineties?"

"Of course," she said. "You found the evidence that got him released. I have to say, I was impressed when you stepped across from the dark side."

"He's in trouble again," Novak said, ignoring her barb. "I'm convinced he's innocent."

"Now I'm intrigued," she said. "Let's take a walk."

The three left the room and crept down the hall, slipping into a small, darkened viewing room. Novak fumbled until he found a light switch. To avoid attracting the attention of anyone who might pass by, he turned down the dimmer until they could just see each other. "This about the Tifton murder?" she said.

"Yes. You may recall he helped put Walsh behind bars. The county suspects he killed Tifton. As far as I can tell, they have only circumstantial evidence, but no one has a better motive. Jeffrey's looking at no one else."

"But you don't buy it," she said.

"Walsh misled me when I first interviewed him; the lead detective knows it. I'll have a helluva time on the witness stand, if it comes to that. But I know the man. He swears he had nothing to do with Tifton's death."

"What do you want me to do?"

"Represent him, at least at the outset. Keep him out of jail. He says he can't take going back. I fear what he'll do to himself if they try."

She pulled the green frames of her glasses into her mop of red hair. "I have a full caseload now. My cup runneth over, and I'm not sure I have the goodness and mercy to take on anything more. Tell me," she said, gripping his forearm in her fist, "why are you doing this?"

"I think he's innocent. He doesn't have anyone else."

"But why you?" she demanded.

Rather than answering, he looked at Barbara, whose expression showed she, too, was curious. "I don't know," he said. "It just seems the right thing to do."

She looked off to the side and scratched her scalp. "All right," she said, "I'll talk to him. You're a strange man, Karol Novak."

"Yeah," he said with a chuckle. "I guess I am."

LYDIA BARNWELL PADDED to the kitchen in her slippers and robe, poured raisin bran into a bowl, and prepared a latte. She stared at the steady rain pelting the glass. Her phone told her it would be in the low 40s all day. Wet, cold, and nasty, she thought. A perfect day for a funeral.

She paged through the electronic version of the *Post-Gazette* while she thought about the events of the previous evening. Detective Lyle Jeffrey had first expressed his condolences. "I didn't realize you were close," he said.

She didn't know where he'd gotten his information. Their relationship was common knowledge at Boyleston PD. Perhaps some loudmouth had told him. Her money was on Mark Ewer. How had he ever become a detective? The previous chief's mistake, she thought, one of many. Novak would never have put Ewer in a position of trust.

"We once were," she'd told Jeffrey, "but we remained friends."

"Still," he said, "it must be rough for you."

"It's tough on all of us," she said, hoping that closed the matter.

He'd continued to engage her in small talk, or what passed for it among police officers, chatting her up long past the time they both should have moved on. He had something on his mind, and she was curious to know what. She saw Novak looking at them, perhaps worried Jeffrey was trying to recruit her.

As indeed he was. "Why don't we get together for coffee sometime?" He posed it as a suggestion rather than a question.

So there it was. In the space of five minutes, he'd moved from sorry-for-your-loss to now-that-you're-free. And wasn't the man married? She wasn't positive, but thought she'd seen him squiring an attractive woman around at a police function some time back. Was this why he'd included her in suspect interviews? It wasn't his respect for how she'd handled the investigation into the missing child, she decided. He was hitting on her.

And with that, she strung him along. Two could play the same game. "I'm always up for coffee," she said. As long as he thought he had a chance, he might continue to involve her in the investigation. She'd learn what she could while keeping him at arm's length.

"How's the investigation going?" she asked.

He cupped her elbow and steered her further into their corner of the room. "Confidentially," he said.

"Of course."

"We have enough to arrest Walsh. If it weren't for the holiday, we would have done so already, but the Assistant DA is back in the office Monday. That's when we'll file charges."

"That was quick," she said. "I heard you got a search warrant. Did you find anything at his house?"

Jeffrey shook his head.

"No bloody shoe?" she said. "No stained clothing?"

"We came up empty, but that means nothing. He's had plenty of time to get rid of incriminating evidence."

"Nice work," she said.

"You're part of it, too," he replied. "You interviewed the others, allowing us to focus on Walsh. And we found enough to confirm our suspicions."

He'd given her a shit-eating grin and strolled away. As she finished her breakfast and prepared to leave for headquarters, she considered how much to tell Novak.

Li Wan, his wife, and their two children lived in an apartment above his restaurant. Novak hated to bother the man since he suspected he worked late, but he rang their doorbell and waited until he heard steps descending the staircase. "Yes?" he said, peering at Novak through thick lenses.

As Novak introduced himself, Li interrupted him. "I know you, Chief. How can I help you?"

Novak smiled. People who offered to provide information were too rare. "You remember the night Fred Tifton was murdered?"

"Yes," Li said. "He'd come in for takeout just an hour beforehand. I explained all this to the officers from the county."

"I know," Novak replied, "but I'm asking about someone else. Do you know a man named Thomas Walsh?"

"Ah, yes," he said. "Mr. Walsh. Poor man. He's been through so much. He and his wife used to dine here when my father owned the restaurant. I was just a teenager, but I worked in the kitchen and remember him well."

"The night of Tifton's murder," Novak said, "do you recall if he came in?"

Li thought for a moment. "I'm opening the restaurant," he said. "Can you come with me?"

Novak followed the man out the doorway of the walkup and took the dozen steps to the restaurant's entry. He was surprised to find it unlocked. Li stood aside as Novak entered, taking in the fragrant smell of something cooking in the kitchen. Clean cloths and settings adorned the tables. Novak remembered the restaurant served both lunch and dinner. Li said something in Chinese, and a woman's shrill voice answered.

Mrs. Li emerged from the kitchen, wiping her hands on an apron, gave him a slight bow, and said hello. Li Wan said a few words to her, to which she responded with a wide grin, a vigorous nod of her head, and a stream of Chinese. "He here," she told Novak.

Li translated for his wife, who'd been born in rural China and had met her husband when he returned to visit his extended family years before. "Hua says he came in around eight o'clock and picked up two dishes and an order of egg rolls."

"How can she be sure he came in on that specific night?" Novak asked.

Li and his wife exchanged a few more words. She turned to Novak and said, "He cold."

"She remembers him because he was shivering when he came in. He was hugging himself and moving up and down on the balls of his feet. When she asked if he was ill, he told her he was just cold, that he'd been standing out in the weather for more than an hour. She understands more than she can speak," he added before Novak could ask how she'd gotten so much out of him.

He thanked them both and left. This didn't disprove Walsh had crossed the street and entered Tifton's office, but whenever Novak ordered takeout, he took it home to Barbara before it grew cold.

"We have nothing," Gordon Horvath said as Novak entered his office, shaking rain off his coat. The chief was seldom late, but he offered no explanation for his tardiness as he called on the other two to join him.

"We've confirmed every alibi and come up empty-handed," Barnwell said. She added that Craddock and Stuart had only their spouses for confirmation, "but there's no way to disprove Shiela Craddock's story, and I believe Joan Stewart."

Novak absorbed this information without comment.

"Meanwhile," she said, "Jeffrey is about to arrest Tom Walsh."

At this, Calvin Mayfield spoke up. "Who told you that?"

"I got it from the horse's mouth," she said. "He told me in confidence, so, of course, I'm telling the three of you."

Novak drummed his fingers on his desk and leaned back in his chair. So Walsh wasn't being paranoid. "Did he mention what evidence they have?"

"No. Their search of Bridey's house turned up nothing, but Jeffrey suspects he got rid of his shoes and bloody clothing. He's relying on circumstantial evidence, but plans to arrest him Monday." She hesitated, as though she had more to say.

Novak waited, but when she didn't continue, he decided not to pursue it. "About the funeral," Mayfield said. "Pittsburgh PD is closing off the area around the church from East Liberty down to Penn."

"Locals won't like that," Horvath said.

"They'll have to get over it," Mayfield responded. "We're expecting a blue wave from the commonwealth and six states. The Governor and both US senators are coming, and they may want to say a few words."

"Since Eastminster is streaming the service, you can count on it," Horvath said, making no attempt to hide his sneer.

Novak tugged at his ear. "They can't not."

Mayfield reviewed who would provide coverage to the borough during the service. "We'll be spread thin, but Crafton and Carnegie have agreed to help if needed."

The three rose to leave, but Barnwell stayed behind, closing the door to his office. "Someone took it upon himself to share with Jeffrey that David and I once had a relationship," she said.

Novak nodded. So that was what she was about to say when she'd hesitated moments before. "Any idea who?"

"Yes," she said, "but I can't prove it."

Novak closed his eyes and expelled air from his lungs. "I'll have a talk with him."

"Please don't," she said. "I'm just letting you know. He's not to be trusted."

Novak agreed. If he were to confront Ewer, it would put Barnwell in a box. But he had to stop his leaking if he was indeed the source. He doodled on a notepad as he considered what to do, but before he could act, his cell phone rang. He didn't recognize the number, but answered it anyway.

"This is Bridey O'Connor," a woman's voice said. He asked what he could do for her. "Thank you for finding that attorney for Dad."

"I spoke to her about the case," he said, "but I'd appreciate it if you'd keep this to yourself."

"Okay." She drew out her response in a puzzled voice, uncertain why he wouldn't take credit for his good deed. "Only, she's a little weird, isn't she?"

"Ceil Adams cuts quite a figure," he replied, "but she's a top defense attorney. A bit of St. Joan and a lot of St. Jude."

"You think Dad's a lost cause?" she demanded.

"I only mean that she takes on hard cases. I know. I've been up against her a few times."

"Because," Bridey said as though he hadn't spoken, "The county detective claims he found dad's prints on the sign used to kill Tifton. I know how they got there. We were out for a walk in the neighborhood a few weeks ago. It was right after that windstorm, you know? A For Sale sign had blown over in a neighbor's front yard. Dad picked it up and drove it back into the ground."

"Why would he do that?" Novak asked, suspecting Bridey had cooked up the story.

"Not for Fred Tifton," she said, "but for that agent of his, Walt Dwyer. He and Walt go way back. Dad was also looking out for our neighbors. Luke and Mary Varga are trying to sell their home. He's had a stroke, and she's too frail to give him the care he needs. They need to move into a senior living facility, but can't afford it until they sell their place."

"Have they found a buyer?" Novak asked, reasoning that if Tifton's sign was still in the front yard, it couldn't be the murder weapon.

"No," she said. "It's been on the market for months. That's why they've changed agents."

If Bridey was telling the truth, this explained why the sign had been returned to Tifton's office. "I assume you've told Ms. Adams about this."

"Dad did. I'm not sure she was paying attention."

"I'm sure she was," Novak said. "She doesn't miss much. At the moment, her priority is keeping the DA from charging him."

Bridey thanked him again and disconnected. Inevitably, Jeffrey would learn he'd recruited Ceil Adams to represent Walsh. As he thought about the county detective, he had an idea. He left his office, entered Horvath's cubicle, and took a seat. "I need your help with something," he said in a confidential tone.

AFTER HE'D SPOKEN to Horvath, Novak closed his door while debating whether to follow up on something that had bothered him the night before. Taking a deep breath and shrugging as if the decision made no difference, he called his friend on the borough council. Bernie Jackson picked up on the second ring. "Morning, Karol. What can I do for you?"

"What makes you think I want something?" Novak said with a slight laugh.

"Because you're calling on your personal phone," he said.

"You should have been a detective," Novak replied.

"At least I would have had job security." Jackson was a professional photographer whose primary sources of income, business, family, and school portraits, had been undermined by the growing popularity of cell phone photography. Working through Barbara,

Novak had helped restore his business of taking class portraits, but it wasn't enough to keep him going. "So what's on your mind?" Bernie said.

Novak rose and stared out the window where the rain washed the colors from everything it touched, rendering the world in shades of gray. "I ran into Stan Sabol at the viewing last night," he said. "We spoke briefly about David, and then he moved off without another word. It was almost as if he wanted to avoid me."

Novak waited for Jackson to say something, to ask a question or make an excuse, but he was silent. "What's going on, Bernie?"

After another pause, Jackson said, "I've been meaning to talk to you."

"Talk to me now."

"Peter Watson, the facilitator the state sent?" Jackson asked.

"What of him?" Novak said.

"He's suggested someone younger should lead the regional force."

When Jackson again hesitated, Novak went into interrogator mode. "And Sabol agrees with him?"

"He's done an about-face. I've been trying to turn him back around, but..."

"He's one of three votes, Bernie. What aren't you telling me?"

The council member emitted a long sigh. "He has Lentz with him."

Novak took it all in. In the spring, when Novak had insisted on his long-delayed retirement, Lentz and Jackson had urged him to stay to oversee the merger. Lentz had made his priority clear: he wanted Boyleston to be the lead player in the troika. With Novak heading the department, he figured he'd get his wish.

But they were at cross-purposes. Lentz thought a regional force would save the borough money. while Novak envisioned an enlarged force to improve the quality of law enforcement for the three communities. Had their diverging goals caused Lentz to change his mind?

"What are you thinking?" Jackson asked.

Novak studied the barren branches of the oak trees lining the opposite side of the street. "I'm not sure."

"I've done my best, Karol. I've told Lentz I'll resign if he doesn't support you."

"Don't fall on your sword, Bernie. It's not worth it."

"Lentz went behind my back," Jackson said. "He'd discussed this with Sabol for days, but never told me. I was blindsided."

"I understand," Novak said. "Do whatever you have to do. I'll do the same." At the moment, however, he didn't know what that might be.

NOVAK HAD one more task to complete before picking Barbara up to attend the funeral. He parked his cruiser before a duplex on Melbourne Street, took the front steps while holding the handrail, and rang the doorbell. Hearing no ringing inside, he waited ten seconds, then knocked on the door. A young Black woman answered, dressed in tight leggings and a loose sweatshirt bearing the logo of Bluefield State College.

"Hello, Nia," he said. "Is Norville here?"

"About time you came here," she said. She stepped aside and allowed him to ascend the stairs ahead of her.

Norville Chastain was spread out on a sofa watching the Ohio State-Michigan game. A beer can rested on a round hassock in imitation leather before him. He reached for the remote lying beside him and muted the audio. "Hello, Chief," he said.

"Norbert," Novak replied. "How are you doing?"

"I'm okay," Chastain said. One look at the young officer told Novak he was not doing okay.

Novak removed his hat, perching it on his knee as he settled into an armchair upholstered in red placed at an angle to the couch. "How're your meetings with Dr. Grady going?" he asked.

"The head doctor? She's all right, but she doesn't talk much. It's kind of awkward."

"I know," Novak said. "I've been through it. She's there to listen rather than speak. It's a little unnerving."

"Yeah." Chastain stared at the screen as an Ohio State player ran toward the end zone for a pass but dropped it. "The funeral's today," he said.

"At two," Novak said.

"I suppose I should go, but I don't feel up to it." Novak let the silence fall between them, hoping Chastain would fill it. "All those eyes on me," he said.

"You think others blame you for what happened?" Novak said. "They don't. They blame the shooter and, to a certain extent, Kimrey himself for leaving himself open. I ask myself why he acted as he did. I have an idea, and if I'm right, I'm the one who should feel guilty."

He leaned forward in his chair, bringing himself closer to Chastain. "But I don't, Norville. David knew better. He made a poor decision, and it cost him his life. There's nothing you could have done about it."

"I should have stopped him," he said.

"You told him to wait for backup, didn't you? Suggested he wait for the SWAT team?" The officer nodded. "Then you did what you could. You're a rookie. He was supposed to be training you, not the other way around. You didn't cause his death, Norville. You did nothing wrong."

Chastain studied him for a moment, and tears welled in his eyes. "I'm not sure I'm cut out for this."

"Well, I am," Novak said. "I fought council this summer to fund the vacant position. From the start, I wanted you to fill it. I saw your record at the academy and your outstanding test results. You impressed Mayfield and me during your interview. Everything you've done since joining the force has confirmed our judgment. You've worked all your life for this. Don't throw it away."

Through all this, his girlfriend stood at the entrance to the kitchen, her arms crossed. "The chief's right," she said. "You can't let some madman with a gun kill your dreams."

Chastain looked from one of them to the other. "Okay," he said at length. "I'll try."

Novak thanked him, repeated his words of encouragement, and took the stairs to the entrance. "And you're right," he told Nia as he grasped the doorknob. "I should have come sooner."

"At least you came," she said.

Eastminster Presbyterian Church is an imposing stone structure on Highland Avenue in Pittsburgh's East End. Its tall steeple dominates the local skyline, shared by the mostly white neighborhood of Highland Park and the largely Black East Liberty neighborhood below it. The congregation reflects this racially mixed community, which struggles with the benefits and challenges of changing demographics. Young, well-educated workers for high-tech companies like Google have transformed the once-blighted fringes of the neighborhood.

Novak stepped aside to allow Barbara to enter the reserved pew before him, but when he knelt, she reached for his arm and pulled him in behind her. This was not his first time in a Protestant church, so he knew better, but the habit of kneeling and crossing himself was hard to break. Unchurched though he was since leaving the faith, he still found Protestant services too informal for his taste. It was as though they didn't take worship that seriously, although too many priests he'd encountered took a similarly casual approach to their vows.

A lectern and pulpit stood at opposite sides of the raised platform, framing an altar he assumed was used for communion. Above the stage, a large frame meant to represent organ pipes held a barren cross, the structure displayed against an illuminated purple background. The pews, forming an arc facing the front of the sanctuary, were filled with uniformed men and women. More sat in the choir loft beneath the wooden beams of the church. The organist played a litany of funeral music, most of which Novak recognized: "Rock of Ages," "Nearer My God to Thee," and "Abide with Me."

Wayne and Janet Kimrey sat alongside their children in the front pew, two rows ahead of the Novaks. Alongside them were other friends and family members he didn't recognize. One figure stood out, Lydia Barnwell, dressed in black. While David's mother dabbed her eyes, Novak couldn't tell if Wayne betrayed any emotion.

The organist ended the litany, and a pastor, wearing a black robe with a red shawl bearing what appeared to be representations of the cross, stood at the pulpit. "We have gathered today to celebrate the life of David Kimrey, devoted son, companion, friend, and a dedicated public servant," he said. "David died doing what he loved, serving and protecting. He died while trying to help the family of a disturbed man. Like Christ Jesus, he gave his life so that others might live. We honor him today. Let us pray."

The pastor raised his arms, indicating that those able to do so should rise. A sound like muted thunder filled the sanctuary as they did so. He prayed for David and asked God to welcome him into his heavenly family. When he prayed for comfort for his mother and family, Janet Kimrey's sobbing vied with his words.

Barbara gripped Novak's hand as though afraid he would drift away from her. Every officer's family fears their loved one can be taken at any moment. Barbara's sense of dread had lurked in the background since her husband was a young patrol officer, but now it dominated her thoughts.

As the pastor intoned an Amen, the creaking of pews as hundreds of fannies settled back into their seats sounded like trees groaning under the weight of a storm. A man approached the lectern and read the Twenty-third Psalm. A Black woman followed him, her "Amazing Grace" echoing the song's roots in the slave trade. Novak saw Barbara raise a handkerchief to her eyes and wrapped his arm around her shoulder.

One of David's high school friends followed. He brought a measure of levity to the proceedings, recounting antics he and David had conducted during their years together, the most memorable being stuffing Limburger cheese into the vents in the English classroom one cold morning, producing odors so strong the class was dismissed to the school library. "I did this," the young man said, "but David put me up to it, demonstrating his leadership skills at an early age."

A parade of others spoke, including the governor. As Horvath had suggested hours before, his words of praise to "the men and women in blue" seemed aimed more at his constituents than David's family.

Then it was Novak's turn. He took the red-carpeted steps to the pulpit and looked out to the congregation. For a moment, his words deserted him. He had never been comfortable speaking to people, but that wasn't what affected him at the moment. Instead, the field of blue uniforms brought home to him the enormity of what had occurred. He recalled how, after David and Lydia had split, the young officer had gone into a tailspin, how Mayfield had tried and failed to redirect him, and how, when Novak had assigned him to discover who was raiding the alms box at St. Cyril and Methodius Church, David had redeemed himself by camping out at the church for two days.

Novak had brought the young officer back. He was studying to become a detective, and Novak didn't doubt that, given time, he would have become a good one. As he began speaking, Novak recalled his own transition from patrol officer to detective over three decades before. All the cases he had worked, all the crimes he had solved, all the human misery he had witnessed passed before him. David would experience none of that.

As he felt the eyes of over six hundred officers on him, the words he'd rehearsed before the mirror over the past forty-eight hours fell away. "David was an outstanding officer," he said, "but he was a better man. Let me tell you a story about a young boy he found taking money from a collection box at our local church." He related how, through Barbara, he'd learned Antone had stolen the money to buy food for his aging grandparents, his caregivers who themselves needed care.

"We let the young man off with a warning," Novak said. "Father Murray let him keep the money. 'After all,' he explained, 'it's for the poor.' But that wasn't enough for David. I later learned he bought the family groceries out of his pocket and delivered them to them personally. He befriended this boy, taking him to Steelers games, attending his school performances, and becoming the father he never had."

From a side pew came a low moan, rising and falling like a mourning dove. Novak stopped and peered to his left. He'd been unaware the young boy was sitting alongside his grandmother in a pew beneath one of the three round stained-glass windows. "Antonne," he said, "David loved you like a son. And all of us—all his friends and fellow officers—will continue to look after you. That's my promise."

WITH THE SOUNDS of "O God, Our Help in Ages Past" echoing in their memories, Karol and Barbara joined the funeral procession as it made its mournful four-mile journey onto Penn Avenue, arriving a quarter hour later at Woodlawn Cemetery. Novak's cruiser followed four black limousines trailing the hearse. Behind them, a long line of patrol cars stretched for blocks, their flashing blue and red lights reflected in the rain-slick streets. Mounted motorcycle patrol officers leapfrogged each other, blocking access from side streets and forcing the occasional vehicle ahead to the side.

As they passed a major intersection, a driver honked his horn, inching his car forward as though to break through the line. Novak slowed, lowered his window, and glared at the man until he stopped. "He can't spare five minutes to honor a fallen officer," he said.

"The whole country seems self-absorbed," Barbara replied. As her husband muttered agreement, she said, "That was a moving tribute you paid to David, nothing like what you'd rehearsed."

Novak gripped the steering wheel, staring straight ahead as he spoke. "Father Murray called this morning to tell me what David had been doing for Antonne. It took me by surprise. David never mentioned it. When I looked over those faces, I threw away my prepared remarks and told the story."

"You did well," she said. "Did you see how Lydia reacted?" He shook his head. "She began sobbing. It was the first time she showed any emotion. I'm surprised you didn't notice."

"I was watching Antonne," he said. He rapped his fingers on the steering wheel. "With David gone, we have to do something for him."

Barbara agreed as they entered the cemetery on Highland Way. The hearse crept south along the drive, turned at the loop, and continued halfway north, halting twenty yards from a large white tent erected over the gravesite. An honor guard pulled forward and removed the casket from the back of the hearse, placing it on a mechanism erected over the rectangular hole in the ground. Novak and Barbara joined other mourners, who clustered around the site under a sea of umbrellas. A few in bright colors added an incongruous touch to the solemn occasion. It took ten minutes for the visiting officers to emerge from their cruisers and encircle the gathering, standing at attention in their raincoats.

Barbara linked her arm with Novak's as he held their black umbrella aloft in his free hand. A light wind tugged at it, forcing him to grip the shaft in both hands as the ceremony began. It lasted only ten minutes. The pastor intoned a brief prayer, the mechanism lowered David's coffin into the ground, and Wayne and his two surviving children tossed small clumps of earth over it. An Irish officer sang "Be Thou My Vision," and a bugler played taps.

Funeral attendants led Wayne, Janet, and their family back to the limousines, and the mourners departed. Neither Novak nor Barbara spoke for several minutes as the windshield wipers slapped back and forth, punctuating the silence.

As they crossed the Fort Pitt Bridge and entered the tunnel, the wipers stopped. In the ensuing silence, Barbara said. "I worry."

Her husband did not respond. "It could have been you," she said.

"I know," he replied. "It gets worse every year. More people with more problems having more guns. And a great deal more mistrust, not just from Blacks but from everyone. It's not as fun as it used to be. That's not the right word. It was never fun."

"Rewarding," she said.

"Right," he said. "Thank you."

They left the Parkway West at the Greentree exit, headed down the hill toward Crafton, then continued on Noblestown Road toward Boyleston in silence. When they reached their home, he killed the engine and turned toward her. "Something's come up. We have a decision to make."

She said nothing, waiting for him to explain.

"I won't be heading the merged department after all."

"What? Why?"

He took her through his conversation with Bernie earlier in the day. "That's dirty," she said. "You only stayed this long because they begged you to. And now they're taking it away? We lost an entire summer together. Traveling, spending time with Jen, working around the house..." She trailed off, waving her hands as she searched for other things they might have done together.

"What will you do?" she asked. "Can you fight it?"

"I'm not sure I want to. I haven't had time to think about it."

He exited the cruiser and came around to her side, holding the umbrella over her. They stepped onto the porch, and Novak unfurled the umbrella, shaking off the water. A package lay alongside the mat. He stooped over to pick it up and followed her into the house.

Barbara started the water for tea while he sat at the counter. "Unless they change their minds, I'll lose my job. It's a question of how long I stay. Should I take my leave now or stay to manage the transition? It's not like we need the money."

"Your choice," she said as she poured boiling water over the tea bags in their cups. "What's in the package?"

"I don't know." He reached across the counter for the scissors and sliced across the top of the sealed envelope. "It's the yearbook I ordered. That didn't take long." In the turmoil following David's death, he'd forgotten about it.

"You're still after the priest," she said. "I wish you could let it go."

He dunked his tea bag a few times, removed it, and took a sip, not answering her.

CHAPTER NINE
SUNDAY, NOVEMBER 28

AFTER SWAPPING his cruiser for the family car, Novak
returned to the house and drove his mother to Mass. Yesterday's
downpour had turned into a cold mist, so rather than dropping her
off, he parked the car in the lot and walked her to the entrance,
holding the umbrella over her head as she pushed her walker along.
Izabela had long since stopped asking him to join her and did not
do so this morning, but as she entered the narthex, she turned and
gave him a wistful look, as though she were saying goodbye for the
last time.

Returning to his car, he hunched over the steering wheel with his
arms folded. Soon, he would have to say farewell. As she entered her
ninetieth year, Izabela grew more frail by the day. Besides her
increasing deafness, her eyesight was failing.

She had arrived with her mother from Czechoslovakia, weeks
after VE Day, speaking not a word of English. Her father, Novak's
grandfather, had come to the country before the war to work in a steel
mill, saving money to bring his wife and daughter to the new country.
But Hitler's annexation of the Sudetenland and subsequent push east
had trapped them in Nazi-held territory for nearly seven years. The
nuns at St. Cyril's had taught her English, and she had quickly

caught up from years of erratic schooling. She had worshipped here from the time of her arrival.

Novak's revelation that he and others had been sexually abused by a predator priest had shaken her faith and destroyed his. She continued to worship here and would for the rest of her days, but he would not. Could not.

Rather than returning home, he drove four blocks to a doughnut shop, ordered a cup of coffee and a cruller, and opened the package that had been waiting at his doorstep the previous evening. It was a photocopied reprint of someone else's yearbook, a woman named Alice, and the inside front cover was plastered with handwritten endearments: *Friends forever, Norma*; *Always remember the good times, Sandy*; and several others. He read each of them, searching for anything Timothy Dacey might have written.

He paged through the photos of seniors until he found Dacey's picture. His dark hair was parted near the crown and neatly combed, and he wore a solemn expression bordering on a frown as though he were about to celebrate Mass. The knot in his tie resembled a choke hold, his shirt collar bulging as though it were too small for him. Only the shoulders of his regulation blazer were visible in the shot.

While many others had signed their photos, often with a brief note, Dacey had not autographed Alice's yearbook. Had they not known each other, or had she failed to find him on the day the year-books were delivered?

He took out his notebook and began writing the names of those who had signed. Most were girls, and if they had married, they might be hard to find. Several boys had signed. Then he stopped, realizing he was confused. These were not Dacey's friends, but those of the woman who'd owned the original yearbook. Still, he could start here. Novak wrote every name, producing a list that covered two pages.

"Can I get you anything else?" the owner said as she refilled his cup.

"No, thanks, Mary Ellen. Just the bill."

"It's on the house," she said.

He didn't protest. They had conducted this ceremony many times in the past. But as he replaced the yearbook in its padded envelope and finished the rest of his coffee, he left a five-dollar bill and two ones on the table. No one would accuse him of taking a bribe, no matter how small.

———

Two miles away, Lydia Barnwell sat in a Starbucks in Greentree near the county police building. Lyle Jeffrey had called an hour before, asking to meet for coffee. She was reluctant at first, unwilling to get involved with who she had now confirmed was a married man, but her desire to remain close to the case won out. Jeffrey could probe for whatever he wanted, while she could go after what she needed.

She watched him pull into the driveway in an unmarked county vehicle. A line of cars snaked around the building, encircling it in fumes as drivers awaited their turn at the takeout window. Jeffrey found a parking spot and strolled through the traffic, ignoring the mist, with one hand in his pocket as though jingling keys.

He smiled and waved at her, raised his eyebrows and hand as though holding a coffee drink, and nodded when she raised her cup. He placed his order and slid in opposite her. "You got here early," he said. "I was going to buy your coffee."

"I have a gift certificate," she lied.

"I wanted to speak to you after the service," he said, "but you were with the family, and I couldn't get to you." She smiled and nodded. His statement did not seem to require a response. "That must have been difficult for you."

"It was emotional." She kept her voice flat, not inviting further inquiry.

He was not put off. "It's remarkable his family included you. You must have been quite close."

"Like I said at the reception, it was over months ago," she said, "but I remained close to his parents. They asked me to sit with them, so out of respect, I did." She folded her arms to close the topic.

The barista called his name, and he rose to grab his coffee drink. When he returned, she seized the initiative. "You're arresting Walsh tomorrow. What do you have on him?"

He raised his cup to his lips while studying her. "That's what I wanted to see you about. What's this about a false alibi?"

She narrowed her eyes and gave a slight shake of her head. "What?"

"When you interviewed the other suspects, one of them gave you an alibi that turned out not to be true."

"No," she said. "Where did you hear that?"

He ignored her question. "You've cleared all those you interviewed?"

Barnwell took him through the five stories. "For Craddock and Stewart, all we have are the words of their spouses, but they're unshakable."

"Hmm." He took another sip of his coffee and smiled to himself.

"You and I interviewed the two other agents," she said, "and you talked with Amanda Naughton, Tifton's assistant."

"By phone, yes, but she's still in Somerset."

"So, no formal interview?" Jeffrey shook his head, staring at his coffee cup to avoid her penetrating gaze. "What did she tell you?"

"She was so upset I didn't get too much out of her," Jeffrey said. "I asked whether anyone held a grudge against him. She couldn't think of anyone. She seemed more concerned about whether she'll still have a job when she comes home tomorrow."

Barnwell considered that for a moment, but let it pass. "What time are you arresting Walsh?" she asked.

"As soon as the DA signs off on it. Big mid-morning, if possible. We can place him at Tifton's office within fifteen minutes of the attack. Walsh had motive, means, and opportunity. When Novak asked where he was at the time of the murder, he lied and tried to get his boss to cover for him."

"But that's all circumstantial, isn't it?"

"There's more," Jeffrey said. "We found his prints on the murder weapon."

Novak would not be happy to hear this, she thought. Jeffrey drained his coffee and began to speak, but she headed him off. "I'm still curious where you got that rumor we'd disproved one alibi." He looked at her and shook his head. "Not willing to tell me? Whoever it was didn't know what he was talking about." She emphasized the pronoun, having a suspicion as to his source. And if she was right, who had fed him this garbage? Someone was playing games here.

"What will you do now?" he asked. She turned her right palm over and shook her head, not understanding what he meant. "Now that David is gone," he said.

"I'm going to do my job and go about my life," she answered. He raised his eyebrows, inviting further explanation.

"I'll tell you this in confidence," she said. "There is a man. He's trying to start something. He's nice enough, but I'm not ready. And I looked him up. He's married."

She leaned forward, boring into him with her ice-blue eyes. "Can you imagine? A man with a wife and kids trying to strike up an affair with a single woman. And a cop, at that."

He leaned back from her penetrating gaze. "No," he said. "But being cops, we've seen it all, haven't we?"

Her laugh was cynical. "Indeed, we have."

After he left, she opened her water bottle and sat alone, trying to decide what to do. After a few minutes of internal debate, she opened her cell phone and called Calvin Mayfield. "I've just had the most interesting conversation," she said. "Someone told Sergeant Jeffrey we found a hole in a suspect's story. I don't suppose you or the chief know anything about that."

He laughed so hard she had to hold the phone away from her ear.

Once he'd collected Izabella from church, she took control of the TV and turned the volume up full blast. He tried to make phone calls from his basement office, but the racket seeped through the floorboards like water from a broken pipe. After ten minutes, he gave up and joined Barbara in the kitchen. "Anything I can do?" he asked.

"Cut off the power," she said, then added, "I'm just putting turkey leftovers on the table. You can grab what you'd like."

He told her of his plan, and she gave him a plate of food to take to his office. Once at the municipal building, he warmed his dish in the microwave, filled his coffee mug, and closed his door.

Opening his notebook, he looked up the first name on the list and found no phone number. Had the party moved or passed away? He had no idea. Using his personal cell phone, he called the second name and got no answer. On the third try, he reached a man named Charles Stumpf and introduced himself only by name.

"I'm trying to find one of your classmates at St. Francis, Timothy Dacey," he said. "Do you remember him?"

"No," came the answer.

"You graduated in the same year," Novak said.

"Makes no difference. I worked in the family market after school and on weekends. I wasn't in sports or any of the clubs. Unless I'd gone to grade school with a kid, lived on the same street, or sat next to him in class, I didn't know him. A lot of these folks get together for reunions every few years. Not me."

Novak asked if he could think of anyone who might help him. "Maybe Ross Barnes could have. He knew everyone," he replied. "But he's gone now."

It went like that for the next twenty minutes, a combination of no telephone numbers and faded memories. Until, on one call, he found, if not pay dirt, at least something other than sandy soil. "You should try Birdie Solomon," a man said. "She was class secretary and keeps track of everyone."

Novak asked how he could reach her. "She's on Facebook," he said. "Go to the St. Francis Alumni page, and you'll find her."

"You don't have a number for her?"

"No, she's down in Florida somewhere."

"Is Solomon her maiden name?"

"Yeah, but I don't recall her married name."

"And Birdie is her first name?" Novak asked.

"No, but that's what everyone calls her, and that's the name she still uses. Who did you say this is?"

"Karol Novak," he said. "Dacey was my priest years ago. I'm trying to locate him."

Novak didn't want to use the office computer or its bandwidth, so he used his phone to log on to Facebook. The St. Francis page was marked private, so he applied to join it. Asked what year he'd graduated, he entered 1965, hoping whoever was in charge of the page wouldn't check. That done, he made more cold calls, all of them fruitless. Ninety percent of a cop's work was pure drudgery, but since Novak wasn't identifying himself as an officer, the task became even more challenging. But he had the entire afternoon ahead of him.

———

ONE OFFICE AWAY, Detective Mark Ewer faced an unsmiling Deputy Chief Mayfield across his desk. "Why did you call me in on my day off?" he demanded.

"It's my day off, too," Mayfield said, "not that there's such a thing in police work."

If Ewer was contrite by this response, he didn't say so.

"Detective Jeffrey has asked one of your fellow officers to identify the suspect in the Tifton murder case whose alibi doesn't hold up," the deputy chief said.

Anyone else, Mayfield thought, would have realized the implication of the question, but not Ewing. "So," he said, "who is it?"

Mayfield waited a beat before responding. "No one."

"What do you mean? You told me—"

"That we'd discovered one witness lied to us about their where-abouts the night of the murder," Mayfield interrupted.

Ewing shook his head in confusion.

"But that isn't true. I made it up."

"What? Why?"

"Because I wanted to see whether Jeffrey would find out. He did." Mayfield spread his hands across his desk as though putting his cards on the table. "And you're the only person with whom I shared that bogus information."

Ewing nodded. "I told him. What's the harm in sharing informa-tion about an open case with another agency, especially if they are leading the investigation?"

"I suppose not," Mayfield said. "But the reason I did so—the reason Chief Novak asked me to do so—is because other information was getting to him, things that have nothing to do with Tifton's murder, personal matters. We decided to find the leak and plug it."

Ewing stared at his lap for a moment. "I haven't told him anything that would hurt anyone."

"Just office gossip," Mayfield said. "The way we figure it, you're giving him information that's none of his business—none of yours, come to think of it—to ingratiate yourself with the county. I assume you're angling for an open position. Since you've fed Jeffrey incorrect information and wasted his time, I doubt it will further your career."

"I'm not trying to—"

"Nor will it make you look better in his eyes if you tell him how gullible you are."

Ewer protested again but stopped himself mid-sentence. "What happens now?" he asked.

"Nothing. You'll go back to your job as though nothing has happened. But something has happened," he said. "You've lost our confidence. You'll have to work to regain that trust ... if you want to remain here."

"I will," Ewer said. "I promise."

"That's all," Mayfield said. "Dismissed."

———

By mid-afternoon, Novak had found contact information for seventeen St. Francis graduates and spoken to twelve of them. Only four remembered Timothy Dacey, and none had remained close to him. "Kind of a weird guy," one told him. "He was always hanging out with one of the fathers and had no time for any of us." It did not surprise the man to learn he'd become a priest. "I always figured that was his plan."

"Do you recall the name of this priest?" Novak asked.

"Afraid not. And I doubt he'd still be around. He must have been in his forties or fifties. We thought he was old back then." The man snorted as he considered how his own age altered his perspective. "Why are you trying to find him?"

"He used to be my priest," Novak said. He didn't fumble for an explanation. Dacey had been his priest. All he had to do was tell the bare truth and stop.

After they hung up, Novak considered what the man had told him. In his sixteenth year, the young man had made friends with a middle-aged priest and later joined the priesthood. He and Dacey had something in common: Novak had befriended cops at the same age. Both had decided early on what they wanted to do with their lives.

But their paths had diverged. Had Dacey been attracted to young men back then? Had he seen the priesthood as an opportunity? As he considered the question, which might be unanswerable, his deputy chief tapped on the door. "I didn't know you were in today," Mayfield said.

"I'm hiding out," he replied. "My mother is watching old movies. I wish they were from the silent era."

Mayfield laughed and sprawled into one of the guest chairs. "Our fish took the bait."

"Ewing?" Novak asked.

"The same." He recounted the conversation with the errant

detective. "I pinned his ears back, but how long they remain in place is anyone's guess."

Novak cupped his hands and leaned his nose against them. "What should we do with him?"

"Not much we can do," Mayfield said. "He was here when we arrived and may be here when we're gone."

Novak looked up at him as though suspecting he knew something, but his level gaze conveyed innocence.

"Where do we stand with the Tifton investigation?" Mayfield asked.

Novak studied the ceiling tiles before answering. "We've done all we can," he said. "Jeffrey plans to arrest Tom Walsh tomorrow, and we've run through the stories of everyone we know who had reason to kill him."

"You still don't like Walsh for it?" Mayfield asked.

"No, but I have nothing to back it up. Proving a negative is tough." He considered how much to tell his deputy about his intervention on Walsh's behalf. "Ceil Adams has agreed to represent him," he said.

Mayfield whistled. "High-priced talent. How'd he swing that?"

"One for the Gipper," Novak said.

"Okay," Mayfield said, drawing it out. "You are committed."

"Or need to be," Novak replied.

Lydia took a brisk walk in the forty-degree weather, her AirPods playing Fiona Apple's "Criminal," then moving on to others in her playlist before she could get her mind off the irony of the singer's lyrics. She wasn't looking forward to the next few months. This Army brat had spent time in Italy, Texas, and other warm-weather places, and while she loved life in Boyleston, she could do without the gloomy weather. She understood why so many vehicles bore Florida license plates. Pittsburgh was a hotbed of snowbirds who took flight with the first flakes.

She returned to her apartment and turned on the TV, watching a few minutes of football before turning it off again. While she loved living alone, she hated the loneliness. *Speaking of irony*, she thought.

Lydia called Lauryn Carter, their other Black patrol officer. While they shared a bond within the department—two women against the world—they didn't socialize. "What are you up to?" she asked when the officer answered.

"I'm at my parents," she said. "We always have Sunday dinner together. What's up?"

"Nothing. I was just looking for a little company."

"Sorry," the woman said, "but thanks for thinking of me. Next time?"

"Sure," Lydia said. She sat at her kitchen counter for a moment, one long leg tucked behind a barstool rung. She picked up her phone and glanced at it, thought better of it and put it back down, then lifted it again and dialed a number.

"Hey, Detective," Calvin Mayfield said.

"I feel like a pizza," she said.

"You don't look like one."

"Oh, thanks. That's the greatest compliment I've had all week." *Not really*, she thought, but being hit on by a married man didn't count.

"Pasquale's in fifteen minutes?" Mayfield said.

"I'll order it, you pick it up, and come here," she said.

His pause was almost imperceptible. "You're on."

What am I doing? she asked herself. *What does he expect? What do I expect? A little companionship is all.*

A quarter hour later, Mayfield arrived, balancing a white box in one hand while carrying a sleeve of beer in his other. "I'm glad you called," he said. "I was going a little stir-crazy."

"You too?" she said. "There's something about a holiday weekend when you have no family around."

She'd preheated the oven to 325 degrees and slid the box onto the middle shelf. They popped two beers and sat at the counter, making small talk. The Steelers and Penguins. Approaching winter. Anything but cop talk.

Lydia removed the pizza from the oven and slid two slices onto paper plates. They ate without speaking, then had a second slice. "I spoke to the chief about the murder investigation a few hours ago," he said. "He thinks we've done what we can. They're arresting Walsh in the morning."

"I know," she said. She took another mouthful while she thought, then sipped her beer. "I had coffee with Lyle Jeffrey today."

"Yes?" he said, his brown eyes widening.

"He's using David's death to get close to me. Not a chance." Her laugh was tinged with sarcasm.

"He's married," Mayfield said.

"So I reminded him. Anyway, something he said bothers me, and I didn't realize what until just now when you brought it up." She took another sip while she thought. "We interviewed both agents together, but he was to follow up with the assistant, Amanda Naughton. I don't think he did. He spoke to her by phone, but it didn't sound like a real interview."

"You think she knows something?" he asked.

"Trust me, if she was his assistant, sitting outside his office door, seeing everyone who comes in, listening to bits and pieces of conversations, she knows plenty. Whether she knows she knows it," she said.

"Why don't you do so?"

"I don't want to piss him off."

"Do you care?" he said.

Again, she laughed. "Not at all. He told us they were handling Walsh and gave us free rein to interview everyone else, so..."

"Go for it," Mayfield said. "And if you want company, I'm your man."

Raising her eyebrows, she gave him an appraising look, one he returned. "I could use some company," she said.

As HE OFTEN DID ON Sunday evenings, Novak made mushroom omelets that evening. Izabela had prepared a batch of *halušky* dumplings, and Barbara made a fruit salad. As they ate, Izabela took them through the morning Mass, recounting the priest's homily. Her summaries had once included thinly veiled calls for her son to return to the church, most of which, he suspected, were her own retroactive edits. There was none of that today, nor had there been for some time.

"I'm tired, dears," she said as they finished their meals. "It's been a long day."

Barbara led her upstairs to help her into the bath while Novak cleaned up, leaving the last glass of white wine in the bottle for his wife. After being diagnosed with a traumatic brain injury, he'd sworn off alcohol and was surprised to find he didn't miss it.

As he finished, his phone dinged. He opened it to find a message from Facebook admitting him to the St. Francis Alumni page. He logged on, but couldn't wade through the names on his phone.

After scrawling a note to Barbara, he retreated to his desk in the basement, logged on through his computer, and began combing through the list of members. Timothy Dacey was not among them, not that he'd expected to find him. A third of the way through the list, however, he found a Frances Solomon Ingram. Novak stared at her photo and saw from her profile she lived in Florida. Composing his thoughts, he opened the messaging app and wrote to her.

> I understand you were secretary for the class of 1965. I am looking
> for a member of that class, someone I knew well but have lost track
> of. If possible, would you call me so I can explain who I'm after
> and why?

He included his phone number, reread his message, and changed "I'm after" to "I'm trying to reconnect with." He sent the message, closed the computer, and returned to the kitchen.

Minutes later, Barbara joined him, her dark hair dangling and wiping her brow. "She's getting to be a handful."

"Maybe it's time to call in home healthcare," Novak replied. "I don't like your having to do this, and she won't allow me."

Barbara poured out the bottle of wine. "No," she said, peering at him over the rim of her glass, "it's not time yet."

Before he could protest, his cell phone rang. He glanced at the unfamiliar number but recognized the 561 area code as coming from South Florida. Raising his eyebrows to signal Barbara, he answered via the speaker phone. "Hello, this is Karol Novak."

"Birdie Ingram," she said in a musical voice that reminded him of a bird call. So that's where she'd gotten the nickname. "How can I help?"

He thanked her for returning his call and said, "I'm looking for a man named Timothy Dacey. I knew him years ago and—"

"I remember him," she said before he could finish, "but he's never joined up. He's never come to a reunion, isn't a member of the Alumni Association, and isn't part of our Facebook group."

"He became a priest," Novak said.

"I know that." She sniffed as though she'd detected an unpleasant odor. "Those people go into their own worlds, don't they? They live together and aren't allowed to mix with the rest of us."

Novak wanted to tell her it was the most ridiculous thing he'd heard all week, but he couldn't afford to alienate her. "Did he have any friends you can recall? Anyone who might know where he is today?"

"I don't know that he had many friends. Maybe he did, and I just didn't notice. He was an introvert. Not like me," she said with a cackle.

"Well, thanks for trying," he said.

"I'm sure you've tried his sister."

Novak's mouth fell open. He gaped at Barbara, who had followed the conversation. "He has a sister?"

"Yes, she's a few years older than he is. Three years, I think. Really up there," she said and laughed again. "I guess we all are. I just don't think of it that way. Me and Walter, we still go dancing. I'm not one of these people to sit around waiting for the Grim Reaper." She followed this with another chortle.

"What is her name?"

"Marge something. Hold on a minute." Novak heard her shuffle papers. He looked at Barbara with a triumphant smile, but she frowned as though lost in thought. "Marge Jellinek," she said. "She never married, so that's still her name."

"Jellinek? But Father Tim's name is Dacey."

"She's his half sister or something. Something happened to her father. He died, I think. Vietnam was going on back then. Is that where he bit the dust? Anyway, I think their mother remarried, but..."

Novak waited as the woman searched her memory. "I don't think that worked out. Her new husband was into the booze or something. I can't recall. But I know their mother raised Marge on her own, and I'm sure that went for her brother. You should talk to her. She'll know where he is. And she's still in Johnstown. Me and Walter run into her sometimes when we go back in the spring."

He thanked her again and hung up, unable to shake the image of a fatherless boy whose mother worked long hours, spending all his free time with a priest. His thoughts were leading him somewhere, but Barbara said something that drove it from his mind. "I wonder why George left Indiana?"

"George?"

"George Rollins, my teacher," she said. "During the interview, he told us he was moving here to be near his parents, but he told another teacher they live in Florida."

"Perhaps his parents moved south after he got here," he said.

"No." She shook her head with ferocity. "This was last year, shortly after we hired him. I had a conversation with the Spanish instructor about people born and raised here packing up and moving to Florida. Her parents had done so, and they were miserable. They didn't know anyone."

Barbara put both hands to her temples, leaving the rest of her wine glass untouched. "I remember it as though it were yesterday. 'George says his parents love it there,' she said. I asked her a few questions and learned they'd left a few years before. And they hadn't moved from Pittsburgh but from Harrisburg."

She reached out and gripped his hands with an intensity that surprised him. "It's one of those things you hear and file away, not realizing its significance. He lied to us," she said. "There's a reason he left Indiana. He's hiding something."

DECEMBER, Novak thought, was the least productive month of the year. People returned from Thanksgiving, some having traveled hundreds of miles over the holiday, only to turn their attention to Christmas. The approach of winter, with its three months of gray gloom, strengthened the belief that there was nothing much to do and no urgency in doing it.

There were exceptions: crime and politics, which were often indistinguishable, and the wheels of justice, which moved slowly but could crush anyone caught beneath them. Thus, Novak was not surprised when Ceil Adams called before he reached the police station to convey bad news.

"The DA's issued a warrant for Walsh's arrest," she said. "They wanted to arrest him at his home, but I've promised he'll turn himself in by eleven. They still wanted to make a public spectacle of it, but I raised holy hell with them. He'll walk in under his own power without cuffs."

"How's he taking it?" Novak asked.

"How do you think?" she said. "He's frustrated and pissed off. Thinks the world is out to get him. Mostly, he's scared shitless. He doesn't want to return to a cell, and I'm going to do my goddamnedest to see he doesn't."

Pulling into the parking lot, Novak asked when Walsh would be arraigned. She told him two o'clock. "I'll be there," he said. "I don't know if I can be of any help."

"The only way you can help is by finding the evidence to exonerate him," she said. "And thanks for sending him my way."

Thinking she was being sarcastic, he apologized. "No, I'm serious," she said. "I believe this guy. The courts have screwed him over once, and I'm damned if I'll let them do it again. I love a good fight."

Novak laughed despite himself as he entered headquarters. "That's why I thought of you," he said.

They disconnected, and he opened the door to his office, hanging his windbreaker on the hook behind the door. Before he could take his seat, Mayfield and Barnwell entered, carrying coffees from a local bistro. "Got a minute, Chief?" his deputy called.

They followed him in, and Barnwell shut the door. "We want to run something by you," she said. "Jeffrey hasn't formally interviewed Tifton's assistant, Amanda Naughton. She left for Thanksgiving the night Tifton was killed. They've spoken to her by phone, but it sounds like the conversation was cursory."

"Do you think she knows anything?" Novak asked.

Mayfield chuckled. "Detective Barnwell says we underestimate what a woman sitting outside an office door knows or can guess."

She smiled at him, and Novak guessed she'd given his deputy chief the sort of schooling he got from Barbara. "All right," he said. "We should speak with her, get her story, whatever it is."

He told them about Ceil Adams's call. "Walsh is having a rough time. When he called me last week, he was nearly hysterical. If she can learn anything that keeps him out of jail..." He waved his hand, letting the implied permission finish his sentence.

"Should we alert Jeffrey before we speak with Ms. Naughton?" she asked, her tone implying she hoped not.

"Should we?" Novak repeated. "Yes. Will we? No. He told us he was focusing on Walsh and we were free to interview everyone else.

Now he's making an arrest. If we seek his consent, he might say no. Let's get her on the record."

The pair thanked him and exchanged a smile as they left the room. *Those two are pretty cozy*, he thought. *They must be as anxious as I am to keep Tom Walsh out of prison.*

***

AMANDA NAUGHTON APPEARED to be in her early thirties. Tifton's assistant was a tiny woman, not a hundred pounds by Mayfield's estimate, her jet-black hair streaked with reddish highlights. She wore beige tights and a green double-breasted jacket over a white blouse and peered at the two officers over her glasses. Her eyes were red, as though she'd been crying, and tissues sprang from a box on her desk like a volcanic eruption.

"I don't have time for this," she said. She rose from her chair as though to block their questions. "We'll have to talk some other time." Despite her diminutive size, her voice was deep, husky, and intense. She wasn't seeking permission to delay the interview; she was informing them.

"I'm afraid this can't wait," Barnwell said. "We should have taken your statement days ago."

"I've already told the other officer everything I know."

"We'll keep this as brief as possible," she said and took a chair to emphasize she was staying.

The assistant gave her an exasperated look. "I have nothing to tell you. Mr. Tifton was alive when I left last Friday. He said he was working late and didn't even wish me a safe trip." She snickered as though his showing any concern was a joke. "The first I knew about his murder was when Walt Dwyer called on Saturday." She snorted again. "I think he enjoyed sharing the news. Always the first to know. You know the type."

Barnwell did. "How long had you worked for Tifton?" she asked.

"Three years."

"And did you enjoy it?" Barnwell asked.

Amanda gave a little shrug. "It was a job. It brought in money while I studied for my license."

"You want to become an agent?" Mayfield asked.

"Yeah." She folded her arms and spoke to them as though they were children. "That's where the money is, not sitting at a desk directing traffic and filling out contracts."

"Did Tifton encourage you?" he asked. She pulled her eyeglasses forward on her nose and stared at him. "I take it that's a no," he said.

"You have great insight. Has anyone ever told you that?"

Barnwell had taken enough sass. "Ms. Naughton," she said, "you must have seen and heard quite a lot in your position. Did Tifton have any enemies?"

"Enemies? Apart from his ex-wife and former employees, members of his condo association and contractors, former buyers, and the three of us, everyone adored him."

"That's quite a list," she said. This was the point where she would have asked where the woman was at the time of the murder, but Jeffrey had already confirmed this. But just for the record and to establish that this interview was serious, she asked.

"On my way to Somerset to spend Thanksgiving with my parents," she said. "I use EZ-Pass, so I'm sure you can confirm this. And it was snowing up in the Highlands, so there's no chance you'll catch me speeding."

"Anyone in particular have it in for him?" Mayfield asked.

"The TV says you're making an arrest," she answered.

"The county has a person of interest, but we're tying up loose ends," he said. "Is there anyone else you can think of?"

She dropped her insolent demeanor and seemed to think about it. Her voice deepened as she said, "When I heard what had happened, my first thought was a contractor named Craddock. He's—"

"We know who he is," Mayfield said. "Why did you suspect him?"

"He was in here last year sometime, and they had one hell of a row. You could hear the whole thing. Something about Tifton canceling his contract and making him lose his business. Craddock called him a bastard and said he'd get what was coming to him."

"A threat?" Mayfield asked.

"Just what I said. 'You'll get what's coming to you.' If you consider that a threat, yeah."

The pair glanced at each other. Craddock had the motive, but his wife was covering for him. Could they break her?

"Anything else?" the assistant asked. "I have to pack."

"Going somewhere?" Barnwell said.

"Well, yeah," she said in a where-the-hell-have-you-been tone. "I'm no longer needed."

The two officers looked at each other, thinking the same thing: Who was in charge now that Tifton was dead? "Who told you that?" she said.

"Scowcroft. She's taken charge, even though the deal hasn't gone through."

"The deal?" Barnwell prompted.

"You're the detectives," she said, her attitude returning. "You must know she's buying the agency from him. Or was. She was taking over at the end of the year. Making a lot of changes, she says, and they don't include me. So if there's nothing more..."

AFTER COMPLETING her Monday morning staff meeting and making a tour of the classes, Barbara returned to her office and opened George Rollins's personnel file. She found his résumé and studied his work history. Before coming to Boyleston, Rollins had taught not in one, but in two school systems, both in Indiana.

She called the number listed for his more recent one, a high school in Mayville, a suburban community outside Indianapolis, and asked to speak to the principal. The assistant asked her a few questions and put her through. Barbara identified herself again and said,

"I think we spoke two years ago when we were considering hiring one of your former teachers."

"That wouldn't have been me," she said. "Mrs. Foster retired at the end of the school year. I've replaced her."

Barbara asked if she'd served the school in another position before her appointment. The woman replied she'd been transferred from a middle school. "May I ask what this is about?" she said.

"I'm inquiring into the circumstances of George Rollins's departure," Barbara said. "When I spoke with Mrs. Foster back then, she indicated he'd left in good standing. I need to confirm that."

The pause at the other end was palpable. Barbara wasn't imagining it. She'd experienced it before when a student didn't want to tell her something. "I'm afraid you'll have to speak to the district's human resources department," the principal said.

Barbara asked for the number and dialed it with her hands shaking, convinced she was on to something. It took her ten minutes to reach the director, during which she strolled the office like a caged animal. When the officer came to the phone, Barbara identified herself, changing her demeanor from the open and friendly bearing she usually conveyed to one that was all business. "I'm calling to inquire about the circumstances under which a former Colfax High School teacher left your system. George Rollins," she added without being asked.

"Just a moment, please," the man replied. After another five minutes, he returned to the line and said, "I need to confirm your identity." He had her repeat her name, school, and community. He didn't take her phone number, saying he would look it up himself.

Another ten minutes passed until her assistant advised her the man was on the line. "I'm sorry for the delay," he said, "but I need to make certain who I'm speaking with. Anyone could call and tell me they're a school principal."

"I understand," she said. "What can you tell me?"

"Not much, I'm afraid. Mr. Rollins left to look after his parents during the 2018-19 school year. That's all I can tell you."

"Did he leave on good terms?" she asked.

"That's all I'm allowed to tell you."

"Is he eligible to be rehired?" she asked, searching for another way to get an answer.

"I'm afraid I can't say."

Barbara thought for a moment. "Are you bound by an agreement of some sort?"

The director's pause was even longer than hers. "That's all I'm permitted to tell you."

"Got it," she said. She thanked him and ended the call, knowing the man was trying to send her a message. But how was she to decode it?

AFTER BARNWELL and Mayfield reported the results of their interview with Tifton's assistant, Novak asked them to re-interview Evelyn Scowcroft. "Have her come here," he said. "I'll be back from the courthouse as soon as possible."

As he grabbed a bite at a local sandwich shop, Barbara called to relate her discussion with the human resource director. "He left under a cloud," she said. "He told the school district the same thing he told us, that he was moving here to care for his parents. We know that's not the case. The director gave me the Texas Two-Step, but he all but said they're covered by a non-disclosure agreement. I'm not sure what my next step is."

Novak gave her his best advice between bites of a chicken pesto sandwich, then wished her luck. He drove across the Liberty Bridge and parked behind the courthouse, climbing the stairs of the nine-teenth-century granite building and slipping into the courtroom minutes before the preliminary arraignment began.

The process was straightforward. Walsh would appear before the magisterial district judge, who would advise him of the formal complaint, read him his rights, decide whether to release him on bail, and schedule the formal arraignment a week or more away.

The judge gaveled the court to order, the clerk announced the case file, and a guard led Walsh in, wearing an orange jumpsuit and handcuffs. The bailiff released his bonds, and the judge read the complaint. Assistant district attorney Dawkins rose and presented the bare facts of the case—that Tifton had been killed, the medical examiner had classified the case as a homicide, and that Walsh had both reason to kill him and the opportunity. "We can prove the defendant was in the neighborhood when the victim was murdered. We have physical evidence showing he'd held the murder weapon."

Ceil Adams rose to object. "The state has no evidence my client handled the object when it was within the building," she said. "The murder weapon is a portable sign used in various locations where the deceased offered property for sale. We will show my client came in contact with it days before the murder. The state has only circumstantial evidence."

"You can make your case at trial, counselor," the judge said. "The prosecution has presented a prima facie case. The defendant will be held for trial."

"I ask the court to release my client until the formal arraignment. As you know," she said, turning to the Assistant DA, "the state wrongly accused Mr. Walsh of the murder of his wife in 1999. He served twenty years on death row for a crime he did not commit. Since his release, he's been a model citizen, as he was before he was incarcerated, but two decades of incarceration traumatized him. Mr. Walsh is psychologically incapable of returning to prison. His psychologist attests to that."

Asking permission to approach the bench, she handed the judge a document, which he studied for a few minutes.

The prosecutor countered the argument, insisting Tifton's role in Walsh's arrest and conviction provided him with the motive. "The defendant killed the deceased out of revenge. He acted in anger and is capable of doing so again."

The two attorneys traded arguments, with Ceil continuing to press her case on humanitarian grounds. "The state has created an untenable situation for Mr. Walsh," she said. "His wrongful imprisonment makes him fear small enclosures. He sleeps on his daughter's sofa, unable to endure the confines of a bedroom. It's all in the statement, Your Honor. Returning Mr. Walsh to a cell would cause irreparable harm. We must not exacerbate this wrong."

The judge looked at the two of them. "If I were to release the defendant from custody, I'd want to know someone was supervising him. What do you suggest, counselor?"

"As I said, he lives with his daughter, Your Honor."

The judge folded his hands and stared at her. "I'm not convinced a member of his family can provide sufficient supervision."

"If it pleases the court..."

"Who are you?" the judge said as Walsh turned and stared toward the back of the courtroom.

"This is the chief of the Boyleston Police Department, Karol Novak," Ceil said. "Two years ago, Chief Novak found the evidence exonerating my client."

The judge brought Novak forward. "Your Honor, I ask that you release him to me."

"You're willing to take on this duty?" he asked.

"I am," Novak said. "I've known Tom Walsh since I began investigating his case. I'm convinced he's innocent. He poses no danger to the community. Until his arrest for his wife's death, he was a successful businessman, an outstanding citizen of Boyleston, well-liked by all who knew him. He's suffered enough."

The judge held out his hand as though weighing what Novak said. "In that case," he said, "I'll set bond at $100,000."

Novak knew Bridey O'Conner would put up her house against the bond. Walsh would go free, at least until his formal arraignment. But the chief wondered what Barbara would make of his impetuous offer.

Evelyn Scowcroft arrived at the station a few minutes before four o'clock, wearing a black skirt and a three-quarter length lavender lambskin coat against a gray blouse. An older, silver-haired man accompanied her. "I don't know what more you think I can add," she said, "but bringing my attorney seems a necessary precaution."

She sported the same pearl earrings and double strand she'd worn on the day Barnwell had first encountered her. Her platinum blond hair looked cut and styled. Mayfield raised his eyebrows as she passed, and Barnwell suppressed a smile, expecting him to let out a whistle at any moment, not at her appearance, for she was a handsome woman, but at the odor of money that trailed her with every step.

"Thank you for coming in," Barnwell said as she led the agent into the interview room.

"You didn't give me much choice," she snapped, rubbing one hand over the other, then reversing the action as though removing grime.

"We've learned a few things we need to clarify," Mayfield said as he sat alongside Barnwell, facing the agent and her lawyer.

"What *things*?" she said.

Mayfield had hoped Novak would return in time for the interview, but he'd called to say he'd been detained. Barnwell was happy to take the lead. "When we spoke the day Tifton was found murdered," she said in response to Scowcroft's question, "you neglected to tell us he was preparing to sell the agency to you."

"Where did you hear that?" she demanded.

"Is it true?" Mayfield asked.

"It must be that Amanda, the girl with the golden ear, listening to everything that goes on."

"Why didn't you mention it during our first interview?" Barnwell asked.

She sniffed. "You didn't ask. And what difference does it make?

He'd signed a purchase agreement, but the sale wasn't completed. No money changed hands."

"But he'd agreed," Barnwell said. "Why didn't you just close the sale? Did something change his mind?"

She shook her head, but her attorney answered for her. "No, and if he had, we would have sued to recover damages. He knew that. It was all but wrapped up. He'd set the date for the closing, January 2nd. And we were fine with it. It created fewer tax complications."

"Why was he selling?" Mayfield asked. Barnwell hadn't finished her line of questioning, but she made a note and allowed him to continue.

"No one thing," she said. "The agency isn't doing well, and he didn't have the energy to fix it. He spent more time managing the condominium where he lives. I'm sure you've learned about that."

Mayfield nodded but did not speak.

"He'd formed a management company and planned to expand it to other associations. To do that, he needed money. That's why he'd agreed to sell the agency."

"Now that he's dead, I suppose the deal is off," Barnwell said.

The attorney answered. "No, the agreement is legally binding." He withdrew a copy from a leather folder and slid it across the table. Barnwell pretended to study it, but despite her master's degree in criminology, she was neither an attorney nor did she play one on TV.

"At the moment," Scowcroft said, "no one knows who inherits the estate. Tifton's attorney is trying to determine that."

"But if the new owner doesn't want to sell," Barnwell asked, "what then?"

"We'll sue the estate," he replied. "The purchase agreement obligates Tifton's estate to complete the transfer. The bill of sale is a mere formality."

He raised his chin, looking down at her. Barnwell decided he was making a legal argument that might or might not hold water.

"Besides," Scowcroft said, "I have a lot riding on this. If the estate doesn't honor the agreement, I'll not only try to force the sale, I'll sue for damages."

Mayfield leaned forward, picking at the missing thread. "There's something you're not telling us. What's riding on this?"

Drawing in her breath, she turned toward her attorney, who opened his mouth as though to speak. Mayfield didn't give him a chance. "Don't give me a song and dance about relevance," he said. "This is a murder investigation. Everything's on the table."

Scowcroft crossed her arms and looked away. "This must stay in this room for the time being," she said.

Despite herself, Barnwell smirked. "You're flipping it," she said.

"Who told you that? Amanda," she said, nearly spitting the word out. "Yes, I've agreed to turn the agency over to Bradley Real Estate once the sale is complete."

"And make a nice profit," Mayfield said.

"There's nothing wrong with that. I'll still head the office. It's the best of both worlds."

Barnwell frowned as she put the pieces together. "Why didn't Tifton sell to them?" she asked. "You acting as a middleman."

She looked at her attorney, who gave a slight shrug. "To him, Bradley was the enemy. He felt he'd built Boyleston into a valuable community and Bradley had profited from it. Fred would never have sold to them."

"Did he know you were doing so?"

"I doubt it. It would have killed the deal." Her lips turned down. She looked away, frowning as she considered it. "But who knows? Only the two of us were supposed to be aware he was selling to me. Amanda," she hissed, shaking her head.

"No one at the agency?" she said.

"Neither of them. Neither Amanda nor Walt."

"And your deal with Bradley?"

"No one," Scowcroft replied. "How many times must I say that?"

"What would have happened if the deal had gone through?" Barnwell asked.

"Don't say if. It will go through. It must."

"What happens then?" Lydia said.

"We're doing a top-to-bottom transformation. New office and computers, a complete rebranding, and we'll join the Bradley network that connects to every real state agency in the area."

"What about staff?" Mayfield asked.

She hesitated, again turning to her attorney. "Nothing's been decided," she said.

"Now, Mrs. Scowcroft, you've planned everything else, down to new computers," he said. "Don't tell me you haven't decided who you're keeping and who's to go."

"All right," she said, "only it isn't my doing. Bradley wants a complete turnover."

"That's why you've fired Amanda," Barnwell said. "What happens to Walt Dwyer?"

"They want nothing to do with him. They looked at him once and turned him down. Troy Stuart tried to arrange that." She gave a short, derisive snort.

"And where will he fit into the picture?" Barnwell asked. "Troy already works for Bradley."

"He'll be fine. He'll report to me instead of the Dormont office, but he's a star. Troy will be an important part of my new team."

Lydia took a long swig from her water bottle as she considered what they'd learned. "Does he know about this?" she asked.

"Troy? Not unless someone at Bradley told him. Not that it matters. He'll be fine with it. We've worked together before. There's no better salesperson. He has no interest in running the business."

But Lydia now knew enough about commission structures in the real estate game to have her doubts.

Since examining George Rollins's work history earlier in the morning, something had nagged at Barbara: why he'd moved from a high school to a middle school. She recalled posing the question during their interview two years before. He'd replied that he'd taught ninth and tenth graders at Colfax, and moving to a middle school wouldn't be much different. Besides, he'd said, the only open teaching position in the district was here at Washington Middle School, and he needed to be near his parents.

She now knew the latter wasn't true. And moving from high school science to teaching middle graders was a substantial change.

Barbara wished her antennae had picked up the same signals before Rollins was hired, but what good would it have done? The district had wanted a male teacher at her school, "providing role models for all students," as the strategic plan put it. For one of the few times since she'd become principal, they'd overruled her, choosing Rollins over her choice of an experienced teacher returning to the classroom after raising two kids through their elementary school years.

Now, facing silence from the principal at Colfax High, she faced a dilemma. Mayville district's HR director had dropped hints that something lay behind the curtain. How could she raise it?

She went online and found the school's website. As she suspected, it didn't provide a comprehensive list of teachers. Gone were the days when educators were among the most revered members of a community. Now, they were targets for harassment from anyone with an agenda. The site did provide web links to four brave teachers, three of whom also listed telephone numbers. For a fleeting moment, she hoped she could contact them directly, but then noticed that the phones listed were those of the school's main number.

Under the Administrators tab, she found listings for the directors of special education and IT. She had five names, but how to contact any of them without going through the school? As she stared at the list she'd written on her small notepad, she gave thanks for ethnic surnames. There couldn't be that many Paul Robiskies in the Indi-anapolis area. She entered his name and the city in the internet browser and found two listings. The first was estimated to be in his sixties, the second in his forties. She selected the younger of the pair and dialed the number.

A woman answered, and Barbara asked for Paul. "Who is this?" came a suspicious response. Barbara could hear two children arguing in the background.

"I'm a school principal in Boyleston, Pennsylvania," she said. "I'm reaching out to your husband for information on a former teacher."

"It's not Paul you want," she said. "It's his dad."

Barbara thanked her and asked for the man's telephone number. It rang until it went to voice mail. Should she leave a message? Following her husband's advice to take people by surprise, she was wary of telegraphing why she was calling. While she hesitated, the automated message asked if she was satisfied with her message. She deleted the dead air she'd recorded and waited for the tone. She introduced herself and said, "I'm trying to get information on a fellow teacher you may once have worked with. Please call me if you have a moment." She gave her cell phone number and disconnected.

She searched for matches for the other four names on her list but came up empty. Pushing herself away from her desk, she shook her head in frustration. Maybe she'd have to follow the advice she'd given Karol and find a recent school yearbook.

"You did what?" Barnwell said. But she'd heard Novak perfectly well and didn't need him to repeat that the court had released Thomas Walsh into his custody. "Jeffrey won't be happy," she said.

"I'm not on this earth to make Lyle Jeffrey happy," Novak replied.

"You're that convinced he's innocent?" Mayfield asked.

Novak combed his hair back with both hands, reminding himself he needed a haircut. "I'm convinced of only two things. He won't run anywhere because he has no place to go. And if he's forced to go into a cell, he may do something to himself. As to his guilt or innocence..." He spread both hands out in a gesture of helplessness.

"Well," Barnwell said, "we may have something for you." She recounted the conversation with Evelyn Scowcroft. "She was about to close a deal to buy the agency and resell it to a larger firm, which would keep her as the broker."

Novak leaned back in his chair to study the ceiling tiles, where he often found inspiration. He jerked forward as a wave of vertigo washed over him. The other two waited as he stared at a point beyond them. Although neither suffered from the same malady, they knew the signs. After what seemed like a minute, he said, "We should have discovered this a week ago." He paused again, lost in thought.

"Given what we know," Barnwell said, "let's ask ourselves who benefits from Tifton's death. We'd ordinarily look at who inherits the agency, but that remains a mystery. Who might have wanted to derail the sale?"

"Amanda Naughton may be key to all this," Novak said. "Circle back to her. Find out if she was the source of the information, as Scowcroft suggests, and whether she was aware of her plan to sell to Bradley. And if she knew all this," he added, "find out who she told."

"I'm on it," Barnwell said. She bolted from the office, wielding her cell phone like a weapon.

Novak rose and stared at evening's deepening gloom. "It may come to nothing," he told Mayfield. "This may have no connection to Tifton's death." And if that were the case, they both knew Thomas Walsh might stand trial and be convicted.

His cell phone rang. He glanced at it and raised his eyebrows to Mayfield. "Oh-oh," he said. "Hello, Sergeant. Deputy Chief Mayfield is with me. Do you mind if I put you on the speaker?"

He listened to the response, then clicked the icon so Mayfield could hear the conversation. "First off," Jeffrey said, "I understand you're responsible for Walsh until the formal arraignment. I hope you know what you're doing."

"He's not going anywhere," Novak said.

"I suppose I should thank you. It takes the pressure off us. If anything had happened to him while he was being held..."

Novak arched his eyebrows again. "That was my thought," he said.

"Anyway, something's come up I think you should know. Tifton's attorney has located an heir. You won't believe who it is." Without waiting for his reaction, the county detective forged ahead. "It's a fifteen-year-old boy."

"What?" Both Novak and Mayfield erupted in unison.

"Tifton's son fathered a child years ago. He never married the mother, but he accepted responsibility for the boy, even making provisions in his will for the child's education. That's how the attorney tracked him down."

"Any chance that...?" Novak began, seizing on the possible motive.

"No. The boy and his mother live in North Carolina. That's where Tifton's son lived and where he died. There's no sign she or the boy had anything to do with Tifton's death. She didn't even know the man."

"So, who runs the agency?" Mayfield asked. "Not the kid, certainly."

"Technically, the mother's in charge until he reaches eighteen years of age, but she's seeking legal advice on how to manage the process."

The pair thanked Jeffrey for the information and ended the call as Barnwell entered the office. Rather than taking a seat, she stood in the doorway, phone in hand. "Amanda claims she told no one. When I asked her what Scowcroft intended to do with the agency, she acted surprised. 'She'll run it,' she said. I didn't tell her about the Bradley Real Estate deal. I just probed around the edges. But either she's an accomplished actress, or she knew nothing more than what she told us this morning."

Barnwell shoved the cell phone into her hip pocket. "And she swears she kept the information to herself," she said. "'I need this job until I get my real estate license,' she said. 'Why would I endanger it?'"

The three stared at each other, uncertain what more to ask. What had seemed a powerful motive for someone to kill Fred Tifton hours before had come to nothing. If no one knew about the deal, no one had reason to prevent it.

And that left Thomas Walsh in Jeffrey's crosshairs.

CHAPTER ELEVEN
TUESDAY, NOVEMBER 30

LYDIA HAD BEEN awake for hours, intrigued by a snatch of
conversation she'd recalled from the week before. Standing at the
kitchen counter, she answered her cell phone on the first ring. "Hello,
Wayne," she said to David's father.

"Pardon me for disturbing you so early," he began.

"I'm already up. What's on your mind?"

"It's Howie," he said. "He's in mourning."

Did dogs mourn? She recalled the story of a dog in England who
went to the railway station every evening, waiting for her master to
step down from the car as he always had at that hour. He'd suffered a
heart attack at his desk more than a year before and was never returning, but the dog continued her vigil.

"What's wrong with him?" she asked.

"He just lies around," Wayne said. "He won't eat. When I take
him out for a walk, he does his business and strains at the leash to
come back inside."

In this weather, she thought, *I'd do the same.* "I'm sorry to hear
that, but I don't know what I can do for him."

"The only sign of life he's displayed since David's death was
when he saw you on Thanksgiving Day."

"So you want me to come over?" she asked. "I'll try to get away this weekend, but until then—"

"Lydia, please consider taking him."

"Oh, no," she said before she could censor herself. "No way. My apartment owner doesn't allow pets."

"Perhaps if you explained the situation, he'd relent."

"It's a she, and she won't."

"Howie loves you." It was less a statement than a plea.

"I'm afraid it's out of the question. It's not just the house rules. My job is demanding and unpredictable. I'm gone for hours at a time. It wouldn't be fair to Howie."

"If I don't find a solution, he'll die. I had to carry him out last night. He's losing weight. I can feel his bones."

Lydia shook her head, knowing where David had inherited his obstinacy. "Look, Wayne," she began.

"Please do this," he said, "for David."

One last hug. That's all he'd asked of her. And she'd denied him. "Tell you what I'll do," she said. "I'll pick him up Thursday evening, take Friday off, and care for him over the weekend to see if he perks up. But I cannot keep him."

Wayne's sigh was like an old locomotive releasing steam. "I knew I could count on you. You're always such a kind person. That's why I talked David into giving it another chance. You were right for him, and he was such a damned fool."

His voice quavered. *Please don't let me cry*, she told herself. *I've already agreed to take the dog.*

As she poured herself another cup of coffee, ignoring her shaking hands, she asked what she'd gotten herself into and how she would get out of it. The damn dog. Why had David even owned a pet when he couldn't care for it?

She shoved the thought from her mind and replayed the line that had awakened her at four in the morning: *And things weren't about to get better for him where he was.*

She called a number she'd saved to her contacts. "Troy," she said when he answered. "This is Detective Barnwell. I need to speak with you. When can we meet?"

She listened for a moment and poured her cup into the sink. "Starbucks in a quarter hour? Perfect."

Lydia jumped into her clothes, ran a brush through her curly hair, and was out the door eight minutes later.

THE WEATHER HAD TURNED from unpleasant to nasty. Izabela shivered by the fireplace, even though Novak had the thermostat at 80 degrees. "We have to stop this," he told his wife. "Gas prices are going through the roof. She'll heat us out of house and home."

"Hilarious," Barbara said. "But as you'll recall, you promised to bring the space heaters down from the attic two weeks ago."

Since had had no answer to that, he didn't attempt one. "Have you considered what I told you last night?" he asked.

"About Thomas Walsh?" Barbara said. "What is there to think about? You made the offer, and the court accepted it."

"I should have asked you first," he said.

She held out her hand and placed it on his arm. "You didn't have a chance. If you hadn't spoken up, the magistrate would have held him until the formal hearing. You've said yourself he might not have survived that. You did what was right. Besides," she said, "it's not as though he's living with us."

"Good thing, too," Novak replied. "We couldn't afford another mouth to feed. All our money goes up the chimney. Meanwhile, what's the latest on your project?"

She told him about her search for information on George Rollins's departure from Colfax High School. "They're hiding something, but no one will tell me what." She described how the HR director had thrown hints at her feet, "but just crumbs," she said. "He signals there's something he can't tell me, but he won't say what."

"You said he'd taught at another school before moving to Mayville. Try researching it," he said.

"As if I have the time." She stared into space, then finished her coffee in one gulp. "You're right," she said, rising from the table to carry her cup to the sink. "I have a duty to find out what happened and why. I owe it to my students."

She donned her parka, kissed his forehead, and left for school.

As Lydia entered Starbucks, Troy Stewart rose from the table he'd commandeered near the window. "What can I get you?" he asked.

"Nothing, thanks. I've had enough coffee for a week." She placed her water bottle before her and looked him over. He still looked like he'd stepped out of a soap opera, his clothes tight against his athletic frame. A look of boyish curiosity had replaced his more serious expression of a week before. Or was it a look of appraisal? Despite his song and dance about being a family man, Lydia suspected he was a player.

"You said something's come up," he prompted, glancing at his watch.

Barnwell would not be rushed. She'd come for a purpose and would go about it in her own way. "I'm curious," she said. "What do you think Tifton intended to do with his agency?"

"Do?"

"Everyone says he spent more time managing his condo project than pushing real estate. The agency was failing. What was his plan?"

Stewart leaned back in his chair and glanced out at the parking lot, averting her gaze. "This wasn't out on the street yet," he said, "but I've heard he was selling it."

"To whom?"

She heard a thumping sound. The table shook, and she realized he was tapping his heel against a leg. "It was a complex deal," he said. "He was selling to Evelyn Scowcroft. His agent?" he asked to make certain she was following him.

Barnwell nodded. "But she'd struck a deal with Bradley, the firm I work for." He allowed himself a wry smile. "She was flipping it."

"And how did you take this?" she asked. "Would you have reported to her?" His eyes narrowed, and Barnwell feared she'd made a mistake, signaling that she knew Scowcroft would head the agency. "Or was she reporting to you?" she added.

He drained his cup before replying. "Every agency is led by a broker. Evelyn was to hold that position, but if you suggest I resented it, I didn't. I have no time to run the agency. I sell."

"But the broker does better than the salespeople. They get a slice of the pie, don't they?"

"Okay," he said, parting his hands as though conceding the point. "But she'd made a deal with Tifton, so she held the cards. I can live with it."

"What happens now?" she asked.

"That I don't know. The deal hasn't closed, so will the new owner abide by the agreement? I'm not sure."

"How did you know about this?" she asked.

"Bradley told me. He ran the whole thing by me to make sure I'd stay. 'We know you should head the agency,' Bradley said. 'In time, you will. But she's part of the package. Either we make her the broker, or she won't sell to us.'"

Lydia took a swig from her water bottle while she thought. "When we interviewed you last week, why didn't you mention this?"

When he hesitated, she answered, "Don't say it's because we didn't ask. You're smart enough to know everything is relevant in a murder case. And this is no small thing."

Stewart shifted in his seat and lifted the coffee drink to his lips, but he'd already finished it. He was buying time. "Bradley told me to keep it to myself. He said it would queer the deal if it got out."

"Because Tifton would back out?" she asked.

Stewart nodded and pretended to take a sip. "Are you sure I can't buy you a cup?" he asked.

"No, I want to finish this conversation. Tifton was dead, so there was no reason to keep it a secret, especially not from us. Why didn't you tell us?"

"I was afraid you'd think I'd killed him to scotch the deal."

"And did you?" she said.

Stewart looked from side to side as though others might hear their conversation. "No," he said. "I was at home that night. My wife has already confirmed that."

"Had you told anyone else about Ms. Scowcroft's plan?" she asked.

Barnwell was accustomed to detecting pauses, those moments when a witness decides how much to say. Fixing him with a stare from her penetrating blue eyes, she acted on a hunch. "I know you told one person, but how many?"

"Just Walt," he said.

"Why? You'd been told not to share this with anyone. Why tell the other agent in this office?"

He rotated the paper cup between his fingers until he mangled it. "I don't know. To warn him, I guess. Give him a chance to find something else before the ax fell."

"You knew Bradley wouldn't keep him?" she said.

He crushed the cup, then wiped milk foam from his hand with a paper napkin. "They'd looked at him once and didn't like what they saw, so no, he was going to be out."

"How did he take this?"

"His voice shook," Stewart said. "I thought he was going to cry. He pleaded with me to intercede for him, but I told him I'd done what I could."

"And that's why you didn't share this tidbit with us," she said. "You thought we'd make him a suspect. You were protecting him."

"Maybe so, but Walt wouldn't hurt a fly." He snorted as he

considered those words. "That's what makes him a poor agent. He doesn't have a killer instinct."

Barnwell asked him a few more questions, thanked him, and stood, ending the conversation. She'd gotten what she'd come for and more.

———

After Barbara left, Novak opened his computer and searched for a name. He found no Marge Jellinek in Pennsylvania. Assuming her given name was Margaret, he tried again and still got no hit. Using the driver's license database would have been more straightforward, but he could only access that in an official capacity. Using law enforcement resources for personal business was illegal and, almost as important to Novak, unethical.

He searched for all those with the surname Jellinek in Johnstown and was rewarded with the name M. Jellinek. Her estimated age was 76, and the site listed no prior addresses. If she was Father Timothy Dacey's sister, she had lived in Johnstown all her life. He'd have to pay the site $39 to find her address and phone number. Barbara hadn't complained about his taking responsibility for Tom Walsh, but she'd blanch at the cost of this search. He did so anyway.

As he entered the data, he thought about his next step. He would use their home phone, not his cell, enter *67 to block caller ID, and dial her number. If the woman answered, would he ask for Dacey? He didn't know. Though not given to impulsive behavior—though he had acted impulsively in asking the judge to release Walsh—he'd play this by ear.

It made no difference. For his $39, Novak got only an address. Either the woman had no home phone, or it was unlisted.

Now Barbara would be truly pissed.

———

BARNWELL DROVE to police headquarters with details of the conversation churning in her head. Tifton had been about to sell his agency to Evelyn Scowcroft, who was reselling it to Bradley Real Estate. Three people had known about the arrangement: Amanda Naughton, who appeared to have a solid alibi; Troy Stewart, whose wife insisted he'd been home the evening of the murder; and Walt Dwyer.

Dwyer claimed he'd been having dinner with his girlfriend. What was her name? In the turmoil following David's murder, had anyone bothered to check Dwyer's story? No one on their side of the table, she knew, and Lyle Jeffrey was obsessed with Tom Walsh.

Barnwell entered the bullpen without saying hello to anyone, dashed into her office without taking off her jacket, and pawed through her notes. Sonya Obolensky was her name. Did they have an address for her? Of course not. Lyle Jeffrey and Bill Thurmond had allowed her to participate in that interview. How had they been so sloppy? Startled that they'd included her at all, she'd let the two men take the lead, sitting back as an observer. Had she asked Dwyer anything at all? She couldn't remember, but thought not. *Stop making excuses*, she told herself. *It makes no difference who failed to check Dwyer's story. I need to do it.*

She found Sonya in DMV records. She lived only eight blocks from here. Barnwell poked her head into Mayfield's office, but he wasn't in yet. Neither was Horvath. At the coffee pot, Mark Ewer stood with mug in hand, flashing his silly grin. She needed a witness. He would have to do.

"Put that down," she said, "and come with me."

Ewer did as he was told. Five minutes later, they pulled to the curb before the woman's house, Barnwell having given him the briefest of briefings. It was a lower-middle-class neighborhood, a row of narrow two-story homes on a brick street that sloped downhill. While most homes on the road had white aluminum siding, number 314 was cloaked in brown wooden slats, and the windows were trimmed in green. Rows of low bushes lined either side of the walkway, and snow rimmed a now-fallow garden in the middle of the lawn. Barnwell imagined a riot of color in spring that lasted well into fall. Sonya Obolensky might not be wealthy, but she took care of what she had.

She knocked at the door, hoping the woman was home, then noticed the doorbell and rang it. Big Ben chimed inside. Barnwell felt, rather than saw, an eye examining them through the peephole. The door opened a crack, a chain restricting anything more. "Yes?" a tremulous voice asked.

"I'm Detective Lydia Barnwell," she said. "This is Detective Mark Ewer." She thrust her ID toward the crack, angling it so the woman could see at least a part of it. "We have a few questions. Do you mind if we come in? This will only take a minute." She was unused to groveling but wanted to put the woman at ease.

"What's this about?" the voice asked.

"This would be easier if we could sit down somewhere," Lydia answered. She wanted to look the woman in the eye, see her reaction to their questions, observe her body language.

"I suppose..." the voice said. She didn't finish the thought, but closed the door. Barnwell heard the bolt at the end of the chain slide across the track. The door inched open, revealing a small, round woman with thinning, straight hair and a cherubic smile. "You can't be too careful."

As Barnwell followed the woman down a narrow hall, Ewer stayed behind. "Ma'am," he called out.

What now? Barnwell thought. *Why have I brought this fool along?*

"If I were to push hard enough," Ewer said, "I could tear the clasp out of this wood. A swing bar lock is more secure. If you're around this afternoon, I'll pick one up at Busy Builder and install it for you."

The woman beamed. "That would be so kind," she said. "I live alone and..." Her hands fluttered in the air in an unspoken conclusion to her sentence.

"Let's look at your rear door," he said.

"Oh, the door onto the back porch has a sliding bolt," Sonya answered.

"Just to be sure," Ewer said, following her into the kitchen. He knelt before the door, swung the bolt into place, and back out again. "Yes, this is fine. I'll just take care of the front door. We want to keep our citizens safe."

She thanked him profusely, leaving Barnwell standing outside their intimate circle. She'd never seen this side of him before. "Is there a place we can sit down?" she asked.

"Let me brew us some tea," Sonya said.

Barnwell was about to refuse, but Ewer said, "That would be lovely."

Lovely? Barnwell thought. But she held her tongue as the woman puttered around. She poured boiling water into a tea service, placed it on a long tray, added three cups, lemon, and a small sugar bowl and creamer, and prepared to carry it into the living room. "Let me get that for you," Ewer said.

"That would be so nice of you," she said.

The woman led them up the hallway into the living room, directed him to place it on a round table alongside her chair, and motioned them onto the sofa. Only when she had served them did she say, "Well, now."

"I believe you're acquainted with Walter Dwyer," Barnwell said.

"Walt? Oh, yes. We've been friends for as long as I can remember. He sold us this house years ago. My husband, Jonas—he's gone now—" And she launched into the story of her life.

"Did you always live in Boyleston?" Ewer asked. Sonya stepped back another generation. Barnwell was ready to wring his neck, but she had to admit he'd charmed the woman.

"You and Walt sometimes have dinner together," Ewer said.

"Oh, yes. We go out most Fridays to Eat 'n Park. They have this fish dinner. 'Whale of a Cod,' they call it. It's scrumptious. More than I can eat at one sitting. Have you ever tried it?"

Ewer broke in to extol its virtues.

"But we always go Dutch," she said. "We're not dating or anything. We're just friends. Two lonely old people." Sonya giggled, and Barnwell noted this description was close to how Dwyer had described it. "What you might call a girlfriend," he'd said.

"Did you go out last Friday night?" Ewer asked.

"Yes, because we'd skipped the previous few weeks. I spent one weekend with my sister, and Walt took ill the following Friday."

"This would have been on November 19th?" Barnwell asked, the first time she'd spoken.

"I can't tell you dates, but it was two Fridays ago."

"The Friday before Thanksgiving," she said, and the woman nodded. "You said he was ill. What was wrong with him? Did he say?"

"Walt called to apologize just before I was leaving to meet him. He's such a kind man. He said he'd gotten hold of bad food at lunch and couldn't keep anything down. I offered to come fix him some soup, but he told me not to bother."

"That was thoughtful," Ewer said.

"Well, we try to take care of each other."

It took another ten minutes of badinage before Barnwell could extricate herself from the conversation. "You won't forget me?" Sonya said to Ewer at the door.

"No way. I'll be back by five with a new security lock for you."

In the cruiser, Barnwell said, "If you ever tire of police work, you could become a paramour."

"Not me," Ewer replied. "I enjoy fixing things, but I could never do it full time."

<hr>

DURING THE LUNCH PERIOD, Barbara closed her office door and asked the assistant to see she wasn't disturbed. She reopened George Rollins's résumé and found the Indiana high school where he'd taught after graduating from college. After identifying herself to the assistant, the school's principal came on the line.

"I'm seeking information on a teacher who was with you for a year," she said. "George Rollins."

She heard a sharp intake of breath at the other end. "What's your interest in him?" she asked.

"He teaches here now, and, to be frank, we're having some issues. I'm trying to decide whether it's George or me."

The principal snickered. "I'm sure it's not you," she said. "As you've noted, George spent only one term with us."

"Why did he leave?" Barbara asked.

"I didn't renew his contract. You may not operate under the same rules, but I can refuse to renew at the end of a teacher's first year, and the union has no recourse. I'm not required to state a reason. I just tell the teacher we're not keeping him."

"And why didn't you do so in George's case?" Barbara persisted.

"Hmm," she said. "I take it there's a problem there."

Barbara wished to God people would stop dancing around the subject. "I wouldn't have called if there weren't."

"Does it involve young girls?" the principal asked.

Barbara sucked in her breath. *Young girls?* she thought. "He's acted inappropriately with boys in his class and with two of our female teachers. But girls? Not that I'm aware."

"Perhaps he's learned his lesson, then."

Barbara didn't conceal her exasperation. "I'm concerned enough with what he's saying around the boys. If he has a history of inappropriate behavior around girls, I need to know that."

"Is this between us?" the principal asked.

"No, it is not. I won't broadcast it from the heavens, but I'll have to share anything you tell me with our superintendent."

She was met with silence. "Look," Barbara said, "if George does something illegal to one of my students and I have reason to know he might do so, I will be sued, as will the district. And if you know something that could have prevented it, I'll drag you into it."

"There's no need to threaten me," the woman said. "I just need to be cautious. I wasn't required to state why I wasn't renewing his contract, so I didn't. Making an accusation at this late date puts me in the middle."

"Anything you tell me will be between me and the district," Barbara said.

"All right," the principal replied, but she followed it with a long pause. "George spent too much time with one of our freshman girls. He met with her after class, drove her home from school, and, on one or two occasions that I know of, took her out for ice cream following class. Her parents came to me distraught. They demanded to know how I allowed this to go on. I told them I was unaware of it, but promised to end it."

"Was this a sexual relationship?" Barbara asked.

"No. The parents took her to a psychologist and came away convinced it hadn't gone that far. But he kept telling her how pretty she was, making her feel special. There's no question he was grooming her."

Barbara thanked her, but couldn't resist asking the million-dollar question. "I'm assuming Colfax High asked for a reference before they hired him. Did you share what you knew?"

"No," she said. "I had a heavy discussion with him, as did the superintendent. I thought he'd learned his lesson."

"Not well enough," Barbara replied.

WALT DWYER ARRIVED AT HEADQUARTERS, trailing an attorney. "I don't know what you want to ask me, but I thought I should have counsel," he said.

"That's your right," Novak replied.

"My client has told you everything he has to say," the attorney said.

Novak repressed the urge to say, "but not everything he knows."

Instead, he began with a casual approach. "We have just a few questions. If he doesn't care to answer them, that's also his right."

He escorted the pair to the interview room and sat alongside Barnwell, who started the recording device. She stated the date and time, named the participants, and asked the opening question, as she and Novak had agreed while planning this confrontation. "Since we first spoke to you the day following Tifton's murder, we've learned some new information. Were you aware he was preparing to turn the agency over to Evelyn Scowcroft?"

Dwyer looked first at his attorney, then seemed to make his own decision. "Yeah," he said. "Troy Stewart told me."

"Why did he share that information, do you think?" she asked.

"I dunno. Maybe he just thought I should know."

"Did he tell you this in confidence? Did he instruct you not to tell anyone else?"

"Yeah," Dwyer replied. "He said it would get him in trouble."

"So he stuck his neck out for you," she said. "He must have explained why he let you in on such a big secret."

"Naw, he just wanted to tell me." Before Barnwell could pose another question, Dwyer added, "You know how some people like to let on they know something you don't? Troy's like that."

"Did he also tell you Ms. Scowcroft planned to sell the agency to Bradley?"

Dwyer shifted, raising himself out of the chair by pushing his elbows against the armrests, then settled down again. "He may have mentioned it, yeah. I put little stock in it, though. Tifton would never have agreed to it."

"Did you tell him?" she asked.

"Naw," he said.

"Why not?" Lydia asked. "You could have scuttled the whole deal."

"It was none of my business," Dwyer said.

Before Barnwell could follow up, Novak said, "Where were you on the night Tifton was murdered?"

"I already told your detective that. Her and the two guys from the county."

"Tell me," Novak said.

"I'd gone out to dinner at Eat 'n Park with a friend. We do that every Friday night. Except during Lent," he said. "Then we go to the fish fry at St. Cyril's."

"And who is this friend?" Novak asked.

The attorney interrupted. "I understand the DA has charged another party with Mr. Tifton's murder."

"Yes, but Detective Jeffrey asked us to clear up any loose ends," Novak said. He leaned toward the attorney and smiled. "It will help strengthen his case if Mr. Walsh's attorney tries to shift blame to others at trial. You know how that works."

"During our earlier interview, you mentioned Sonya Obolensky," Barnwell said. "We can confirm this with her?"

"Yeah. She'll vouch for me. Does that answer your questions?"

"I spoke with her this morning," she said. "She tells us you called at the last minute and begged off, said you had fallen ill."

"Oh, yeah, I remember now. I was laid up. Food poisoning or something."

"Yet you were well enough to stay in the office all afternoon," she said. "You were there when Amanda Naughton left for the holiday. You seemed fine when Ms. Scowcroft left at five. And when Troy Stewart called you at five-thirty, you made no complaint."

Dwyer seemed to fold in on himself, hunching over and encircling his stomach with both arms. But he said nothing.

"Here's what happened," Novak said. "As you arrived at Eat 'n Park, Troy Stewart called. The cashier knows you and recalls you standing in the entryway. You spoke to speaking to someone for about five minutes, growing increasingly agitated."

Dwyer twisted in his chair as though to leave. Beads of sweat sprouted on his forehead. He looked toward his attorney but again made no response. Sitting at his end of the table, something near the floor caught Barnwell's attention. She frowned for a moment, then smiled.

Novak appeared not to notice. "Stewart gave us his end of the conversation," he continued. "He told you Tifton was selling the agency to Ms. Scowcroft, she was selling out to Bradley, and they weren't keeping you. Stewart urged you to find something else while you had time."

The chief leaned forward, making sure he had Dwyer's attention. "When the conversation ended, the cashier saw you make another call. You called Ms. Obolensky and told her you were sick."

The attorney tried to interrupt the conversation, but Novak wasn't taking his question. "Then you went hunting for Tifton," he said. "He wasn't at the condo. We spoke to the manager an hour ago. She recalls someone matching your description tried to get in to see him. So you returned to the office, heard music blaring from Tifton's office, picked up one of the yard signs from the hall closet, and attacked him with it."

Dwyer stared at the two of them, shaking his head. "Have I left anything out?" Novak asked.

"My client has nothing more to say. He's innocent of any involvement in Mr. Tifton's death. If you try to charge him, you'll make fools of yourselves, and I will sue for false arrest."

"Interview ended," Lydia said for the record, "at 2:48 p.m., Tuesday, November 30th."

After Dwyer and his attorney left, Barnwell leaned against the table, her left hand on her hip, and said, "Did you notice his shoes?"

"Tell me," Novak replied.

Barbara had overheard her husband question witnesses by phone. Having learned why George Rollins had left his first teaching job, she could pretend to know more than she did when speaking with those at Colfax High. She dialed Paul Robiskie, the special education teacher she'd tried to reach the day before. This time, she connected.

"I left you a message yesterday," she said.

"Yes, and I chose not to return it. If you need information about a former teacher, you'd best speak to human resources."

"I've done so, but they're bound by a non-disclosure agreement. A staff member at Colfax High told me you might confirm a few facts for me in confidence."

"Who was this person?" he asked.

"I promised her not to use her name," Barbara said, faking it. "I'm making the same promise to you. This person said you were concerned by what you'd learned. That's all I can say."

"Wilma," Robiskie said. "She thinks better of me than I am. She sees how dedicated I am to my special needs students, but they have no one else."

To put him at ease, Barbara took a few minutes describing her school's special education program and listened as he discussed his own. As they spoke, his suspicion seemed to fall away, and for an instant, she regretted using him. But as she considered the danger Rollins might pose to her own students, her reservations subsided.

"Who is this teacher you mentioned?" he said. His voice carried a note of resignation, as though he already knew the answer and needed her to confirm it.

Instead of answering, she used a technique Novak had taught her. "I'm trying to understand why the girls' parents didn't file charges against George Rollins." Spoken aloud, the "girls" might be singular or plural, and the "parents" might refer to one or more. She'd not been an English major for nothing.

"I've always wondered the same thing," he said. "I suppose her father being so prominent in the community, he was protecting her privacy." He followed this with a contemptuous chuckle. "More likely, he chose to avoid a scandal. It's all about him, you know."

"So I've heard," she lied. "But weren't the school and district obligated to report him?"

"I'm making an assumption here. She wasn't my student, and I was fairly closeted in my role. But from what I've heard, it never rose to that level."

"He didn't have sex with her," Barbara said.

"Not that she admitted, but that was what he was up to. What do they call it?"

"Grooming," she said.

"Exactly. All those hours he spent alone with the girl—'helping get her grades up so she could get into the best colleges,' he said." The man snorted again. "She was already a straight-A student. Who did he think he was fooling?"

"And taking her out for special treats, I'm told."

"There was something to that effect," he said. "Again, I wasn't privy to what happened, but you know how the talk gets around in the lounge."

Barbara laughed. "I do. It causes me no end of problems."

He joined in the chuckling, but had nothing more to offer. Lydia again promised him anonymity, to which he replied, "I don't care. I'm retired now. If you want me to speak to someone in your district, I'm happy to do so. But keep in mind, I only know what I heard."

Novak and Barnwell emerged from the Liberty Tunnel at 4:25, crossed the bridge, and entered Downtown. Although the sun wouldn't set for another half-hour, the clouds obscured what little light remained. At Crosstown Boulevard and Forbes Avenue, a car ran a red light, causing Novak to hit the brake. Barnwell's head jerked forward. "What an idiot," she shouted. "Did he not see us?"

"It was a she, and everyone drives like damn fools between the holidays," he said. "They think they'll make it to Christmas faster."

In other circumstances, he would have pursued the kamikaze driver, but she had to take a back seat to other concerns. Their appointment was only five minutes away, and Novak had pleaded with Lyle Jeffrey and the Assistant DA to make time for them. He found a parking spot, and they bounded up the stairs, Barnwell carrying a file folder under her arm.

Jeffrey was waiting for them in the reception area, his long legs stretched before him as he scrolled through messages on his cell phone. Seeing Novak out of breath, he said, "Relax. She's never on time. Judges have reprimanded her for showing up late for trial." When Novak checked in at the reception desk, however, the clerk said, "Ms. Dawkins will see you now."

"How about that?" Jeffrey muttered as the clerk led them down the hall.

Melissa Dawkins rose to meet them but didn't smile, directing them to chairs with an imperious wave. "You're here about the Walsh case. You know we've charged him. The judge released him into your custody. Is he giving you problems?"

"Not all," Novak said.

Before he could continue, Barnwell said, "He's innocent."

Dawkins jerked back in her chair as though struck, and Jeffrey uttered a sound that sounded like he was trying to halt a runaway horse. Novak put a restraining hand on her arm. "Put another way," he said, "we have evidence a different party committed the crime."

With that, the Assistant DA seemed to relax, resting her elbow on her desk and her chin on her hand as her gaze bore into Novak. "Go on," she said.

"Tifton was selling his agency to one of his agents, Evelyn Scowcroft. She planned to resell it to another firm, Bradley Real Estate."

"How did you learn this?" Jeffrey snapped.

"Through Tifton's assistant," Novak said. That quieted the county detective, who had to realize he'd never sat down with her.

Novak recounted their investigation of the last two days. "When we questioned Dwyer the day after Tifton's murder, he claimed he'd spent the evening having dinner with a lady friend. But she says he called to cancel the date within minutes of the time Troy Stewart informed him of the impending sale."

"Interesting," the Assistant DA said, "but it's circumstantial."

"We interviewed Dwyer this afternoon," Barnwell said. "He was wearing a pair of Bostix shoes, the kind that's built like a trainer but looks like an oxford. That's what the killer wore. The seam between the outsole and the tip on the left shoe is discolored by a brownish substance. It could be blood. He's small in stature, so I suspect he wears a size 10, the size of the bloody footprint the medical examiner found at the scene."

Turning to Detective Jeffrey, Novak said. "Walsh wears a size 11. I'm sure you tried finding a record of Walsh purchasing that brand."

The Assistant DA turned to Jeffrey, who acknowledged as much. "How did you miss this?" she asked.

Novak broke in before the detective could defend himself. "In the days following the murder of my officer," he said, "we all missed things. It's taken a few days until we—until Detective Barnwell here followed up on earlier leads."

Lydia gave no hint of triumph. Novak was trying to absolve Jeffrey of responsibility to get him on their side.

"But you'll follow up now," Dawkins said. The Assistant DA dismissed the three of them, telling Jeffrey, "I expect you to get back to me as soon as you know something."

"And Thomas Walsh?" Novak said as he turned in her doorway. "Where does that leave him?"

"I'll not move to dismiss the charges until I'm satisfied we have the true perpetrator," she said. "This office has suffered enough embarrassment over Mr. Walsh. Before I move, I must be convinced."

Novak restrained himself from pointing out that the DA's embarrassment was nothing compared to what it had done to Walsh.

***

BARBARA SMOOTHED her skirt as she took a seat in the assistant superintendent's office. Alex Northman extended his hand, and

Barbara took it, recoiling from his clammy grip. Why had she never noticed this before?

As he slid into his desk chair, she glanced at the photos of his family on the credenza behind him. Three boys, from the looks of it, at various stages of their lives. An image of one young man had been taken on the Penn State campus. She'd heard rumors the youngest boy was in some sort of difficulty. Alcohol? Drugs? She couldn't recall. What most stuck her was that he had no daughters. Men who'd raised girls tended to be more aware of the dangers they faced than those who had not.

"You said this was urgent," Northman said.

"It concerns George Rollins, the science teacher," she said.

The assistant superintendent folded his hands, lowering his head to look at her over his reading glasses. *Why don't you just take the damn things off?* she thought.

"I've spent two days delving into his history before he came to us," she said. "He claims to have left his first school because it was a temporary position. That's not true. His principal chose not to renew his contract due to an inappropriate relationship with one of his female students."

Now, Northman did remove his glasses. "What does that mean?" he asked. "Was it a sexual relationship?"

"Not yet," she said, "but her parents felt it was headed that way." Barbara took him through the conversation with the high school principal.

"But no charges were filed," Northman said.

"No, the girl's parents wanted it hushed up, so she simply refused to renew his contract."

"Then I don't see—"

"There's more," Barbara said. She outlined her earlier conversation with Colfax High School's special education teacher. Northman nodded and made throat-clearing noises to show he was listening. When she finished, however, he said, "This is all second-hand, hearsay."

"It is," she admitted, "but you'll recall Rollins told us his reason for leaving Mayville was to be near his parents. They were no longer living here at the time. He lied to us."

"That's putting it a bit strong, don't you think?"

"I do not."

"They may still visit here. There may be a logical explanation."

"If so, we need to ask him about it. I'm more troubled about his current behavior, making suggestive comments in the classroom and hitting on women teachers. And I am deeply concerned he may continue the behavior that sent him to us—grooming young girls."

"Have you had any reports he's doing so?" he asked.

"No, we rarely learn these things until it's too late. If he's keeping such a relationship quiet, telling the girl not to discuss this with other students or her parents … That's how these men work."

"That's a lot of ifs," Northman said.

"Are you telling me you're not concerned?" she said, her voice rising.

He frowned and replaced his reading glasses. She recognized this was a deliberate technique. By peering at people over his half-glasses, he looked down on them, just as some executives sat in a higher chair when facing subordinates.

"I'm saying no such thing, Mrs. Novak. We can't take action against someone based on suspicion alone. As the wife of a police captain, you should know that. We'd open the district to a massive lawsuit."

"We'd open ourselves to greater consequences if we knew someone's past behavior was problematic, yet we did nothing. Not only would we face a lawsuit, we would scar a young person for life."

He folded his hands, betraying no emotion. "What would you have me do?"

Barbara leaned forward in her chair, placed her hands on the edge of his desk, and stared at him, demanding his attention. "I want our attorney to investigate. I want her to speak with officials of both Indiana school districts and puncture the cloak of silence in the non-disclosure agreement. They know that if George Rollins repeats his behavior of the past and goes beyond it, concealing it puts them at legal risk."

"All right," he said. Barbara realized she'd given him an out. Passing the problem to the district's lawyer meant Northman wouldn't have to act on his own. "I will do so," he said. "And thank you for bringing this matter to our attention. I know you have the best interests of your students at heart."

WITHIN HOURS of the meeting with the Assistant DA, Jeffrey obtained a search warrant and descended on Walt Dwyer's home with an evidence team. The real estate agent wore the same pair of shoes, and when the detectives seized them, he demanded, "What do you want with them?"

His attorney tried to silence him, but the man would not be mollified. "Those are my work shoes, the only pair I own. What am I supposed to do now, take clients around wearing sneakers?"

The attorney pulled him aside and spoke in his ear, holding his elbow to restrain him. While he may not have known what the shoes signified, he knew they were important and that Dwyer's insistence on retaining them was not helping his case.

As the search continued, Jeffrey noted the man had no other pair of what could pass for dress shoes. He was struck by the paucity of his wardrobe and the rundown condition of his furniture. Not only was Dwyer not a wealthy man, he seemed to live on the edge.

The crime lab took records from his desk and seized an aging notebook computer whose cover was emblazoned with the Tifton Realty logo. Dwyer's protests were more subdued, as though his records were not as crucial as his clothing. As the forensic investigators passed through the living room toward the front door carrying a clear plastic bag, his squawks rose in intensity. "You can't take my raincoat. Those are my best wool pants. Am I supposed to go around naked?"

Jeffrey took him in for questioning and called Lydia Barnwell, asking her to join Bill Thurman and himself. The three detectives, Dwyer, and his attorney, sat in an interview room on Greentree Road designed to hold four people. Despite the hard freeze outside—or perhaps because of it—the room was as hot and sticky as a changing room at a gym.

The detective sergeant led the questioning, following the path Barnwell had blazed earlier in the day. By now, the attorney had taken charge, advising Dwyer not to answer the simplest of questions. After an hour of this, the detectives took a break. Jeffrey called the medical examiner's office and urged them to expedite the analysis. When the examiner balked, Jeffrey barked, "Just do it."

As he stood by the phone, rubbing his hands together in frustration, Barnwell asked, "Why did you include me?"

Jeffrey smiled and placed a hand on her shoulder. Although it annoyed her, she didn't flinch. "This is your case, Barnwell. I wandered up an alley and spent so much time poking through trash cans I didn't notice I was in the wrong place."

"Are you sure we are now?" she asked.

"Aren't you?" he said. "When did you first suspect him?"

Barnwell crossed one arm across her chest, rested her other elbow on it, and rubbed her cheek with her hand. "He called us two days after the murder to suggest we question Louis Callon, the home buyer who felt Tifton had misled him. I took it at face value, figuring he was just being a good citizen. But a part of me wondered why he would go to the trouble."

"He was shifting the blame to someone else," Jeffrey said.

"Yeah, it's one of those things that sits at the back of your mind wanting to get out. When we learned about Scowcroft's deal to buy the agency, I couldn't let it go. I knew there had to be a connection." She looked up at the monitor, which showed Dwyer and his attorney sitting in the interview room, not speaking to each other. "When will we start in on him again?"

Jeffrey followed her gaze. "When the lawyer gets antsy," he said.

It didn't take long. The attorney burst from the room and, seeing Jeffrey at the end of the hallway, said, "If you have no more questions for my client, I'm taking him with me."

"Oh," Jeffrey said, "do we have questions." He whispered to Barnwell as he held the door open for her. Detective Thurman was nowhere to be seen.

"At 5:15 on the nineteenth," she said after they'd resumed the recording, "Troy Stewart told you Evelyn Scowcroft was buying the agency and selling it to Bradley. That would put you out of a job."

"On advice of counsel, I have nothing to say," Dwyer said, with more assurance than before.

"You immediately called Sonya Obolensky to cancel your dinner date, saying you were sick."

"Again, nothing to say on advice of counsel."

"But when we questioned you the following day, you claimed the two of you had had dinner," she said. "Why did you lie?"

"Nothing to say," he answered.

Barnwell found another way to pose the question. "You've already asked that," the attorney said.

"Yes, I did. And your client didn't answer. I'm prepared to sit here all day and into the night until I get an explanation."

"And we're leaving," the attorney said. He half-rose from his chair, but Thurman interrupted them, taking the chair at the end of the table Barnwell had previously occupied.

"Three hours ago," he said, "we removed a pair of shoes from your bedroom closet. The crime lab has determined the sole of the left shoe matches the print left in Tifton's blood."

Dwyer studied his hands but said nothing.

"The tip of the shoe bears traces of human blood," he said. "They also found blood on a pair of wool slacks, a raincoat, and a dress shirt heaped in the back of your closet. We don't yet have a DNA result, but when we do, I'm sure it will match that of the victim, Mr. Tifton."

"On advice of counsel, I have nothing to say," Dwyer replied in a high-pitched squeak. His hands shook, and as he had hours before, he seemed to cave into himself.

"I do," Jeffrey said. "Walter Dwyer, I'm charging you with the murder of Fred Tifton on Friday, November 19th. You have the right to remain silent. Anything you say can be used against you in a court of law..."

FIVE DAYS LATER, Thomas Walsh got an early Christmas present. Novak picked him and his daughter Bridey up in his unmarked cruiser and drove them to the courthouse to appear not before a magisterial district judge, but before Judge Judith Cohen of the Court of Common Pleas.

Walsh knew what to expect, but he still twitched in his chair as the clerk called his case. Novak sat in the first row of observers alongside Bridey, who leaned forward in a fruitless effort to place a hand on his shoulder. Judge Cohen donned her horn-rimmed glasses and told the Assistant DA, "I understand you have a motion."

"We do, your honor. The commonwealth moves to dismiss all charges against the defendant, Thomas Andrew Walsh."

The judge asked Ceil Adams if she had anything to say, but Walsh's defense attorney knew when to keep her mouth shut.

"Well, I do," the judge said. "Ms. Dawson, this defendant has suffered enough at the hands of the state. This case should never have been brought. If it had gone to trial based on the evidence you intended to present, I would never have allowed it to go to the jury. Your office has a duty to pursue justice, not just convictions."

"Yes, your honor," the Assistant DA said, not about to engage in debate.

"And to you, Mr. Walsh, I give my personal apology. Our justice system is imperfect, but it's the best we have. I wish you all the best as you put your life back together again."

"Thank you, your honor," Walsh said, "but I don't know if that will be possible."

Judge Cohen blinked several times as though searching for something to say. Instead, she banged her gavel. "Case dismissed."

As Ceil Adams escorted them from the courthouse, reporters rushed forward and asked Walsh for a statement. "This was a travesty of justice," the attorney said. "If it were not for the diligence of the Boyleston Police Department and Chief Karol Novak, the Commonwealth of Pennsylvania would have perpetuated the persecution of this innocent man." Despite the biting cold, accentuated by wind gusts rushing around the courtyard of the old building, she spent another two minutes assailing the district attorney's office. This, Novak figured, was more an advertisement for her services than a response to the question, but it took the pressure off Walsh, who telegraphed his impatience by shifting his weight from one leg to the other.

As Novak drove Walsh and his daughter across the Fort Pitt Bridge toward Boyleston, he called over his shoulder, "I know this has been a nightmare, but I hope you can resume life. I'm happy to call Ralph Norris at Busy Builder and ask him to give you your job back."

When Walsh did not reply, Novak said, "Tom, did you hear me?"

"Yes," he said, "but I mean what I told the judge. I don't know how I can do it. The next time someone in this borough dies suspiciously, the county will come for me. I'll always be a suspect."

Novak thought about what he'd said as he returned to police headquarters. While he hoped Walsh was mistaken, he knew how too many police officers thought. A few would include him in their list of suspects whenever the opportunity presented itself. A handful of others might want Walsh to be guilty of something so they could avenge their embarrassment over their two false arrests.

As he entered the door to the police station, he had no time to dwell on the matter, for Norma Marks looked up and said, "Councilman Jackson is waiting for you in your office."

Novak entered, shut the door, and grabbed the man's hand. "What brings you to this side of the building, Bernie?"

Jackson slumped in his chair and stared at him for a few seconds. Novak waited, knowing his friend would share what he'd come to say in his own time. "I've just submitted my resignation," he said.

"I'm sorry to hear that," Novak said. "And the reason?"

"I think you know the answer. Despite our promise to you, the planning committee is recommending the merged department seek a new chief. When I refused to go along, Doug Lentz replaced me on the committee. I can't serve under him."

He withdrew a folded paper from his vest pocket and handed it to Novak, who read the brief letter of resignation. "Because you have undermined my role as chair of the Public Safety Committee," it read, "I find I can no longer serve on the council."

Novak nodded as he finished the two paragraphs. "I'm sorry, Karol," Bernie said. "I did all I could."

"I'm sure you did, but," he said, brandishing the letter, "I don't think this was necessary."

"It was," Jackson said. "What will you do now?"

Novak held out both hands, palms up. "I'll have to discuss it with Barbara."

Jackson chuckled. "You never make a move without getting permission, do you?"

This wasn't entirely true. When he'd agreed to stay on to lead the transition months before, he hadn't consulted her. He'd acted on his own in asking the court to release Walsh to his custody. But most of the time, Bernie was right.

"Not her permission," Novak said, "her advice."

Lydia lay on her bed, awakened by a loud sigh from the companion curled against her back. "What is it?" she asked. "Having a bad dream?"

Alerted by her words, he scampered over her and licked her face. Lydia giggled for a moment, then lifted him to the floor, swung her legs over the edge of the bed, and sat for a moment before rising to her feet. She went to the bathroom as Howie sat outside the door looking at her. "This is weird," she said.

The Westie wagged his tail as though she'd complimented him. Lydia entered the small kitchen, poured water into the bottom of the Moka espresso pot, a gift from Calvin, poured coffee into the filter, and placed it on the smallest burner on the stove. While she waited, she looked out the front window of the apartment she'd soon have to vacate and groaned as she glimpsed the street lamp illuminate flakes of snow. "We have to brave the elements," she told Howie. He wagged his tail again and jumped from one side of her to the other as she returned to the kitchen.

After gulping down a bowl of raisin bran, she donned a sweatshirt, dressed Howie in his red jacket, and left for a quick stroll through the neighborhood. The dog seemed to love the weather, bounding at snowflakes, trying to catch them. As she walked, she worried. The management company had given her thirty days to find an apartment that allowed pets, and those that did were fully rented. "Maybe we should buy a house," she said aloud. Howie looked up at her with what she took to be a smile.

When her cell phone rang, she cursed under her breath—she didn't want Howie to hear foul language—and stared at the screen before answering. "Hey," she said as she answered it. "What's up?"

"Can you come by headquarters in an hour?" Lyle Jeffrey said. "There's something we'd like to discuss with you."

"What's happened?" she asked.

"We'll tell you when you get here," he said. "Eight o'clock, okay? And don't mention this to anyone else until we've talked."

She agreed and pocketed the phone as he disconnected. *What the hell could this be?* "We have to head home," she said aloud. "I have a meeting." Howie wagged his tail and headed back in the direction they'd come. *God, he understands me,* she thought.

An hour later, she parked behind the ACPD headquarters on Greentree Road and entered the building. Within a minute of giving her name at the desk, Lyle Jeffrey entered the reception area and motioned her in. "Glad you could make it on such short notice," he said.

"Is there something new in the Tifton murder?" she asked as they approached the elevator.

The detective chuckled. "No, that's in the hands of the DA. I suspect they're working to cut him a deal if he pleads guilty to manslaughter or something, but it's out of our hands."

He led her into an office that looked out on Parkway West, jammed with cars inching into the city. "Have a seat," he said, directing her to a round table in the corner. He offered her coffee. She declined, placing her water bottle before her on the table.

"You've seen the morning news?" he said. She had not. "We caught Marvin Milford in the act last night."

Milford was the assault suspect she'd tried and failed to lure into attacking her the week before Thanksgiving. "Actually, a woman took him down. She left a bar in Munhall about ten. He followed and attacked her, but he tangled with the wrong gal. She's a Tae Kwon Do instructor. She responded with a roundhouse kick that sent him sprawling. Bystanders heard him moaning and rushed to her aid. They held him down until officers arrived."

He provided more details as she listened with growing satisfaction. "But you could have told me this over the phone," she said.

"No, that's not why we asked you here." Before she could question him, another detective, Glen Carpenter, entered the room. He smiled and greeted her like an old friend, calling her by her first name. He and Novak were close, and she'd worked with him on the murder of a convenience store owner when she was still a patrol officer.

"You've been with the Boyleston PD for how long?" Carpenter asked.

She answered, and he posed more questions about her background, education, and training. "What's this about?" she asked.

"I don't want to seem like I'm poaching," Carpenter said, "but Detective Jeffrey is impressed with your work on the Tifton case and, earlier this year, your work unraveling the Rose Fallon murder. We'd like you to come work for us."

Before she could answer, Lyle Jeffrey said, "We need more female detectives. You have a way of getting people to open up. Chief Novak mentions it whenever he speaks of you. And you speak Spanish. I barely know English." He gave a self-deprecating laugh while Carpenter looked away, a smile on his lips.

Jeffrey outlined what she could expect regarding pay and benefits. They couldn't offer her the job themselves, he said. She'd have to go through the application process like any other new hire. "But with both of us behind you, we don't foresee a problem. What do you say?"

"I'll have to think about it," she said. "Chief Novak has supported me in everything I've done. I feel disloyal even considering this, particularly since he'll need me as he organizes the South Hills Regional Police Force."

Carpenter and Jeffrey exchanged a glance. She looked from one to the other, knowing they were communicating something between them. "You do that," Carpenter said. "Give it some thought. Talk it over with Chief Novak. I suspect he'll encourage you."

Lydia drove slowly as she headed west toward Boyleston. The offer had come as a surprise. She'd entered the building an hour before, thinking something had gone awry with the Tifton murder case. Instead, she'd been offered a new career path. How wrong she had been.

And then she began laughing. This wasn't the only mistake she'd made. She'd thought Lyle Jeffrey was after her. And indeed, he was, though not in the way she had assumed. *What kind of detective am I?*

NOVAK COULD ALWAYS TELL when Barbara was angry. Her voice tightened, half an octave higher than usual, and her mouth puckered as though she'd bitten into a lemon. She raised her eyebrows as he entered the kitchen, motioned him to sit at their breakfast table while she clenched her cell phone. "This is unacceptable," she said.

As she listened, Novak heard a male voice from the phone, though he couldn't make out the words. "I recognize that," she said, "but the fact I don't have to deal with him doesn't make him any less dangerous."

Barbara listened again, her hand gripping the phone even tighter. He'd already guessed what the argument was about from the context. "I don't care," she said. "You don't need proof he's doing the same thing here. It's enough that he lied to us when he applied."

Another pause, and now her voice cracked as she responded. "I don't care that you're counseling him. Others have done the same thing. It hasn't altered his behavior. By transferring him to the high school, you're not only hiding the problem. You're inviting him to repeat it."

She listened again and said, "No, I will not. Goodbye." She stabbed at the phone to disconnect the call.

"The district's transferring Rollins to another school rather than removing him," he said to short-circuit her explanation.

"Bastards!" she said. Which was unlike her. Novak hadn't seen her so angry in—he couldn't remember when.

"What will you do?" he said.

"I don't know. He told me to keep this to myself. You heard my answer. The problem is, I don't know who to speak to."

"The high school principal, at least," Novak said.

"Of course," she replied, knocking her palm against her forehead.

"I should have thought of that. I'm so pissed off I'm not thinking straight."

"You would have," he told her, reaching for her free hand.

"Why are they doing this?" she said, her voice close to a sob. "Why won't they take responsibility?"

"No one does," Novak said. "Remember Daryl McMahon, the deputy chief when I arrived? He was a campus cop at Norwalk University. He was dismissing drug charges against female students in exchange for sex. When the university discovered this, they swept it under the rug, transferring the problem to a small town in Northwest Ohio. When he got in trouble there, they fired him but kept it quiet. That's how we got him."

Barbara remembered all too well.

Novak peeled an orange as he continued. "The Catholic Church transferred predator priests from one parish to another, even moving them to other dioceses, where they continued molesting children. It's the way of the world. Solve the problem not by addressing it, but by passing it along to someone else."

"And then there's us," she said.

"Yes," he agreed. "Thank God for us."

"Speaking of which," Barbara said as she pulled her coat on, "what's the latest on your priest?"

Novak poured himself another cup of coffee and shoved the last section of orange into his mouth. "A friend, a retired state patrolman, is looking into things for me. I expect to hear from him today or tomorrow."

"And then what?" she said.

He stared into his cup as though it would provide an answer. "I haven't decided. But this is one can I'm not kicking down the road."

She paused at the back door, car keys in hand. "Karol, why are we doing this to ourselves?"

He asked what she meant.

"Working for people who don't appreciate us. You've put in your thirty years and more. I can take full retirement. We'd promised to take Jen to Montréal to improve her French last year, but once Lentz convinced you to stay, you got too busy with the transition to follow through."

Returning her keys to her coat pocket, she placed a hand on his arm. "She's not getting any younger, Karol. Soon, she'll just want to hang out with her friends, and we won't see much of her. Let's take her to France and spend a glorious month there."

"I'll give it some thought," he said.

"You do that."

THREE DAYS AFTER CHRISTMAS, Novak parked behind a vehicle on Rock Avenue in Daisytown, a neighborhood just outside Johnstown. The temperature was ten degrees, but he gave thanks for the cloudless sky that had helped him make his way up the winding road into the Alleghenies.

He turned off the engine, locked his car, and climbed into the front seat of the other vehicle, whose motor was running. He carried a manila folder whose flap was secured with a string. "Long drive?" the man behind the wheel said.

"Not bad. Thank God they've cleared Highway 22," Novak said. "That it?"

"Uh-huh," the driver said, nodding toward a small, one-story ranch-style house with white siding but no porch. A separate garage faced the street. The narrow avenue seemed more like an alley. At the far end, Novak knew, lay St. Gregory Church.

"He's home," the driver continued. "What're you gonna do to him?"

"Just talk to him," Novak said. His friend had cross-examined Novak when he'd asked for his help, wanting reassurance he wasn't aiding an act of violence. "Don't worry," Novak repeated. "I just want to face him."

"And if he's armed?" the friend said.

"I'll take the chance. I'm not carrying."

Novak thanked the fellow officer and told him he could leave, but his friend was having none of it. "I'll stay put. If anything happens, I'm your backup." He flipped open the glove compartment, revealing a Glock 19. Novak assured him he wouldn't need it, but his friend said, "Just in case."

Novak thanked him, but declined. He approached the door with the envelope tucked under his arm, noting the unpretentious facade. Not only did the house lack a porch, it had no overhang to provide shelter during a rainstorm. He took the one step onto the concrete entrance and rang the doorbell. A dog parked, he heard shuffling inside, and a petite lady with straight white hair opened the door a crack. She wore no makeup, and her clouded eyes were sunken into her skull. "Yes?" she said.

"Ms. Jellinek," he began.

"It's Miss."

"Yes, ma'am. I'd like to speak to your brother."

She looked behind her, then returned her attention to Novak. "Why? What do you want with him? Who are you?"

"Father Dacey was my priest years ago," Novak said. "I've come to say hello."

"He's left the priesthood," she said.

"I'm sorry to hear that. Still, he befriended me years ago. I'd like to thank him."

She looked behind her again and seemed to receive permission. "All right, come in. But take off your boots."

"Of course," Novak said. He closed the storm door behind him, braced himself against the jam, pulled off his right boot with the toe of his left, then crossed his leg to take off the other. He saw no sign of Timothy Dacey.

"You can sit in the living room. Do you want coffee or anything?"

"That would be fine," he said, thinking it might let him stall for time if Dacey ordered him to leave. He waited while she fiddled around in the kitchen. Then he heard voices, Dacey's low, hers more shrill as she said, "I don't know. I asked him, but I didn't hear what he said."

Another low conversation and Dacey approached the living room, a perplexed expression on his face. He was hunched over and had a sallow complexion. What was left of his hair was a tangled mess, as though he'd just arisen. But it was mid-afternoon. A nap? Novak wondered.

"Hello?" Dacey said, making it sound like a question.

"Hello, Father," Novak said as he offered the man his hand. "Do you remember me?"

The older man squinted. "I'm afraid not. I've had so many parishioners over the years, and my memory isn't what it used to be."

"Karol. Karol Novak."

Dacey peered at him, then brightened. "Ah, Karol. It is you. After all these years. How are you, my boy?" He collapsed into an armchair, pulled a gray wool blanket with frayed edges over his legs, and smiled.

"I'm well," Novak said.

Marge Jellinek, the half sister, hobbled in carrying a mug of coffee. "I forgot to ask if you take anything in it," she said.

"Black is fine." She folded her hands and nodded, uncertain whether to leave or stay. Novak smiled but stared at her, willing her to leave the room. When she did so, Novak asked, "And you? How are you after all these years, Father?"

"You can stop calling me that. I've left the priesthood."

"And why is that?" Novak said, leaving his coffee untouched.

Dacey looked from one side of the room to the other as though searching for an answer. He pulled the blanket closer to his chest and said, "I was getting too old for it."

Novak affected a solicitous tone. "But doesn't the Church let you retire in peace, take care of you in your later years?"

"Well," Dacey said, "my sister needed my help."

"Uh-huh," Novak said. He stared at the man until he looked

away, then rose and opened his manila folder. "Do you remember this young man?"

Dacey looked at the photograph. "Henry," he whispered.

"Yes, Father. Henry Sutton. Did you hear he's passed away?"

Dacey shook his head. "That was a long time ago."

"He was only eighteen," Novak said. "Do you know he took his own life? That means he'll never get to heaven, doesn't it? Do you know why he did so? What caused him to prefer death over life at such a young age?"

Dacey closed his eyes, covered his mouth with his fist, and bowed his head. He whispered something. "What did you say?" Novak asked, trying to keep the menace out of his voice.

The old man looked away, still covering his mouth. "I'm sorry," he said.

"Sorry," Novak repeated.

"Yes, for all the pain I caused. I didn't mean to—I never intended to hurt anyone."

"Then why did you do it?" Novak asked in a louder voice, unable to conceal his anger.

Dacey muttered something else. Again, Novak said, "What did you say? I can't hear you."

Marge Jellinek burst into the room like a wild animal escaping from its cage. "What's going on here? Why are you questioning him like that? Can't you see he's sick? I want you to leave."

"Not until he gives me an explanation. All these years, I've waited for him to answer for what he did to Henry. And to me."

"I'll call the police," she shouted.

"Lady," he responded in a low growl, "*I am the police.* And I want an answer." Turning to Dacey, who'd sat as though tied to his chair, he said. "Why did you do these things to us? What gave you the right?"

Dacey said nothing, but his sister spoke for him. "Because that's what they did to him," she hissed. "At St. Francis. The priests treated all the boys that way, but Tim was special. They made him one of their own. One of *them*."

He stared at Dacey, who sat with his head bowed, a look of—what? Shame? Resignation? Defeat? Whatever he was thinking, this was a broken man. Whatever he'd done to others, he'd also done to himself. He wasn't worth Novak's time.

"Please leave," the woman sobbed. "Now."

Novak covered his eyes. His body shook. Had he suspected this? Had he known it from the moment a former classmate told him what a loner Dacey had become, how he spent all his time at the church?

He struggled to his feet and reached for his boots, a wave of vertigo sweeping over him so powerful he leaned against the wall for support. "God help us all," he said.

Calvin Mayfield poked his head into Novak's office and said, "There's someone to see you, Chief."

Novak was about to tell Mayfield to send them in, but something in the man's demeanor made him leave his desk and come out into the bullpen. Barbara stood amid the group of officers. All of them were there—Barnwell, Ewer, Horvath, Marks, Lauren Carter, and Norville Chastain. Even Ceil Adams, the defense attorney who had done so much for Tom Walsh.

As Novak studied them in confusion, Ewer broke into an off-key rendition of Happy Birthday. Mayfield tried to settle on a key, using his powerful baritone to impose order, but he failed. This was a police force, not a choir.

Barbara moved aside, revealing a chocolate cake with six candles surrounding a large plastic 60. The men and women showered him with gag gifts, Ewer presenting a plastic specimen cup. "You'll be using this a lot," he said, "but it will take longer each year to fill it."

"It's already happened," Novak said.

"Speech," someone called.

Novak, who'd never been good at off-the-cuff presentations, said, "I'm uncomfortable with all this attention, particularly since I'm leaving you at the end of the month."

"Leaving us high, dry, and leaderless," Mayfield said. This produced laughter from everyone since he had been appointed acting chief through the transition. Novak hoped the three municipalities would take a close look at the man. A Black chief leading a force serving communities with a large minority population might build trust.

"And without one of your best detectives," Novak said. While Barnwell still had a few hurdles to clear, everyone was sure she would soon join ACPD.

They gobbled the cake, washed it with coffee and ginger ale, and Novak retreated to his office with Barbara. "I hope I'm doing the right thing," he said, not for the first time.

"You know you are," she said. "You came out of retirement to turn this department from a disgrace to a model of an effective, small police force. You've done that and more, Karol Novak."

And Barbara, having been disciplined for informing the principal of the Boyleston High School about George Rollins's background, had resigned rather accept a two-week suspension. "You've also done the right thing," he said, "as you always do."

Ceil Adams tapped at the open door. "I'd like a word," she said.

Novak invited her in and introduced Barbara, who reminded him they'd already met. "You're going to have lots of free time now that you're retiring," the lawyer said.

Novak laughed. "I'm told the time gets absorbed quickly."

"I'm serious now," she said, placing a hand with lacquered finger-nails at the edge of his desk. "Everything I know about you tells me you've been on the wrong side of the justice system for most of your life. You spend more time protecting the innocent than finding the guilty."

"Not true," he said.

"Maybe that's hyperbole," Ceil said, "but I'd like you to work with me. Not full time, but on a case-by-case basis. I need a talented investigator, and when tough cases come up, I'd like to call on you."

Novak looked down and rotated his now-empty coffee mug. "I don't know," he said.

"Give it some thought," she said. "The cause of justice needs you."

"I will," Novak said. "I'll consider it."

"We will give it serious consideration," Barbara said, reaching out to grasp his hand.

ABOUT THE AUTHOR

James H Lewis has published seven novels in the mystery genre, a short story on Mystery Tribune, and a historical novel set in World War II Canada. A former journalist whose work has appeared in the Washington Post, on ABC News, PBS, and the Eurovision News Exchange, he works as a storyteller for nonprofit organizations. Lewis lives in Pittsburgh, PA and is a member of Mystery Writers of America, PennWriters, and The Author's Guild.

If you enjoyed this book, please leave a review at your e-store or on Goodreads. Reviews are the primary means by which independent authors alert other readers to our books. To follow future investigations of Karol and Barbara Novak, Calvin Mayfield, and Lydia Barnwell, go to my author's website, jameshlewis.com where you may subscribe to my mailing list. Thank you.

9 7 9 8 9 8 6 3 7 9 7 8 4